Lorraine Wilson writes flirty, feel-good fiction for One More Chapter – a division of HarperCollins – and is unashamedly fond of happy endings.

She splits her time between the south of France and is usually either writing or reading while being sat on, walked over, or barked at by one of her growing band of rescue dogs.

 twitter.com/Romanceminx
facebook.com/LorraineWilsonWriter

Also by Lorraine Wilson

A French Escape Series

Poppy's Place in the Sun

Christmas at the Chateau

Jojo's French Escape

Ski Season Series

Confessions of a Chalet Girl

Secrets of a Chalet Girl

Revenge of a Chalet Girl

Secret Crush of a Chalet Girl

Rebellion of a Chalet Girl

Chalet Girl Plays Cupid

DAISY'S FRENCH FARMHOUSE

LORRAINE WILSON

One More Chapter

a division of HarperCollins*Publishers* Ltd

1 London Bridge Street

London SE1 9GF

www.harpercollins.co.uk

HarperCollins*Publishers*

1st Floor, Watermarque Building, Ringsend Road

Dublin 4, Ireland

This paperback edition 2022

1

First published in Great Britain in ebook format

by HarperCollins*Publishers* 2022

Copyright © Lorraine Wilson 2022

Lorraine Wilson asserts the moral right to be identified

as the author of this work

A catalogue record of this book is available from the British Library

ISBN: 978-0-00-836314-7

Printed and bound in the UK using 100% Renewable Electricity by CPI Group (UK) Ltd

For the friends who helped to encourage and inspire me during the writing of this book – John Prentice, Kate and Bernie.

Also for the real and very much missed Squeaker and Pickle – may your tails continue to wag within the pages of this book and your memories live on.

Author's Note

If you're new to the French Escape series or simply need a reminder, here's a who's who of the main characters, both human and canine to refresh your memory.

Humans

Daisy – a new arrival in St Quentin sur Aude seeking a fresh start in France. Friend of Poppy's. Has an unusual talent she tends to keep quiet and is an incurable romantic, though she is, ironically, trying to cure herself of that.

Anton – antiquarian bookshop owner and expert appraiser. Local widower. Writing a history of the area's folklore. Has a sexy-professor vibe going on but is completely unaware of it.

Poppy – children's book illustrator, artist, and owner of the farmhouse now converted into a guesthouse, Les Coquelicots, in St Quentin sur Aude. A little scatty but has a very big heart. Lives with her husband, Leo, in his nearby barn conversion.

Leo – husband of Poppy, heir to the Dubois estate including the chateau and the vineyards. Veterinary surgeon and partner in the local practice. Adores Poppy and her entourage of tiny dogs.

JoJo – runaway ex-reality star now living her French dream, browsing the markets and catering for guest-house visitors as she puts the past behind her. Girlfriend of celebrity chef Cal.

Cal – celebrity chef splitting his time between France and London. Boyfriend of JoJo. More passionate about food than about being a celebrity.

Mme Dubois – mother of Leo; lives at the Chateau St Quentin. Mayor of St Quentin sur Aude. Always dressed immaculately and secretly wishes her daughter-in-law would spend more time thinking about babies than rescue dogs.

M Dubois – husband of Mme Dubois, father of Leo. Also residing at the Chateau St Quentin. Art collector who's very fond of his new daughter-in-law.

Dogs

Peanut – tiny chihuahua and smallest of all the dogs in St Quentin, but probably the bossiest. Rescued by Poppy. Likes disco dancing, particularly to ABBA, but also has a fondness for reggae. According to Poppy she is part meerkat, part baby kangaroo, part fruit bat and part dog, but one hundred per cent loved. Oh, and quite as nutty as her name suggests.

Treacle – slightly timid chihuahua who is as sweet as his name suggests. Friend of Peanut and also rescued by Poppy. Loves cuddles once he gets to know you and has been slowly discovering his inner chihuahua cheekiness since his rescue from an abusive home.

Pickwick – miniature Yorkie with quite a lot to say for himself. Inherited by Poppy from her grandmother. Loves cuddles, sticking his tongue out, and doesn't let his crooked little legs stop him from bouncing around the garden like a baby lamb, chasing balls, sticks, or anything anyone has been foolish enough to throw for him.

Flump – chihuatriever (chihuahua-golden-retriever cross). Also rescued as a puppy by JoJo. Full of character. Kleptomaniac mischief-maker with the mysterious ability to open closed doors. Loveable canine rogue and loyal friend to canines and humans alike.

Barney – blind ex-hunting-dog, rescued from euthanasia by Poppy and living out a very comfortable retirement in the farmhouse. Part hearth-rug, part griffon, part beagle. Extremely happy and unfazed by his disability.

Maxi – Pyrenean Mountain dog belonging to Leo. Very sensible and well behaved except when Peanut, whom he adores, is around, when he will roll about like a puppy and do his best to impress her.

Pickle – depressed cairn terrier cross belonging to Anton. Grieving the loss of his mistress when we first meet him. Likes to take objects and hide them. A real water baby. Enjoys swimming so much that getting him out of a river or lake is a challenge.

Squeaker – Mixed terrier of unknown parentage. Also belonging to Anton. Still very young and puppyish. Lives with Pickle but was a tiny pup when their mistress died.

Molly – a papillon dog who seems to believe she is part cat. Likes her independence and refuses to cooperate where baths or getting wet are in any way concerned.

Chapter One

"To love is to be vulnerable."
C. S. Lewis

FROM: *Daisy*
TO: *Poppy*
SUBJECT: *Urgent!!!*

Hi Poppy,

I don't suppose you need an extra pair of hands at the guesthouse this summer do you? I'm cheap to keep, I promise, and I really, really need to get away. Not in a 'I've just robbed a bank and I'm fleeing the country' kind of way but an 'I've humiliated myself and urgently need a change of scene' way. I don't suppose there's any way we can just leave it at that is there?

No, I didn't think so!

Well... you know how you kept telling me to be brave and seize the day and how I'd regret it if I never found out if Scott felt the same way as me? So I did it. I made the grand gesture, the symbolic race to the airport, the kind of act that's always rewarded in romcoms with the object of the heroine's desire.

I didn't quite chase him to the airport, but I did leave my post at the hotel reception desk and sort of chased him to catch up with him as he was leaving the hotel. My skin is prickling with horror at the thought of it but in my defence, he has a really long stride! I'm not entirely sure what came over me, but he'd said goodbye and given me one of those lingering looks I was telling you about and had turned to go. I was watching him leave the reception desk when I suddenly felt I couldn't bear to let another wasted opportunity go by so I raced after... ahem, I mean I followed swiftly to catch him up.

He seemed lovely, surprised but pleased. I think he was genuinely happy when I asked him out. He said 'yes' after all. He said he'd meet me later that evening for a drink. So far so good. Then we might have, erm, indulged in some very unprofessional behaviour on my part, given I was still on my work shift. Not that unprofessional, before your imagination goes into overdrive! Still, it was bad enough to have got me into serious trouble if my boss had seen. I wasn't that unlucky but unfortunately it was witnessed by one of my colleagues. You remember me telling you about Becca? She was coming into work to take over for the night shift and she's always been angling for my job. I could never understand why she hated me so much until someone told me that she'd interviewed for my position as head receptionist and failed to get the job.

As if that wasn't bad enough, I then subsequently found out that he's married. Seriously, after all these months of flirting, waiting to walk me to the tube station when my shift was over, opening up to me, asking my opinion about things… I feel so naïve! I mean, I've had married men hit on me before at work but this felt different. It was *different. There was this intense connection whenever we locked eyes – you know, that sensation of the world around you fading out because of the intensity of the moment. I know I've always been a bit of a romantic but it felt like the real deal.*

Obviously I had checked his hand to see if he was wearing a wedding ring, and no, he never did. Some men don't I suppose, or maybe he lost it, but the point is I feel like I don't know if I can trust my intuition any more. I followed it, possibly put my job at risk given that sleeping with the hotel clients is a definite no-no, and for what? For a man who wasn't what I thought he was.

Plus I've got the whole incident looming over me now. I'll just be waiting for Becca to start the rumours, or maybe even go direct to Gina, my boss. Angie, the other receptionist who I'm friendly with, knows and I'm sure I can trust her but I think it's only a matter of time before what I did gets out and it's far better to jump before I'm pushed.

So… I need to get away. This was only ever meant to be a temporary job but I got comfortable and coasted. Also, and this is embarrassing to admit, but I really don't want to see Scott again. Married or not I think he does have some feelings for me and I'm concerned he might wear me down with his charm. He never actually said he was single and I was the one who asked him out. All he's really guilty of is flirting when he wasn't in a position to do so. I do feel strongly that I would never want to have an affair with a married man but given there's a strong sexual attraction between us, I'm concerned my resolve might weaken if he turns on the charm. It's best to put temptation out of reach. Way out of reach. Which gets me to the point of my rambling email (sorry!).

I was hoping that maybe I could come and stay with you in France for a bit? You've been saying how busy you are since the chateau art gallery and The Barn restaurant opened on top of all the usual guesthouse work. You wouldn't have to pay me – I'd be happy to work in return for bed and board. I promise not to bore on about Scott either. Coming to France would be a chance to put it all behind me, maybe even find a new direction in life. Like I said, the hotel reception work was only ever supposed to be a temp job until I found something better.

Then I got the promotion and it was too easy to stay where I was comfortable. Maybe this could all work out well for me if I can turn this into something positive? From now on no more moping over a man. No more unrequited love. I need to get myself sorted out first and work out what I really want in life.

And you have my permission to slap me if I fall for someone unavailable again!

What do you think?

Love from Daisy

xx

FROM: *Daisy*
TO: *Poppy*
SUBJECT: *You're a total star!*

Thanks Poppy, I really appreciate this.

Is this where I admit I've already handed my notice in at the hotel? I've even found someone who wants to rent my room in the flat-share. There's someone I met who's working at a café near work — she's Australian and wants somewhere decent to stay for the summer, before she moves on with her travels. She's sleeping on someone's sofa at the moment so is keen to move in asap. My flatmate, Vicky, is fine with it as

5

long as my half of the rent still gets paid so it's all worked out perfectly.

JoJo sounds lovely. I can't believe you live with an actual real-life celebrity! I love the sound of the barn you're converting into gîtes. I'm sorry you've had builder hassles but it's good luck for me that it's not going to be ready for guests this season so I have somewhere to stay that won't mean you losing out on any rental income. I'm fairly good with a paint brush if you want me to help out with the decorating.

I can't wait to meet the new additions to the St Quentin muttley crew and to see Peanut, Treacle, and Pickwick again. I bet they're loving life in the country. I've seen Peanut's disco dancing on YouTube – she's a natural born star!

I've been giving some serious thought to what I could do in France if I stayed longer than just the summer. It seems that setting up my own business might be the way to go and I was wondering, do you think there's a market for pet sitting or dog walking? I've so missed not being able to own a dog because of my long hours, not to mention the leasehold conditions regarding pets. When I was growing up our family was never without at least one or two dogs, plus our very own grumpy cat before grumpy cats became a social media phenomenon.

Anyway, thanks a million for being my Escape Plan. Oops, make that my New Dream Life Plan obvs! Running towards, not away from, lol.

See you soon.

Love and hugs to the fur babies,

xx

FROM: *Daisy*
TO: *Gran*
SUBJECT: *Changes*

Hi Gran,

I hope this email reaches you okay. I know you said there'd be no way of contacting you at the ashram but that if you could get to an Internet cafe you would. How is the ashram? I can't wait to hear all your news.

So, anyway, here's my news: I've left my job at the hotel and I'm moving to France. Well, maybe moving to France. I'm going for the summer at least and then we'll see.

I'm staying with my friend Poppy, the artist – do you remember her? She's married now and has this beautiful guesthouse she renovated from an old farmhouse.

The catalyst for the change is not so good. Something embarrassing happened with that guy Scott I told you about – you know, the guest who stayed at the hotel regularly and was always really flirty, chatting to me for ages. The one I'd felt such a connection with.

7

Honestly I'm so confused, Gran. You always said to trust my intuition and I had such a strong sense of connection with him. I told you when we locked eyes there was this sense of knowing each other already? Which is why I'm so confused because in this case my intuition was leading me astray. I listened to my instincts and got myself into a mess.

One day, when he was checking out of the hotel, I decided to try to take things further — all the lingering looks and accidental hand brushes were driving me to distraction. So I hurried after him, deciding to take the plunge and ask him out. He said yes and it was all going great except when he managed to get his watch caught in my hair. Don't ask why that happened — you probably don't want to know! It was when I was disentangling it that I touched the watch and had one of those odd experiences we used to talk about.

As soon as I touched the watch I knew his wife had given it to him, that despite his not wearing a wedding ring he was married. I haven't had an experience like that for a while and blurting out that I knew he was married didn't exactly go down well. Obviously I couldn't explain how I knew and I think he thought maybe I was trying to honeytrap him or something. It was all horribly awkward and there was no chance to try to talk things out because at that very moment one of my colleagues, who happens to want my job, walked past us into the hotel, sneering at me and making it very obvious she'd seen the whole thing.

There were a few snide comments when I went back in to formally hand over to her for Reception night duty and I felt I couldn't stay on after that. There would have been all the gossipy rumours, not to mention the kind of talk about me being weird or freaky – the labels I've had to cope with my whole life and the whole reason I do my best to hide the times when I do touch an object and get a flash of insight. The fact I keep it quiet and have never charged any money for anything like that has never stopped people calling me a fake and a fraud, out for attention or their money – or both. I know I don't need to tell you how bad it was for me at school, before I became better at masking my reactions. You were always the one who helped me through it and that's why you're the only one I've told the whole story to.

Obviously I haven't told Mum. She'd be furious, but then she never understood like you do about not exactly having control over incidents like that. It's not like I enjoyed making myself a target to be bullied at school. But then you said she rebelled against your interest in anything spiritual or paranormal by trying to be as normal as she possibly could and refusing to introduce you to her friends. And then I came along and even when I was very young started to tell her friends the history of their jewellery or antiques. They thought it was charming and I was a natural born story teller. Only you know that she used to punish me for doing it and I'm so sorry that my confiding in you led to you becoming further estranged from her. I know you've said I shouldn't feel guilty about it but I still do. Let's say it's a part of me I'm still not entirely comfortable with. Though it did let me know that Scott was married so… oh, who knows! I guess you can tell I'm still really confused about, well, everything.

I'm keeping my story simple. I'm saying I asked a guest out while I was still technically on shift and that's a sackable offence. That I decided it was better to jump before the rumour mill made its way to my boss.

I hope you're having a great time and I really do long to hear all about your adventures and travels, plus any wisdom you might have for me!

For now I'm going to focus on my trip to France and hopefully building a life for myself there.

Lots of love from Daisy xx

———————————

FROM: *Daisy*
TO: *Angie*
SUBJECT: *Miss you!*

Hi Angie,

You know I'll miss you too. I'll miss our lunches in the park and our nights out but… well, you know why I have to go. Becca is probably already practising her interview technique as I type. I really hope you go for the head receptionist position and get it instead of her. You'd be much better. You should definitely go for it.

A break is the best thing and who knows? Maybe, after I've sorted myself out of course, I'll meet a tall, dark, and handsome Frenchman like my friend Poppy has. Ooh, that reminds me, I have gossip: you'll never guess who I'll be staying with? Poppy has moved out of the guesthouse to stay with Leo in his barn conversion and I'll be in a conversion-in-progress, another outbuilding belonging to the guesthouse. But living in and running the guesthouse and restaurant is JoJo, who used to be in Sex in the Suburbs *and her boyfriend, celebrity chef Callum O'Connor! At least, he's there most of the time, I think, when he's not filming in London.*

So… it should be interesting.

Wish me luck

xx

As I wait outside the arrivals hall at Carcassonne Airport, trying not to get jostled by the crowd of holiday makers, I'm not feeling quite as upbeat about my new opportunities as my email to Angie might have suggested. The sun is warm on my skin and a trickle of sweat runs down between my shoulder blades. The jeans and shirt outfit that were perfect for London weather are now overheating me and I wish I'd worn a T-shirt underneath so I could take my shirt off.

One of the wheels of my suitcase is decidedly wonky and as usual I've put too much in my shoulder bag so now the strap is digging into my shoulder. I had no idea how long to pack for. It could just be for a few months or maybe, hopefully, longer, if I can work something out.

When I see Poppy walking towards me my spirits lift. I was starting to feel like a child waiting at school for a non-appearing mother. I am excited but I'm also a bit freaked out; this is a big step to take. I've been living in my comfort zone for too long, suppressing any restlessness that arose when I questioned if I was really happy. I stop feeling freaked out when I see Poppy though. She is one of those people with natural warmth who make you feel better just by being around them.

"Hi!" she waves frantically and makes her way through a small crowd of tourists waiting in line for a taxi.

She envelopes me in a hug and I feel some of my tension dissipate.

"It's been so long since I saw you," Poppy exclaims.

"I know." I return the hug with equal warmth.

"Thanks so much for putting me up. I really appreciate it, honestly, I can't tell you how much."

"You might change your mind when you see your accommodation." She laughs. "Would you like me to take that bag? No? Well, I'm afraid summer is obviously our busiest time. You're lucky we haven't been able to get the extra accommodation finished for the season. Don't worry, it's habitable, just not paying-guest ready."

We head off towards her car.

"I'm still grateful."

"No, honestly, you'll be doing us a favour. We'll be grateful for the extra pair of hands this season – it's been hectic." She waves away my thanks and helps me get my suitcase into her car boot.

It's the first time I've been to this part of France – I couldn't get leave to come to her wedding last summer. I look out at the countryside as we take the road to St Quentin sur Aude and see that it's every bit as gorgeous as Poppy described it. Green and verdant vineyards are interspersed with field upon field of golden sunflowers and patches of dark, wild forest.

"There's wild boar in those forests," Poppy says, noticing my looking. "You have to be careful driving at night. There's even been the odd wolf spotted but normally the wolves and bears keep to the higher mountain slopes of the Pyrenees."

The Pyrenees are an imposing sight, despite their distance.

"Have I moved back in time to the Middle Ages?" I joke. "I had no idea there were wolves here."

"Not many here exactly but one was caught on camera not too far from here."

We pass through tiny villages and quaint hamlets, all with their own ornate *mairie* and village school building. There's a mixture of modern villas and traditional French shuttered houses with ornate metal work, vibrant window-boxes, and hanging baskets. I don't see any chain shops, just individual *boulangeries* and the odd grocer's and butcher's shops.

"From what I've seen so far it's lovely here. I can see why you like it," I say, staring out of the window at the latest village we are passing through where a typical market is in full swing, stalls laden with fresh produce.

"Yes, it's great. I don't regret moving here for a minute," Poppy replies. "The countryside is beautiful but the towns and cities are also lovely to visit and within easy reach – Toulouse and Carcassonne especially, but also Mirepoix, our nearest town, is lovely and people come from all over to visit the Monday market. There's also the medieval walled *cité* of Carcassonne which you have to visit. It's going to be a bit hectic this season but we'll find time to do the fun stuff, I promise."

"Do you really think I could make a go of living here long term?" I muse aloud. "Start my own business, I mean? Obviously I've got experience with hotel work but I've been thinking it might be time for a change, to work out what I really want to do with my life."

"Sure. I don't see why not." Poppy shrugs. "Lots of other people manage it so why not you? You have some French, don't you?"

I nod. "Yes, to A-level and I've been using it at the hotel a little with our French guests so hopefully I'm not too rusty."

"That will definitely help. So…" She pauses and I worry she's going to bring up the subject of Scott. I'm not feeling up to talking about my confused emotions surrounding Scott or why I felt so strongly that I had to get away, not now anyway. She knows a little bit about my ability to sense things about the objects I touch but in typical Poppy fashion takes it totally in her stride and thinks it's fascinating. I haven't talked to her about the history of bullying, of being punished by my mother or of the friends or boyfriends I've lost because of it. She's so accepting of everyone I'm not sure she'd understand and it would only upset her.

"So…?" I ask warily when she doesn't finish her sentence.

"Have you had any more thoughts about what you might like to do?" she asks. "Did you read the feedback I sent you from Leo?"

I relax. "Yes, that was really helpful thanks. It's good to know there's some demand out there and really kind of him to offer to put a card up in his veterinary practice. The more I think about it the more I'm sure I'd love to do some pet sitting and dog walking, that sort of thing. I always wanted to work with animals when I was younger and spend more time outdoors. My parents talked me out of it though, told me I had to be sensible and get a proper job."

"So what do they think about what you're doing now then?"

"I, um, haven't actually told them," I admit. "I know I'm going to have to. They know I'm here but they may have assumed I'm just taking some annual leave to visit you and I… well, I may have let them carry on believing that."

"May have, eh?" Poppy snorts with laughter. "Don't worry, I'm not judging you. Parents can be tricky. Trust me, I know from personal experience. I get on far better with my mother now we live in different countries. It helps."

"Gosh yes, your wedding. I remember your emails from last year. I'm really sorry I couldn't get leave to make it over, by the way."

"It's fine, no worries. Honestly, life's too short." She smiles widely. In fact, she positively glows with health and happiness. The slight air of anxiety she used to carry with her in London has disappeared.

"Both being married and living here obviously suits you. You look fantastic."

"Fresh air, sunshine, good sex… you can't beat it as a beauty regime."

"True," I agree. "I'll have to take your word for it about the good sex. It's been a while and I'm not exactly looking at the moment."

My words run out and suddenly I feel tired again. I didn't get much sleep last night and the train and tube trip to the airport with my wonky suitcase was a bit of an ordeal this morning. What with all the queuing at airports and waiting for trains, it seems amazing how long travelling a short distance can actually take you, door to door.

"I understand. I wasn't exactly looking when I met Leo, you know. You never really know what's around the corner though."

"Hmm," I reply noncommittally. Okay, so things worked out for Poppy but I'm not sure how often you get a chance at love in one lifetime. I'm not someone who believes we only have one soulmate and if we mess it up that's it. But… the kind of instant mind-blowing sense of attraction and connection? Well, that's only ever happened to me once and I know enough from what Poppy has told me that she never really had that with her ex, Pete. Could it be true that we only get one real chance at the kind of love that sweeps us off our feet?

I hope not.

Not that I'm comparing what I felt for Scott with how Poppy feels for Leo. It just felt like the startling connection I had with Scott had the potential to develop into something wonderful.

I can't help replaying the first time I saw Scott: the wide, easy smile he flashed at me that somehow lit me up inside, and the sense that when we locked eye contact, we already knew each other. I'd been transfixed, my own lips mirroring his smile, standing stock still until Angie had cleared her throat and nudged me in the ribs.

How often does that come round in a lifetime? Just my bad luck that my 'one' turned out to be married, unavailable. That's not how it's supposed to work out. If there's even any 'supposed to' about it. I can't contain a small sigh. I'm not heartbroken, of course not, but I'm disappointed and confused and wish I had the answers. But then that's one of the reasons I'm here, to work out what I want in life and to sort myself out. As much as my heart yearns to know a deep love connection, I do know that focusing on romance isn't exactly a very solid foundation for life.

"It'll all work out, Daisy, you'll see," Poppy asserts confidently, touching me lightly on the arm. We've pulled up in front of the guesthouse while I've been lost in thought. I recognise the elegant, old farmhouse from her photos and from paintings on her art journal blog. There are pretty painted window boxes beneath pale-blue shutters and copper planters filled with lavender positioned by the steps to either side of the double front door. The jagged outline of the Pyrenees is just visible beyond the rolling forested hills.

As soon as we let ourselves through the gate to the front garden, a cacophony of barking erupts from the house and the front door is cracked open, letting a stream of dogs of all shapes and sizes barrel towards us.

"Peanut!" I recognise one of Poppy's chihuahuas and am gratified that she remembers me too, she's jumping excitedly up and down on her hind legs. I get down to my knees on the path and soon the other chihuahua, Treacle, has joined Peanut and they're both using me as a climbing frame. Pickwick, the miniature

Yorkie, isn't far behind them and deposits a slightly soggy tennis ball on my lap.

"Ignore him or you'll be doing that all day." Poppy rolls her eyes but greets them all with as much enthusiasm as they do her.

"I don't mind. You know how much I love your dogs – I've missed them." I can't resist Pickwick's hopeful little face and throw the ball for him.

A sandy-coloured dog a bit bigger than the chihuahuas pushes forward and takes the space on my lap vacated by the tennis ball, clearly not willing to miss out on the action, or rather, miss any fuss that might be handed out.

"Hello, who are you?" I stroke the back of his head and he tips his nose up towards me, watching me.

"Flump, stop mutt-mobbing the poor girl!" Joanna Grant makes her way towards us now. "Hi, I'm JoJo. You must be Daisy. That little reprobate on your lap is called Flump. Watch him, he likes to steal things, mostly because he wants you to chase him to get them back but it has led to some… um… interesting moments."

Her cheeks flush pink and I wonder what she can possibly be referring to.

"Er, okay, thanks. The mind boggles." I smile back at her. "Flump is such a little sweetie; those big brown eyes make him look like butter wouldn't melt."

"It's how he reels you in, makes you lower your defences, forget to lock your bedroom door, that sort of thing. Sorry, he gets a bit enthusiastic." She groans as Flump wriggles back against me and nestles his head into my cleavage.

"It's not a problem, honestly. I love dogs." I continue to make a fuss of the chihuahuas and Flump. "What breed is he?"

"A Chihuatriever, we think."

"A what?" I ask, bemused.

"A cross between a chihuahua and a golden retriever. Or possibly a Labruahua. And yes, it really is a thing." JoJo laughs at my raised eyebrows. "And before you ask, no one seems too clear on whether it's a naturally occurring phenomena or, you know, a test-tube thing."

Before I've had time to digest this rather odd trivia I notice Poppy's blind dog Barney ambling towards us across the grass, tail wagging lazily. She described him to me as her part-griffon, part hearth-rug crossbreed dog, and I notice he really does look like a nice, cosy rug.

"And this is Barney." Poppy makes her way over to him and gently guides him towards our group. "He knows his way around okay but sometimes he likes to feel your touch. He's just happy to know there's someone nearby."

I reach out and let Barney sniff my hand before stroking his large velvety ears. It's slightly awkward given Pickwick has chosen this moment to deposit his tennis ball at my feet again.

"You're certainly in demand," Poppy giggles. "It's your own fault for mentioning you wanted to do dog sitting and pet walking on the ride over; they obviously tuned in with their supersonic hearing and heartily approve."

"I'm sure the dogs think you've come to stay purely to see them," JoJo adds.

"Oh but I have. Sorry, did I not make that clear?" I laugh and it occurs to me that I haven't felt this… light in a long while. Pet therapy is definitely good for the soul.

"That's Maxi lying over there by the front door." Poppy points out the Pyrenean mountain dog gazing at us impassively. "He's Leo's dog and he's far too sensible to get involved in a doggie scrum, which is just as well given his bulk. Unless Leo's been away, that is, then he can be every bit as nutty as this lot."

Poppy reaches down and takes Pickwick's ball away. "Later, Pickwick. Give Daisy a chance to unpack at least before you start harassing her."

"I don't mind, really I don't. It's lovely to be around dogs again. We always had dogs when I was growing up but because of my hours and live-in shifts at the hotel, plus the lease at my flat not being dog friendly, it's just not been possible."

"Well you'll certainly get your dog fix staying here." JoJo's smile is warm. I love her dog and therefore she approves of me.

"I'm sure I heard there are more dogs in St Quentin than there are people," Poppy says, scooping one of the chihuahuas off me before it gets caught in my hair.

"Sounds like my kind of place." I reluctantly get to my feet before I get pins and needles.

"Shall I show Daisy around?" JoJo suggests. "Haven't you got to get back to the gallery?"

"I should, yes." Poppy nods. "I'll see you later though. We all eat together early, before the guests who've booked for an evening meal. You're in for a treat. Cal's cooking is out of this world. I mean, JoJo's is great too…"

"Don't worry, I knows me place." JoJo puts on a mockney accent. "Go on, go. Stop stressing."

She shoos Poppy away.

"I really do appreciate this," I say to JoJo as we

head for the house. "I hope I won't be getting in your way."

"You're doing us a favour actually. I'm not just saying that to be polite. I could really use another pair of hands around the place," JoJo says, her tone serious. "Plus, if you're up for some dog walking and dog entertaining when we're at our busiest, please go for it. I always feel bad if I haven't had time to give Flump a long walk – he has so much energy."

I'm glad that the arrangement is going to be a reciprocal one and I'm looking forward to getting some quality 'dog fix' time.

———

The converted *gîte* in the old barn behind the farmhouse is perfect for me. Okay, it still has bare plasterboard walls and the tiling in the en suite isn't done yet, but the missing work is mostly cosmetic. It's perfect because it gives me my own private space to decompress.

Space to take a breath.

Clear country air at that. All the avenues of trees lining the roads here are obviously doing a good job of limiting any pollution.

I sit down on the bed, a nice double with a new

mattress that's already made up with crisp white bedding. I'm searching through my case for something cooler to change into and realise I haven't thought about Scott or my life in London since I arrived here. I ignore the wave of depression that threatens to sink me. I'll be fine. I'm just going to have to deal with it.

I pull out my comfy denim shorts and a pretty floral shirt and stuff the emotions back down in much the same way that I'm stuffing discarded clothes back into my case.

Once changed, I emerge out into the warm sunshine again to be greeted by an inquisitive Flump who wags his tail enthusiastically, even though it's only twenty minutes since I last saw him. I stroke his velvety soft ears and smile, remembering my childhood Jack Russell, Ella, my best friend in all the world. She had the same kind of mischievous streak that Flump clearly has. I've definitely missed having doggy friends in my life.

JoJo isn't far behind.

"Ah, there you are Flump." Her face relaxes into a smile. "He's such an escape artist that I'm never really happy if I can't see him. Open the door to take a parcel in and he'll be off like a shot looking for new adventures."

She scoops him up in her arms. She's even more

beautiful than I remember her from TV. Happier and healthier, all sort of shiny and glowy. Crap. I've just realised I've moved in with two loved-up couples. Great way to get over my unrequited love. I'm even more glad I've got my own space in the barn.

"I promise I'll keep an eye out for him," I say.

"Thanks, I'd appreciate it. He's given me a few scares in the year I've had him. He's still quite young, I suppose. He can open internal doors by the way – I wasn't joking about locking your door, unless you want an unexpected cuddle from a kleptomaniac pup."

"That sounds quite nice actually. I was just thinking how much I've missed having a dog."

"Well, Flump is very good at giving cuddles and he seems quite keen on you too which is good enough for me. He's a good judge of character," JoJo says and I'm not entirely sure she's joking. "Poppy said you needed to get away. To start over."

"Yes…" I hesitate.

"Well, if you ever want to talk about starting a new life here, or leaving an old one, well, I've been there and done that, as they say; I'm the queen of reinvention." JoJo smiles self-depreciatingly.

"Thank you," I reply and decide to move the conversation to more solid ground. "I would like to set up my own business here if I can."

"Ah yes, pet sitting or dog walking or that sort of thing?" she asks. "I think that could work. I'm always seeing people online asking if anyone can recommend a pet sitter. It's often hard to find someone local because most people who like animals tend to have plenty of their own to look after already."

"That's good to hear, thanks."

We walk back to the guesthouse kitchen. The sun is deliciously warm on my bare arms and legs.

"Well, you can definitely get some practise in with our lot. There's a lake in that direction, down that foot-path over there." She points in the opposite direction to the chateau towards some woods that back onto hills and the Pyrenees beyond, framing a clear blue sky above. "Leo's barn conversion is over there, between here and the chateau. Oh, and don't be surprised if you get woken by donkeys, geese, pigs, goats or cockerels. Angeline has pretty much everything in her animal sanctuary. She's the other partner in Leo's vet practice."

"It all sounds great."

"And if you need any help setting up as a micro-entrepreneur for your business, just let me know. The French love their paperwork and Poppy isn't the person to ask – she's allergic to it. I think she assumes the paperwork fairies do it all while she's painting."

"And you're the paperwork fairy?"

"You got it."

"So if I clap my hands and say I believe in fairies you'll help me too?"

"Or you could buy me a drink sometime – that works too." She giggles. "Shall I show you around the guesthouse and explain the routine now?"

By the time my tour is finished I'm in no doubt that I'll have plenty to take my mind off Scott and the life I left behind in London.

I take Poppy's dogs out for a walk as my first task the next morning and learn the art of how to put their harnesses on when they're dancing about. "I think someone is excited about going for a walk," Poppy says, putting Treacle's harness on once he's stopped spinning in circles. He then immediately goes to Pickwick's harness and tries to step into it. "Do you think he thinks he'll get twice as many walks if he has two harnesses on?" I ask. "Who knows what goes on in their minds?" Poppy rolls her eyes. "You know we had to switch our home pod off in the barn because Barney's barking kept setting it off and all of a sudden the fan would switch on and we'd have obscure music start to play." "At least he wasn't ordering things online. I've read about pets doing that." Poppy puts her hands over

Barney's ears. "Shh, don't give him ideas. I'm fairly sure we've disabled any devices that can do that. I'd better check with Leo. The annoying thing is, the pod would never acknowledge my voice.""Definitely a conspiracy," I laugh. "Or maybe it just picks up lower register sounds more easily.""Maybe," she shrugs. "Oh, I forgot to say, if you come across men in ditches with sub-machine guns don't worry about it.""Er, what now?" I ask, attaching the triple coupler to a lead and hooking up the three little ones so they can't get too tangled up. I can't help wondering if I've heard her correctly."Men with guns.""Yes, I got the men with guns bit, and I know you told me hunting is still very popular in rural France but are you sure about the machine guns?" I ask doubtfully. "That really doesn't sound right.""Okay so we may have had a little... incident." Poppy's cheeks turn a little pink. "If you object you can put it in writing with the local *mairie* – you know, they're like the village council, only they have a lot more power in France. Basically, it's then in writing that you object to having hunters on your land and they're supposed to abide by that. So, when I saw men with guns, I assumed they were hunters and kind of lost my temper a bit." "You lost your temper?" I ask incredulously. "I'm not sure I can imagine that." "I can when it comes to some-thing that might threaten my dogs. There have been a few fatal accidents in the past with dog walkers, not to mention the danger to any dogs being walked.""So what happened?" I understand now. Poppy is one of the gentlest people I know but if her dogs were ever threatened, I know she would fight ferociously to protect them."Well, as I said, I got a bit worked up and these men were just staring at me like I was some sort of annoying wasp. It was at that point that Leo came along and whisked me away." She pulls a face. "He explained that the Foreign Legion's barracks are based not that far away and they were on an exercise. I did point out that that was information it might have been handy to know beforehand but to be fair to Leo I've only actually seen them twice. The second time I saw them I tried to smile and nod, but they just gave me these blank-eyed stares. Leo says they don't have a sense of humour and I must pretend they aren't there if I see them again.""Okay then, consider me warned. I'm still confused as to what exactly you thought they were hunting with machine guns?" I head out of the door with the three littl'uns in tow. "Funny, that's what Leo asked me. I don't know – hunting isn't exactly my thing." She shrugs. I somehow wished she hadn't mentioned it. Now I'm going to be searching for armed men instead of just admiring the scenery and playing with the dogs. "Anything else I should know?" I ask,

30

reaching down to stroke the chihuahuas who are wondering what the hold-up is about. "Yes. Avoid Cat Alley," Poppy answers thoughtfully. "Avoid Cat Alley?" I raise my eyebrows. "The village is mostly populated by dogs – in fact, there are actually more dogs in the village than there are people – but there's one road down by the chateau where there are at least six resident cats, possibly more. We call it Cat Alley." "So what's it really called?" I ask. "So I know which street to avoid." She looks blank, as though the real name of the road has never occurred to her. "Not sure. But there's a cat who basically waits for you to drive along and then dashes out in front of the car at the very last minute. He's a ginger tom. He likes to wind up any dogs he meets too; he jumps out at them, says rude things in cat for all I know. We call him Kamikaze-cat or Kami-cat for short."

"Uh-huh. Anything else I ought to be forewarned about?" I ask, thinking the countryside sounds a lot more dangerous than I'd imagined.

"Erm… well, I suppose I should mention Paul," Poppy shrugs. "He works on the vines. He'll try to hit on you, no doubt about it. He tries it on with pretty much any new female in the area. He's good-looking and he's charming but he's trouble."

"Trouble I can do without." I grimace. "I did

mention I'd come here to get away from those kinds of complications, didn't I? I'm here to build a new life, not get taken in by another charmer."

"Of course, I know that," Poppy places a placatory hand on my arm. "I just thought you ought to be warned about him, you know, if you're feeling a bit, umm… fragile. He's very charming but it's kind of always all about him, you know?"

"Yes, I know the type, don't worry. I'm not planning on falling for anyone – it's too much hassle."

"It can be, sometimes, I suppose, if it's with the wrong person," Poppy says, her brow creased. "I haven't offended you, have I?"

"Of course not," I say and manage an encouraging smile. "Beware of men with machine guns, cats who want to run you off the road, and charming villains twirling fake moustaches as they plot having their wicked way with you. Got it."

Poppy smiles back and I head for the back door, much to the dogs' relief that they are finally going out for their walk.

"Oh," Poppy halts our progress and I can practically feel the small dogs twitching with impatience. "If by any chance a man turns up with a trailer full of psychotic goats, trying to return them again, on no account let him leave them here. It's probably not very likely to happen. I think they've been happily re-homed this time by Angeline – you remember, I mentioned her? She's the other vet in Leo's practice and she runs the small animal sanctuary on our land. The goats haven't been sent back to us for a while now but just in case anyone does turn up with some goats, please phone me or Leo immediately and do not under any circumstances try to unload them or sign to accept their delivery."

"Um, okay then," I pretend to make a mental note, feeling slightly bemused. I had no idea things were so lively in the countryside. "Beware of psychotic goats. Is that it?"

"Sure, now that the donkey enclosure has been doubly reinforced and extra locks put on the gates. I mean, the donkeys are clever but they can't manage those bicycle-lock combinations; they just don't have the dexterity."

I look for a sign that she's winding me up but she seems totally sincere.

"Okay, got you," I reply, slightly baffled. "Well, I'd better take these three for a walk now before they self-combust with impatience."

And before I wonder exactly what kind of place I've actually moved to.

Chapter Two

"Love makes your soul crawl out from its hiding place."
Zora Neale Hurston

I walk towards the chateau with Flump on his lead. Barney is getting a bit old for long walks, particularly in the summer when he'd rather be lying on the cool tiles of the guesthouse kitchen or pottering slowly around the garden.

JoJo is welcoming new guests this morning and wanted me to take 'that furry trip hazard otherwise known as Flump' somewhere out of the way. I'm happy to oblige – he's a real cutie, full of mischief but a lovely, affectionate dog. I'm planning on taking him down to the lake where I can put him on his longer extendable lead as I don't think JoJo trusts him off the lead without her there – or maybe she doesn't trust me, but that's fine. I get how precious he is to her and know trust needs to be earned. First though, I fancied a nose around the chateau grounds and wanted to take a peek into the animal sanctuary.

We take a route that leads us round by the donkey paddock and I stroke the warm, furry muzzles of the more inquisitive ones who push their necks out over the fence. Flump sniffs suspiciously but doesn't bark, obviously used to their proximity but not entirely trusting these non-dog animals. It's then that I hear a frenzy of excited barking and some shouting coming from the direction of the chateau. A ginger tom streaks past me, startling Flump, and flies up a nearby tree. Two dogs follow him, tongues lolling, excited for the chase. They look like terrier crosses, one a sandy-gingery colour and the other chocolatey brown. The terriers we had when I was younger used to be terrors for chasing cats too. I wonder if this is the cat Poppy warned me about who likes to take risks, like running in front of cars and baiting dogs?

Flump tugs hard at his lead and I tighten my grip and head over. I pick up the smaller chocolatey terrier as she seems friendlier, an assumption she proves by giving my neck an enthusiastic lick. The ginger dog looks askance at me, so I feel in my pocket for Flump's liver training treats. I hand one to the chocolate dog in my arms and she gulps it down without chewing before giving me another lick. Then I put a few on the floor for both Flump and the ginger dog in an attempt to distract them from the cat. Looping Flump's lead over my wrist, I use my spare hand to take out his extend-able lead and quickly clip it onto the ginger dog's harness while he's snuffling around in the grass for more treats.

Then I shepherd my little flock away from the cat and back up to the chateau where I presume someone must be missing them. I hope the owner won't mind me interfering. I know I'd want someone to help me out in a similar situation but I know it's more common for the French to let their dogs roam the countryside unsuper-vised – at least that's what Poppy tells me. Hopefully I've done the right thing. I haven't seen these two dogs around for the past couple of days so perhaps they're visiting.

As I turn into the chateau gates I almost bump smack into a man running towards me. From the harassed expression on his face I assume he must be the dogs' owner. He rattles off something in French so fast I can't understand him; the accent is thick too, different from the French I learnt at school. I've been warned about this, that the local accent here is very strong, strains of the Occitan tongue still present in the dialect.

"*Désolée. Je n'ai pas compris.*" I explain hesitantly that I haven't understood, just about holding onto the chocolatey pup who is wriggling in my arms and attempting to leap straight into the man's arms.

"*Vos chiens?*" I add hopefully.

He nods and takes the chocolate terrier from me, some of the tension seeping out of his features.

"English," he says, more of a pronouncement than a question. "Thank you."

Now I'm not so encumbered by wriggling dog, I'm able to appreciate her owner is actually rather attractive and smartly dressed in jeans, shirt, and jacket.

I hand him the lead attached to the ginger dog and he takes it.

"I had a spare lead with me. I was just dog walking," I explain inanely.

"Ah, you are a dog walker?"

"Um, yes, amongst other things."

"I am very surprised that Pickle let you catch him. He can be, how do you say it, a bit of a pickle sometimes."

"Pickle? That's not a very French name." There's

something about this man, the harried look in his eyes, the sadness in Pickle's eyes that's tugging at me.

"My wife… she… was English."

Was…

Oh dear.

I feel bad now. I've accidentally stumbled into something very personal.

"Oh, I'm sorry," I say totally inadequately.

"You are sorry that my wife was English?" His mouth quirks into an unexpected smile that somehow lights me up inside.

"I… er…" At least he's assuming I'm discomforted by the topic and not by his smile. "You know what I mean. I assume she hasn't just changed nationality or something?"

I cringe. Did I really say that out loud? What's the matter with me today? I close my mouth before I can dig an even deeper hole.

"Died, yes." His reply is matter-of-fact, but not curt.

"I'm sorry," I say and this time manage not to add anything weird.

"We are too," he replies a little awkwardly and I find I'm missing that lovely warming smile he flashed at me before I took the conversation into a downhill trajectory. "Pickle hasn't really recovered from it. He's been very sad and… grumpy I think is the right word."

"Poor boy." I crouch down and offer him another liver treat, which of course means I have to offer Flump and the little chocolate dog another treat too.

"And what's her name?" I stroke the chocolatey terrier's ears, which are velvety soft.

"Squeaker," he replies, a glimmer of a smile reappearing on his face. "Yes, my wife chose her name too. It was not long before she died so Squeaker was just a puppy and is not so affected as Pickle. She is full of trouble."

"She's adorable." I straighten up. "I'm Daisy by the way, as we seem to be doing introductions. And this is Flump."

Flump introduces himself by sniffing at the man's trousers and then wagging his tail. Clearly he has Flump's seal of approval. And mine too. Anyone who loves their dogs this much has to be okay and he's also got that sexy-professor look going on, though obviously that observation is completely irrelevant. I haven't come to France to make a fresh start only to instantly fall for yet another unavailable man. Or any man at all for that matter.

"Well, I'm Anton and perhaps, as we're doing introductions, we had better shake hands," he replies solemnly and I think from a slight twinkle in his eye that he's mocking my Englishness with the hand shake, but in a gentle, teasing way, not unkind.

"Nice to meet you, Anton." I take his hand to shake and instantly I'm hit by an energetic jolt that startles me and leaves my hand tingling. "Should I shake paws with Squeaker and Pickle too?"

I hope the joke will detract from the charged moment as Anton looks a little dazed. Did he feel that charge too? It felt like sexual electricity but something else too, something more, a little like when I pick up energy from touching objects only much more powerful. It's certainly left me feeling shaken. I settle for stroking the dogs instead.

"Do you have a card?" Anton asks.

"A card?" My mind goes instantly blank. Like a calling card?

"For your business. You said you are a dog walker, yes?"

I'm sure I'd just said I was dog walking but I'm not about to let a minor cultural misunderstanding get in the way of a potential new client.

"Yes, I am," I reply confidently. I have a dog and I am walking therefore I am a dog walker. The logic is impeccable.

"Do you dog sit too?" he asks and I have to bat the

image out of my mind of me sitting on top of a pile of dogs.

"Yes, of course, any pet-care needs," I assert with confidence. "Well, cats and dogs mostly. If you have an elephant or tiger that might be a little out of my skill set."

Anton laughs and I feel ridiculously happy that I made him laugh.

"No elephants or tigers, no. Just the two dogs. I did have a neighbour I paid to watch them if I have to leave them for a job but she is unreliable. She let me down today in fact. If I leave the two of them alone they howl, and my other neighbour complains. Bringing them with me to a job doesn't always work out so well."

He shrugs and his rueful expression makes me smile. While it's a pain for him, I'm exceedingly glad his previous pet sitter is so unreliable.

"I'm afraid I don't have any cards on me," I reply, though I intend to remedy that as soon as I can. "But I can give you my number if you want to put it into your phone?"

I'm determined not to let my first potential paying customer get away for the lack of anything so trivial as the lack of a business card.

Juggling leads and dogs we manage to complete the phone number exchange.

"What is your job exactly?" I ask nosily, curious as to what has brought him to the chateau.

"I examine and appraise old documents and I also own a shop in Mirepoix for old books. Antiquarian books."

I'm about to comment on how fluent his English is but that would bring us back to the dead English wife and I'm not making that mistake when everything is going so well.

"Ah," I say, curious about his reason for visiting the chateau, but as he doesn't volunteer any further information I'll have to wait and ask the others later. "I'd better let you get on, I suppose. Just let me know when you want me... need me, I mean."

Yep, I have a definite case of foot-in-mouth syndrome today. Heat creeps up my neck and warms my cheeks but I'm hoping the nuance of that particular expression has escaped him.

"It was very nice to meet you Daisy," Anton replies formally.

"You too Anton," I smile. "And your lovely dogs."

As I walk away, I can't help feeling an inner tug back towards them, like an invisible cord is drawing me in. Feeling decidedly unsettled, I turn my mind to the more practical problem of how I'm going to get around the area for the jobs I pick up. Never mind. I'll find a way, I'm sure. I'll consult the hive mind at the guesthouse. To be honest, I hadn't envisaged picking up jobs this soon but I'm not going to turn it down.

JoJo doesn't know much more about Anton when asked, but Poppy fills me in when she pops in later that day.

The chihuahuas go into their ecstatic welcome routine which involves a lot of dancing on their hind legs and chattering to me, and Pickwick nudges forward slightly more sedately. Flump also joins in the rapturous welcome despite the fact he's been with me all day. Their unalloyed joy is very bolstering for the self-esteem. I have a mental flashback to Pickle, the depressed ginger dog, and feel a tug at my heart again.

"Anton? Yes, his shop in Mirepoix is gorgeous. I love browsing in there. He's very passionate about his work."

"Why was he at the chateau?"

"He comes from time to time, whenever we unearth new documents in the attic or find something that looks rare in the library. We've had some very lucrative finds in past years, so we get anything promising checked out now."

"Ah, well it looks like he might be my first paying customer. He's sort of offered me some work."

"Oh?" There's something a little too innocent about her tone but thankfully she doesn't tease me. After all, she knows I'm here to avoid making life decisions based on unavailable men and Anton is still clearly grieving. It's the strange tug I feel towards him and his dogs that's driving my curiosity. Perhaps it's just an empathy thing. I sense they are in need and maybe I have a part to play in helping them. That's all.

"He mentioned his wife too," I add casually, trying not to betray just how much I'd like more details. I don't think I pull it off though. I'm not sure people trying to sound casual and uninterested ever do.

"Ah yes, that was so sad. Claire was very much a part of the community and it was such a shock because she wasn't ill. A car accident eighteen months ago involving an icy road and a bridge. She helped us with raising money for Angeline's animal sanctuary – it's not just Anton who still misses her.

"Good that he's going to offer you some work though," Poppy says, examining me thoughtfully.

"Where does he live? In Mirepoix itself above the shop?" I turn my mind to more pertinent information, to the things I really do need to know, not the stuff that's none of my business.

"No, if I recall, he has a house between here and Mirepoix on the edge of a hamlet."

"I'm just wondering how I'm going to get to my jobs," I shrug. "I really hadn't expected to get a job so soon or appreciated the distances involved between the villages, but I certainly don't want to turn down my first paying client, especially as it could turn out to be a regular job. I'm assuming public transport isn't exactly an option? I haven't noticed many bus stops or buses for that matter."

"You assume correctly but don't worry, I can always give you lifts to start with," Poppy replies.

"Yes, with all that free time you have Poppy!" I reply dryly. "No, you're too busy as it is. I'll have to find another solution."

"Well, there are some spare bikes at the chateau I suppose," Poppy says with all the enthusiasm of a non-cycler. "I think a couple are in good shape and Leo's sister had one that might be the right size for you."

"That would be fine," I say. "If you really think it would be okay for me to borrow it."

"Of course. I'll ask Leo later but I'm positive it will be fine."

I remember belatedly that Leo's sister also died in tragic circumstances and have a lingering doubt whether it will be okay for me, using her bicycle. Sometimes my ability to pick up other people's energetic residue from objects can be a little disturbing…

Chapter Three

"We need not think alike to love alike."
Francis David

There's a technical name for it. It's called *psychometry*, this phenomenon of picking up energy or memories from objects, usually objects that have a strong emotional significance to the owner. Most people don't believe in it and that's fine with me. Well, mostly fine.

I wasn't really given a choice about whether to believe it as it started when I was very young, before I knew there was anything unusual about it. I'd pick things up and say they felt happy or sad when I was a toddler. When I got a bit older I'd tell stories about the people who used to own the objects I was holding. That was when my parents started to freak out a bit. Maybe other parents would've assumed they had a budding author in the family but because of my mother's history with her own mother it was a very contentious issue.

My grandmother had a similar gift to me, as well as a few others that my mother refused to let her talk to me about. If it was in our genes I don't know, but the gift – or ability or phenomenon, depending on how you view it – completely skipped my mother who took herself off to the local church youth group, became more and more religious, and increasingly viewed all such things as works of the devil. She refused to let Gran talk to me about it so we simply stopped talking in front of Mum and talked in secret instead.

Personally, I could never understand how feeling energy could be evil because it just happened naturally. It's not like I joined a cult or a coven or anything. My mother's assumption that I'd been born evil, or was wilfully doing things just to upset her, hurt me. I'm not sure how sensing energy is any different to being an empath, sensitive to other people's moods and feelings. We're all beings with electromagnetic fields after all. I see what I can do as a kind of extension of that. Because I grew up able to do it, it's not a weird phenomenon to me. Unfortunately I learnt the hard way that it's extremely weird to most people.

I quickly learnt to stop sharing if I picked something up, unless someone actually asked me. I'd try to control my facial muscles to conceal I was experiencing anything at all. I didn't like feeling that I had to bury this part of myself, this gift that was as natural as breathing, yet I didn't like being punished by my mother for something I couldn't control, or being bullied and ostracised at school.

Ever sensitive to the accusations that I must be a fraud, it has never occurred to me to try to profit from my 'gift' or whatever it is – I'm never sure how to classify it really. It's just kind of a part of me, that's all.

In my teens I did a bit of reading about psychometry and tried to read about energy generally, including quantum entanglement and quantum biology and lots of science that was way beyond me intellectually but which left me with a sense that maybe I wasn't a freak. Perhaps one day science may have an answer to explain how I can do what I can do. It certainly left me believing that we aren't totally separate living beings, adrift on a world of dead matter, but that everything is interconnected and everything is energy.

In the absence of an explanation that made sense to me, I made up my own definition: that in picking up the sensations attached to a treasured object it is a little like I'm sensing an energetic memory, a kind of residue of energy left behind. People often say they feel 'atmospheres' in rooms where events connected with strong emotion have occurred and this isn't that much different. All the same, I rarely get the same reaction from touching people. The memory of the energy surge I received when I took Anton's hand still reverberates through me, distracting me from all other thoughts. I can't help wondering if it's meant to mean something.

Anton. Hmmm. My preoccupation with him and his dogs lately, the strange tug I'm feeling, is just compassion, that's all. He's clearly still living in the aftershock of his wife's death. He's unavailable.

Which is irrelevant because so am I.

I can appreciate his sexy-professor attractiveness and charming smile that makes me feel warm inside without romanticising him. It's just an objective observation.

Still, my thoughts stray to him more over the next few days of dog walks, bed making, and laundry than I'd care to admit, and when I finally get a text from him one evening asking for my help, I'm surprised by the depth of the relief I feel. Relief because it's my first paying job but also because I'm curious to see him again, to understand why I had that strange reaction to him.

I've enjoyed the fast pace of the guesthouse work and living in a busy household with lots of people and dogs coming and going at all hours. It means I don't have time to become too introspective or worry if I've made the right decision coming out here. Taking the dogs for walks to the lake has been even more enjoyable because it's given me time to think, while the peace at the lakeshore and laughing at the antics of the dogs has made me feel like I'm slowly unwinding inside. I hadn't realised how tightly wound I was when I left London. This feels like a good place to try to stop doing and being what everyone else expects me to be, and to work out what it is I actually want in life. If it isn't sensible or 'normal' then so be it. I'm too old to care if my parents don't approve. Well, okay, maybe I still care a bit what they think, otherwise I'd have told them the truth about quitting my job already, but I'm determined I'm not going to live my life by what they think I should be doing anymore. I still feel uncomfortable when I remember what happened with Scott but I've decided to do my best to put all that behind me.

On the whole there has been so much going on, though thankfully no Foreign Legion soldiers in ditches with machine guns yet, so I haven't let myself get too self-indulgently morose about it. Meeting Callum O'Connor left me a little starstruck but I'm gradually coming around to the idea that he and JoJo are actually real people. Really nice people, in fact. They're the first celebrities I've really met, or at least known well enough to have a cup of tea with.

It's after the guests have gone to bed and I've helped JoJo with the clearing up that my phone pings with an alert for a text from Anton.

I can't help the smile that spreads over my face when I read it.

Dear Daisy, this text is from Pickle and Squeaker. We would very much like you to come to our house to play with us and take us for walks and things. The 'things' mostly involve giving us treats, in case you didn't realise. Anton will tell you we only get two treats each day, but it's actually supposed to be four each. He's always forgetting so we thought we had better text you so you don't forget too. Can you come to look after us tomorrow for the day, starting at 9am? There are more dates too which we expect Anton will tell you about but we thought you really needed to know about the treat thing most of all. Regards and licks from the dogs.

"Hot date?" Cal enquires casually, leaning back in

his kitchen chair and resting his arm around JoJo's shoulders.

"That would depend on your definition of a hot date," I reply, smiling. "It's a text from my first client actually."

"Anton asked you out on a date?" JoJo's eyebrows shoot up.

"No…" I feel my cheeks warm up. I could have phrased that better. "I mean, it's not a date at all; it's work."

"It's like that, is it?" Cal teases me, chuckling, and my cheeks burn a little hotter. I'm still a little in awe of him to be honest, which isn't helping on the blushing front.

"Stop teasing her." JoJo rolls her eyes and swats him playfully on the arm.

"It's not like anything," I reply as patiently as I can manage. "In fact, the text isn't even from him; it's from his dogs. Well, you know, him writing as though it's from his dogs."

"Aw, how sweet," JoJo coos, and I can't help smiling my agreement. Now it's Cal's turn to raise his eyebrows sceptically as if to imply there is definitely more to this than I'm admitting.

"It should be a good job for me. It's going to be at least one or two days a week hopefully and I might get some jobs through the cards and flyers Leo says I can put up in the vet practice reception area." I try to shift the focus of the conversation onto growing my new business and ignore the undeniable frisson I'm feeling at the thought of seeing Anton again. I'm not going to let anything derail my plan to rebuild my life. He's attractive, fact. I'm a young woman with hormones, fact. Neither of those facts actually signifies anything.

"So what brought on the idea for a change in career then, Daisy?" Cal asks.

I pretend not to notice JoJo subtly nudging him in the ribs. I'd assumed she would've got all the details from Poppy and filled him in but he wasn't here when I first arrived and I'm sure they have more important things to talk about than me. Or should that be, more important things to do than talk, if the radiant glow on JoJo's face is anything to go by.

"I just fancied a change of scene. A fresh start and all that, you know," I say vaguely.

And I totally humiliated myself in my last job by literally chasing after a client of the hotel I worked for, kind of a big no-no as far as Human Resources are concerned. Oh, and he turned out to be a married client at that. So I thought I'd better get far, far away before I completely lost all my marbles and I'm trying desperately to hold on to the remaining few I have… is what I don't say.

"Yes, we know what you mean," JoJo says firmly. "It's great that you're picking up work already. The admin fairies are going to have their work cut out to get your paperwork in order."

I smile gratefully at her; her reputation as an organiser and administrative whizz has been firmly impressed on me by Poppy. I'm grateful for all the help I can get, tackling the rules and regulations of a new country. "It's just as well I believe in fairies then. Any particular beverage these fairies prefer?"

"Crème de cassis I believe," JoJo replies solemnly and Cal shakes his head at us both as though we've lost the plot.

"Okay thanks, I'll bear it in mind." I grin. "Right, I'd better be off to bed. I've got an early start tomorrow to get to this job. I'm not entirely sure how long it's going to take me to cycle there so I'm going to allow lots of time. Can I help you with any of the breakfast prep for the guests before I leave in the morning, JoJo?"

"It's okay. You can leave it to me – I won't dock your pay." She laughs. "Seriously, it's fine, Cal's here to help me now. He needs to do some menial work to keep his feet firmly on the ground, especially when he's been filming and everyone is telling him how wonderful he is."

Cal pretends to look wounded but pulls JoJo into a close embrace.

"Just go off to your job tomorrow and enjoy playing with doggies all day. I'm half tempted to quit here and join you," JoJo says.

I know she's not serious. She loves running the guesthouse and helping Cal plan menus for the restaurant, plus she gets time to play with dogs too.

"Well, as I'm not being paid anything I can't really afford to take a pay cut so I'm very relieved. Unless you were thinking of docking the food you give me of course." I pull an expression of mock horror.

"We wouldn't be that cruel," JoJo replies.

"Thanks," I reply wholeheartedly. The food here really is exceptional and as many ingredients as possible are sourced from local farms, and some even come from the guesthouse's own vegetable patch. "Hopefully Leo might have another potential client for me too, someone he knows who needs help looking after her dog when she has to go for medical appointments, but I know it'll take time to get a business established. I'm extremely grateful for food and a roof over my head in the meantime."

"In business terms at least you don't have overheads to speak of," Cal contributes. "Particularly if you're cycling to jobs."

"Apart from insurance I think my main overheads are going to be dog treats." I head towards the back door and my barn sleeping quarters, aware that, as friendly as they are being, they would probably prefer to have some time alone together. "I intend to bribe my way to success."

I was only half joking about the bribery. I'm determined to win Pickle over. I want to comfort him, to make him happy again. I'm cycling towards Mirepoix the next day and lamenting that cycling seems to use different muscles from walking and bed making. Anton's face flashes into my mind as I cross the bridge over the river at Moulin Neuf and follow his directions to his home. The vibrant sunflower fields and bright blue sky do a lot to lift my spirits and the journey isn't that arduous once I get warmed up, at least there are no hills to negotiate.

I turn towards the Pyrenees that loom over the skyline. Comforting will be for dogs only, not for vulnerable, unavailable widowers. I've had a few relationships over the years where I've tried too hard with someone who just wasn't that into me. I deserve to be someone's sole romantic focus, or main relationship focus. That's what Angie tells me and I know she's right. My desire for connection has led me to make mistakes, but doesn't everyone? She always used to say I was a hopeless romantic and I'd retort that it was exactly the opposite and I was a hopeful romantic.

I thought she was wrong when she said I had a pattern and that it was a self-esteem thing. I'm still not totally sold on her theory; I mostly think I've been unlucky, though I know my relationship with my mum has affected my self-esteem. But if she's right that it is a pattern then the way to break it must surely be to abstain from men and focus on myself for a while. I know what it's like to be the one who is more loving than loved.

Not anymore. There's always a choice to be made, a conscious decision to be made. I'm not a helpless victim of my pheromones. Just because I feel attracted to someone doesn't mean I need to, or should, explore that attraction.

I'm so deep in thought I almost miss the turning to Anton's house. It's an elegant, old farmhouse built of soft creamy stone with pale-green wooden shutters. It's the kind of property I'd expect from him. Elegant but unpretentious. I mentally steel myself to avoid touching any antiques. I can shield myself in advance if I make

the effort and I really want to be completely professional for my first job.

Anton is dressed smartly again, his smart jacket and
open-neck shirt revealing a tantalising glimpse of
tanned chest.

His smile seems to hold a touch of amusement but
maybe I'm imagining it because he turns away to call
Pickle. Squeaker has already come running and puts her
paws up onto my legs, only really able to reach my knees.
She extends her nose to sniff towards the pockets of my
shorts for liver treats, her stubby little tail wagging madly.

Pickle, however, doesn't materialise.

Anton's face creases in concern. "I'm sorry, I'm
going to have to leave you now. I have a long drive
ahead. Pickle knows the signs I'm leaving and goes into
a sulk. He's probably hiding under my bed."

He looks so guilty I can't help reaching out to touch
him lightly on the forearm.

"It'll be okay. I'll take care of him, I promise."

Anton looks distractedly at my hand on his arm.
There's a micro expression of emotion that flits across
his face too quickly for me to decipher it. I instantly
remove my hand, feeling flustered.

It's difficult for me to suppress the urge to comfort.
I'm naturally a tactile person as well as being generally

empathic, so I can often pick up on others' emotions. I don't usually feel them quite so intensely though. Or care as much as if they were my own. In the same way I'd initially grown up assuming everyone could feel whether objects were happy or sad, I assumed everyone could pick up on other people's feelings and felt a desire to nurture and comfort. I really wish they did; it would make for a far less cruel world.

Yet the desire I feel to comfort now is intense and primal. Ignoring it is difficult, as it tries hard to push through the need for social propriety and the personal space of a virtual stranger.

Instead I sigh inwardly and stare awkwardly down at the old wooden floor, polished and stained so the natural grain of the oak gleams. Focusing on the wood helps me to let go of the desire to hug Anton. I must get better at filtering myself.

Anton hesitates, glancing towards the wooden staircase and I realise with relief that he hasn't noticed anything odd about my reaction but is worrying about Pickle.

"Honestly, you go, it'll be fine," I say. "I'll take care of them. Did you leave me a crib sheet about the dogs' likes and dislikes?"

"A crib sheet?" Anton frowns.

"Sorry, I mean the information you were going to leave regarding the dogs," I explain. I must remember not to use too many English idioms. "It helps to know when I'm walking the dogs if they hate cyclists or joggers or have a fondness for chasing squirrels, that sort of thing."

"Oh yes, I have it in the kitchen. I'll go then." Anton picks up his old leather briefcase as I stand, wrapping my arms around my body, resisting the urge to hug him goodbye.

"I can text you updates if you like?" I pick up a squirming Squeaker so she doesn't escape out of the front door with Anton. She doesn't seem to hold it against me, turning to give me an enthusiastic lick.

"Yes, texts would be good. Thank you Daisy." His mouth quirks into a semblance of a smile and then, with another backward glance up the stairs to where Pickle is still apparently sulking, he leaves the house.

I exhale some of the tension I'm feeling once the door shuts behind Anton.

"Hi Pickle sweetheart," I call up the stairs. "I'll be in the kitchen with Squeaker eating treats if you want to come and join us."

I decide giving him a little space might be best. To let him come to me.

Though after twenty minutes I'm second guessing

myself and suddenly worried he might be sick or hurt and here I am in the kitchen ignoring him.

I head upstairs, followed by an enthusiastic Squeaker, and push one door open after another ignoring the bathroom, one spare room with an unoccupied feel and one that's clearly being used as a study. Eventually I find Anton's bedroom and try to ignore my curiosity, instead getting down on my hands and knees to peer under the bed.

A pair of baleful eyes surrounded by ginger fur glares at me from the shadows.

"Hey sweetie. How are you today? Bad day, eh? I understand, we all have those. I just needed to know you're okay."

I put out my hand to him tentatively and he retreats further under the bed to where I can't reach him.

I place a treat on the floor but he ignores it. Then I decide to leave a trail of small liver treats going out from under the bed to the door and to the stairs, making sure Squeaker is under my arm and unable to hoover them up.

"Come downstairs when you're ready and we'll go for a nice walk, okay?" I call over my shoulder and then head down the stairs to the kitchen to make a cup of tea. I have no idea if my approach will work but I don't have a Plan B up my sleeve if not so the tea will give me thinking time.

I'll just have to wait. What I really want is to scoop Pickle up in my arms and give him a cuddle, much in the way I feel the urge to hug Anton.

I'm pleased to find Earl Grey tea in the kitchen and a note from Anton to tell me there's fresh milk in the fridge. He's obviously clued up on the weird ways of the Anglais, adding milk to Earl Grey tea.

His note is in English. His texts so far have been in English too, in spite of my replying to him in French. But if I abandon using French and just use English from now on doesn't that look a bit presumptuous? I've been told it's all about 'making an effort' but it seems a bit daft me writing in French and him writing in English.

I've made myself a cup of tea, topped up the dog water bowl with fresh water and I'm on the floor playing tug of war with Squeaker who is surprisingly strong. What she lacks in size she makes up for in terrier tenacity.

It's then I spy a ginger head with floppy ears peeking around the door. He's pretending not to be all that interested but he clearly is. I restrain myself from making too much of a fuss and scaring him off.

"Hi Pickle, want to join us?" I ask casually.

"Squeaker and I are thinking of going out for a nice walk by the river. How about it? It says in your dad's note that you love to swim."

He forgets to keep up his nonchalant act and trots into the room. He still eyes me a little warily but condescends to sit down next to me. He has his back to me but is pressed up against my leg, a gesture I find strangely touching. My heart goes out to this little dog who wants to be loved just as much as he wants to keep everyone at arm's length.

Hmmm... yes, I know how he feels and we sit in companionable silence for ten minutes, just being together while I keep Squeaker occupied with her tuggy toy. I'm reluctant to break contact with Pickle but in the end my left leg goes to sleep so I have to shift.

"Time for a walk I think." I get to my feet and both Pickle and Squeaker trot happily to the door where their leads are kept.

We enjoy a lovely hourlong walk along a riverbank path and through the fields. I keep Pickle on an extendable lead as per Anton's instructions. Pickle is a water baby apparently and can be a bit stubborn when it comes to leaving the river behind to go home. The countryside in this part of France has a wildness to it, in line with the craggy Pyrenees mountain range we keep in sight for most of the walk. I remember what Poppy said about wolves and bears and while I know it's incredibly rare to spot a wolf this far from the high mountain slopes, I'm still alert to the sounds and movements in hedges around me.

The dogs are nicely tired out from the walk and when we get back they stop only for a long, thirsty drink from their bowl before flopping into a dog bed together in the kitchen. There are two beds side by side but they choose to squash in together in one. Sweet. I refill their water and then make myself another cup of tea, ready for a sit-down and catch-up with my messages while the dogs sleep.

I open up the text app on my phone as it's showing new unread messages. One is from Angie.

You know who was in the hotel lobby early this morning, asking for you? He didn't have a reservation. I think he came solely with the purpose of seeing you. I told him you were in France and he asked if you were on your own or with someone. I had to make it clear you'd left and quit your job and he didn't seem happy.

He asked if he could have your contact details and I said I wasn't sure if that would be okay so he's given me his number to pass on to you instead. I'll send it separately. He also asked me to make sure I told you that he's separated from his wife! I think he must be keen on you. xx

My heart is beating rapidly. Maybe I'm not quite as deluded as I thought I was? I'd begun to wonder if I'd just imagined the whole thing. That I'd seen what I wanted to see. I'd even wondered if Scott had said 'yes' when I'd asked him out because I'd put him on the spot and he didn't want to hurt my feelings.

My spirits have surged with reading the text but I deliberately suppress the urge to compose a message to Scott. I sigh and get up, pacing around the kitchen, nerves taut. Nothing has changed; he flirted with me while he was still married.

But what if he's left his wife because he felt a connection with me? a traitorous thought whispers at the back of my mind, and I'm appalled at myself for thinking it.

"Stop it, stop it, stop it Daisy," I mutter. Pickle opens a sleepy eyelid to watch me but Squeaker is lying on her back, all four legs in the air and snoring quietly, occasionally twitching her tail as she dreams.

I wonder briefly if Anton has the dog sitter equivalent of a nanny cam in his house and decide I need to stop talking to myself, just in case. So, how do I reply? Do I let him have my new French mobile number? I'd had to switch to a French network so potential clients can ring me without racking up exorbitant phone bills.

I was right first time though. Nothing has changed. Scott is married. He was married when he flirted with me, when he said yes to going out with me…

It wasn't a lie exactly, more a lie of omission. Still, I can't quite bring myself to reply to Angie just yet. Maybe I'll sleep on it. I can't get it out of my mind though. Typical! Just as I do my best to move forward I feel a cord from the past, trying to pull me back again. Not that I want to go back, but it's unsettling none-theless. I reply to a message about a potential new job and half-heartedly try to read a novel I brought with me. I'm still on the same page thirty minutes later though so after a brief stint on social media, posting the photos I took earlier of the sunflower fields, and some texts to Anton with photos from our morning walk, I take the dogs for another long walk. They have recharged their batteries with their snooze and are more than up for it. Exercise suits my restless mood. What with all this walking and cycling I'm certainly going to be very fit by the end of the summer.

My new life. New possibilities… So why have I bothered to save Scott's number in my phone 'just in case'. In case of what? My irrational behaviour irritates me but the exercise helps me get the frustration out of my system to some degree.

Once we're back in the house I realise Anton is due home soon and then discover Pickle has vanished somewhere. Of course, now Anton is going to think Pickle has been miserable and hiding all day rather than out on walks with me or sitting in the kitchen with me quite companionably. I go looking for him, telling myself I'm not snooping, just looking for Pickle, and it's impossible not to see things as I search. Impossible not to wonder about the man who lives here or the woman who lived here with him who is both absent yet surely present in so many ways – a sofa chosen together, decorating choices, and thousands of other barely perceptible ways. Anton clearly likes to cook and unsurprisingly is a reader with a huge to-be-read pile on his bedside table with books in both French and English.

Eventually I find Pickle not in the bedroom but in the room being used as a study. He's underneath the desk.

"Hi Pickle. Don't worry, he'll be back soon, I promise." I address his solemn eyes. He still feels sad to me but he's not sulking or cross about my being with him at least. "We'll become good friends, you and I. I do understand a little of what you're going through, I promise. We're going to have lots of lovely walks by the river to keep you cool this summer."

I glance at the desk and see papers and books piled up or left open, all of which seem to be on the subject of local legends, folklore, and witchcraft. Interesting. So interesting in fact that I'm only stirred from my perusal by the sound of excited yapping from Squeaker and the front door opening. Pickle and I both make it onto the landing at the same time as Anton, followed closely by an ecstatic Squeaker.

"I was just looking…" My cheeks flush unaccountably. "Looking for Pickle, I mean, checking on him. Though he's been in the kitchen with me for most of the day when we've not been out walking. He's been fine, really."

At that moment Pickle turns tail and trots straight past me back into the study. Typical.

Anton raises an eyebrow and laughs at my consternation.

"It is okay. I could see in your photos that he was happy." He shrugs. "And you are welcome to look around. I am not hiding secrets of the State."

After making a fuss of Squeaker, Anton pushes open the study door and gestures for me to follow him inside. Squeaker follows, tail and bottom both wagging madly.

"Any problems?" he asks, crouching down to encourage Pickle back out from under the desk.

I follow him in. "No it was fine, honestly. I think I made a little progress with Pickle. I suppose it's early days though."

"He likes you, I can tell." Anton looks up at me and smiles that warm smile at me that threw me so much the first time.

"Er… so all this is to do with your appraisal work?" I gesture to the books and papers.

"Not exactly, no." Anton gets back up to his feet. "I'm working on a book about the myths and legends of the area, where they originated and which ones have endured."

"Really? That sounds fascinating."

"I'm glad you think so." He treats me to another warm smile.

"I don't know where you find the time to write a book on top of keeping your shop open and carrying out your appraisal trips."

Anton shrugs. "The shop is only open part-time and we are not so busy. Often I have time to carry out my research there. I sometimes come across interesting material in my work. I started the project to keep myself busy in the evenings. You know…"

He seems more subdued now and I realise the

significance of what he's telling me – or trying to let me know without having to spell it out. This book started out as a grief project, a much-needed distraction from the chasm of nights alone.

"I understand," is all I say in response, trying to fill my voice with as much kindness as possible.

Anton half turns away and picks up a book from his desk, seeming keen to push uncomfortable emotions to one side and move to the firmer, more intellectual ground of his passion for history.

"We can learn so much from the objects of the past," he says, a gleam in his eye. I almost laugh. I want to tell him he's preaching to the converted but as a conversation opener that's never gone down too well. Sceptics don't usually bother me, as long as they don't make a point of haranguing me, but I realise with a pang that Anton's opinion really does matter to me. I really want him to like me.

After all, he's a client; of course I want him to like me. Is there something more to it though? I dismiss the idea. I'm feeling compassion for him, that's all. Yet the strength of my emotions around Anton, on a day when Scott has basically asked for my phone number makes me wonder if what I feel, what I *felt*, for Scott was more infatuation for the man I believed him to be.

I watch Anton showing me some of his recent

acquisitions and find I'm genuinely really interested. He's writing about the things that lie beneath the surface. He's clearly a man of depth and has real passion for his subject. I like seeing him so animated. It's like a snapshot of Anton pre-bereavement.

Also, I already feel that there's something special about this area, more than the sunshine and the sense of community, and finding out about its past, its legends, and ancient, long-buried tales really appeals to me.

"Like this, it's an old… how do you say… botanical book with natural and herbal remedies."

"It looks very old." I eye the volume warily, sensing a kind of energy from it already.

"Here, you can look if you like."

Before I can say anything he's placed the volume in my hands, the swiftness of his enthusiasm taking me by surprise.

I feel a powerful jolt of accumulated emotions – warmth, love, pain, and sorrow, and a deep fear… I blink hard and breathe slowly, trying to let the emotions wash over me without taking any of them on. I carefully place the book back onto the table, shaken; I've felt this kind of energy before.

"It's a grimoire, isn't it? A witch's grimoire?" The question has escaped my lips before I can stop it. I'm too caught up in the moment and the connection to the past.

He gazes at me curiously.

"You know the word grimoire?" I ask, wondering if it's a language issue or a 'me' issue.

"Yes, I know it – it's a French word. You looked very… strange when you held it, like you were reading with your eyes closed. How did you know it belonged to a witch? I didn't tell you." His tone isn't sceptical as such, more curious.

"I felt it." It's my turn to shrug now. I really don't want to be having this conversation, not with an important new client. I've had too many people turn on me in the past, sometimes unexpectedly and very hurtfully so. But, on the other hand, if I'm going to find a way to be my authentic self somehow, I don't want to lie. It feels important to me that I don't lie to Anton. "I've touched similar books before and they have a certain… energy signature. The owner may well have just been a healer – she did good in the community – but I can't shake the feeling she was persecuted as a witch."

I edge back from the book. I don't want to touch it again. There was too much emotion attached to it and properly shielding myself mentally takes time. I wish I hadn't let myself get so caught up in the moment.

"I think we are maybe having a translation issue…"

Anton frowns, puzzled. "How could you feel it? Sorry, perhaps it is an idiom I have not come across?"

I cross my arms over my chest, feeling edgy and wishing I'd never started the conversation. I could just pretend Anton is right, that it was a translation mistake and invent something to make any potential awkwardness go away. Yet there's a stubborn streak inside me that refuses to retract the words. It belongs to the young girl who was fed up with being punished for something she couldn't control, the teenager who had to swallow down her anger when she was spat at and called a weirdo, or the young woman who was rejected by a boyfriend for being too odd; for all those parts of me – and maybe because of the nature of the book I was holding and the persecution its bearer suffered – I am going to stand by what I said and what I felt.

"No, you understood correctly, I meant that I felt it, felt the energy." I continue to hug my body, my arms forming a defensive shield. "I felt the energy of the woman who owned the book. You know archaeologists have sometimes used people like me, psychometrists, to helps them locate relics. It might be an odd concept if you've not come across it but maybe it's not all that surprising when you consider we are electromagnetic beings, and even Einstein came to believe in the end that everything was energy, even matter. If machines can pick up electromagnetic currents from trees and plants then why not objects too?"

"But you… you are not a machine taking a reading." Anton frowns.

I'm not sure if it's the meaning of my words he's struggling to accept or that it's quite a complex translation. I rarely discuss my gift like this. I can't think what's come over me that I am choosing now with my brand new client to talk so openly about the gift I've tried to conceal for much of my life.

The courage I felt is draining away to be replaced with an edginess that propels me towards the door. I need to put some distance between me and this room, between me and Anton.

"Anyway, I really mustn't take up any more of your time," I say, making plain my intent to leave. "I must get back to the guesthouse to help with dinner preparations."

Anton immediately switches into polite and professional mode, pulling out his wallet to pay me and thanking me for coming.

At the front door I make a huge fuss of the dogs, not wanting to meet Anton's gaze, hoping against hope that I won't see any loss of respect there. It upsets me that the smiley, animated Anton, so excited to show me his project, has been replaced by his usual, more measured and reserved persona. It would upset me far more to feel I've fallen in his estimation, which is crazy. After all, I barely know him.

The bike ride home does little to relieve my mood, though being in motion and pedalling hard does help me work the edginess out of my body. The image of Anton and the two dogs on the doorstep seeing me off is niggling at me and I'm having to ignore the temptation to turn back to try to erase the awkwardness, to get back to the easy connection of earlier, before my 'gift' took us to a stranger place.

It's been a strange day. I barely think about Angie's message until I get to bed, yet even then, as I toss and turn, unable to settle down to sleep, somehow it's Anton's face that haunts me, not Scott's, and underlying it all is a sense I'm where I need to be and it's time to stop hiding. When I do drift into sleep, I swear I feel something of the courage of the woman whose grimoire I held. I dream or sense or hear her whispering to me, soul to soul, telling me it's time to grow into the woman I'm meant to be.

Unapologetically me.

Chapter Four

"Trust your intuition and be guided by love."
Charles Eisenstein

Hi Angie, thanks for letting me know. Men, eh? What is it with their sense of timing? I think the sensible thing to do is have a clean break. He might be separated but he's still married and I'm trying to get a fresh start here. I want to make a go of it. I really like it here. Maybe I'll regret saying no but I think it's the right decision. Thanks for passing on his number though.

Anywaaaaay... how are things with you? Did you go for my old job?

D xx

T he next day Poppy, JoJo, and I are all taking an afternoon break in the garden. Poppy and JoJo are having a yoga session and I decide to join in. It's been a while since I made it to a yoga class but I do remember how relaxed they always used to leave me. And relaxed is something I'm definitely not today. I've decided I'm definitely not going to contact Scott. I know it's the right thing to do but still I'm feeling off somehow and kind of out of sorts.

Running out on Anton before he had a chance to fully process what I was trying to tell him yesterday hasn't helped. I still don't understand why I felt the need to go into quite so much detail with him. I'm worried he's thinking I'm really odd now. A bit of recentring is just what I need.

Flump, Peanut, Treacle, and Pickwick have joined us and are having great fun trying to use us as climbing frames. It's a little disconcerting to be in the downward dog position only for Flump to walk between my back legs and lick my nose, but I get why Poppy lets them join in. With the chihuahuas trying to scale her legs and Pickwick throwing his ball onto anyone foolish enough to be in a lying down position, soon we are all giggling.

"I say the humour element of the dogs joining in is just as good for us as the actual yoga," Poppy asserts and flops into a sitting position on her mat, giving up for the moment and throwing Pickwick's ball for him.

"I certainly feel better for it." I sit cross-legged and stroke Peanut, who has hopped onto my lap for a cuddle, claiming the spot before anyone else can.

"Yes, I thought you seemed a bit fed up earlier. Anything wrong?" Poppy gazes at me shrewdly.

"A few things," I say, looking down at Peanut on my lap. "Scott turned up at my old workplace and wanted to pass on the message that he was separated from his wife. Oh, and he wanted to pass on his phone number. Angie, my friend, wouldn't give him my number but it's possible if he asks Becca she might do it, just to stir things up."

"Really?" Poppy asks. "I can't believe you've taken this long to tell us about it!"

"So, have you sent him a message?" JoJo asks.

I shake my head.

"Are you going to?" Poppy joins in the interrogation.

"No." I shake my head again. "I don't think so anyway. But that's not the only thing bothering me at the moment. Something… weird happened yesterday at Anton's."

"Weird how?" JoJo takes a swig of water from her

bottle. I don't know how she manages to look so radiant while Poppy and I are beaded with perspiration.

I hesitate, not sure how much to say. I don't know JoJo well enough to know if she's likely to judge me because of it. Obviously I don't know Anton well enough either but that conversation happened in the heat of the moment.

"Was it to do with your gift?" Poppy asks casually, stretching out her legs. "It's okay – I told JoJo about it."

Seriously? I raise my eyebrows, but don't say anything; there wouldn't be much point. Poppy always errs on the side of giving people the benefit of the doubt which is very nice and all, but my experience of people's reactions have varied from sceptical and patronising to virtually accusing me of being in league with the devil. It's often impossible to know how someone will react. I suppose she knows JoJo very well though, and the echoes of the dreams I had last night about not being afraid to stand tall and be myself, to grow into the woman I'm meant to be, still resonate with me now.

At least, I'm pretty sure it was in my dreams. Last night is still a little fuzzy in my mind.

"It's fine, Daisy, don't worry. I'm pretty open-minded about things like that," JoJo says and I relax a little. "You know Cal is a bit of a science geek on the quiet and he's always telling me about some latest quantum biology or quantum physics experiment that backs up something that previously people have believed but not been able to prove."

"Oh really? That sounds interesting," I say, encouraged. "It would be interesting to talk to him. I've tried reading up about it but I struggle to keep up with the science."

"Be careful. Once you get him going on the subject he'll never shut up." JoJo laughs. "He says the gap between science and spirituality is noticeably smaller than it used to be."

"What sort of things does he say science is now backing up?" I have to admit I'm both curious and pleasantly surprised. Generally, in spite of the reading I've done regarding the possible science backing up psychic phenomena I'm not used to a good reception from the scientifically minded, and they aren't interested in listening to me. They start from a closed-off mindset and don't listen to what I have to say.

"Oh, things like the electrical field around our bodies, that's generated by our heart reaching much further than previously realised, now they've got more sensitive equipment for picking these things up," JoJo says airily. "So I'm sure he'd say there may well be a scientific explanation for your gift, we just haven't found it yet. I mean, you're right aren't you, with the details you give? Poppy said you've always been spot on. Cal would say it would be statistically impossible for you to always be right, particularly if you knew nothing about the object previously. Therefore it's the more likely explanation that you are actually picking up on something, the same way that some people have a superior sense of smell, it's just that we don't understand why."

I like the sound of this side of Cal and I'd love to talk to him about his reading. Both he and JoJo are very down to earth and nice. I can see that JoJo was completely misrepresented by the media and I'm not at all surprised she ran away to France to get away from all the nasty gossip.

"Well I'm glad not everyone here will think I'm weird." I sigh and fill them in on what happened with Anton and the defensive way I'd reacted to try to explain myself.

"To be fair, you didn't give him much of a chance to react, if you rushed out immediately after," Poppy says. "And you don't actually know what he's thinking. Maybe he's more open-minded than you're fearing."

"Hmm, I suppose," I admit. "I've had a few upsetting past experiences that made me unwilling to stick around to find out, but I'm going to have to face him soon."

Peanut tilts her head back up at me, wondering why

the steady stream of fuss has stopped. I resume stroking her and she snuggles back into me.

"So you care what Anton thinks about you." Poppy smiles.

I shrug, rattled that she's picked up on it.

"He's my biggest client, so of course it matters what he thinks of me," I reply, my words sounding more than a tad defensive, even to me.

"Uh-huh." Annoyingly she just smiles and exchanges a look with JoJo.

"You should've heard what Cal thought of me when we first met," JoJo says. "I actually overheard him talking about me and let's just say it really wasn't good. He'd read all the bad press about me and even though he knows how the media works he was still sucked in by some of it."

"Really?" I raise my eyebrows. "And you forgave him?"

"Well he really is a god in the kitchen." She shrugs and beams. "Not to mention a few other rooms too. To be fair, we both misjudged each other a little at first and he did apologise."

"And look how they ended up," Poppy adds, her eyes gleaming a little with mischief.

"Stop what you're thinking right there. There's nothing like that going on. I just meant it was

83

awkward," I warn her. "For one thing, he's still a grieving widower. Secondly, I'm definitely focusing on myself for a while and can do without any messy complications. Oh, and thirdly, he's an important part of my business. He's probably going to be my biggest client." I pretend not to notice the looks exchanged between Poppy and JoJo. Instead, I get up to play with Flump and Pickwick who are always up for a bit of active play, chasing balls or toys or playing tug of war, while the chihuahuas and Barney tend to prefer cuddles on the whole. I don't know why their teasing is bothering me; I know they're only messing around but for some reason I feel deeply unsettled. I probably didn't do enough yoga.

"I expect Paul will view your 'no men' agenda as a challenge. Has he asked you out yet?" JoJo calls out after me.

"Oh yes, pretty much every time he bumps into me. He seems to know my dog walking routes and manages to be having a break at opportune moments," I say. "He really is thick-skinned, isn't he? At least out of all the dangers you warned me about I've only come across him and the Kamikaze-cat. No psychotic goats or Foreign Legion soldiers with guns. Not yet anyway."

She and Poppy laugh.

"Give it time," JoJo replies. "It's still early days."

"Won't he ever get tired of it?" I turn back and ask, while Pickwick drops a ball on my foot in case I've forgotten what's really important around here, namely a miniature Yorkshire terrier in need of a stick throwing machine, or failing that a human with a high tolerance threshold for terrier antics.

"If you mean will Pickwick get tired of you throwing his ball for him, the answer is no, not ever," JoJo says.

"And if I mean Paul asking me out?"

"The answer is still no," JoJo replies. "You're a challenge now. The only way to stop him is to get a boyfriend. Although that's not always a guarantee he'll stop." "Great," I mutter. At least Paul isn't a real threat to my mental equilibrium. He doesn't have hidden depths like some antiquarian booksellers I could mention; instead he has plenty of not so hidden shallows.

Putting aside my concerns about Anton's opinion of me and the nuisance of being considered a challenge for the local lothario, I'm actually starting to enjoy my life here. Over the next week I begin to discover just how much I love being able to work outdoors a lot of the time. I still get to have contact with people and I enjoy meeting and chatting with the guests here at the guesthouse. They tend to be a lot more laid-back than the stressed-out London business travellers I saw a lot of in my role as a hotel receptionist. The relaxed holiday vibe from the guesthouse clientele is catching.

Sure, some of the behind-the-scenes work is hard but doing it alongside Poppy and JoJo feels like hanging out with my best friends. Although Poppy and JoJo already have a very close bond, they have accepted me in as an equal third without question.

I'm also discovering that while I always considered myself to be a people person, I'm actually happier having some quiet time to myself working with dogs. I'm enjoying their uncomplicated company, their unconditional love, and the unrelenting enthusiasm they bring to everything they do. It's infectious, and uncomplicated is definitely what I need right now.

Though I'm unlikely to start spinning in circles and jumping up and down before I go out for a walk, I find I'm looking forward to our daily excursions more and more.

I know once we get into the really hot temperatures of late July and August I'll have to do most of my walking in the early morning or evening but for the moment the weather is just perfect. Blue skies all the way, and lakes and forests on my doorstep with the impressive peaks of the Pyrenees in the distance. What more could I ask for?

The sunshine feels like it's actually seeping through my skin and into my bones. Tension I didn't realise I was holding onto has begun to evaporate from my muscles, leaving me feeling lighter. I find I'm walking more slowly, no longer driven by the frenetic pace of London living, or someone tutting behind me in a shop because I'm taking a millisecond longer over my transaction than they think I should.

In short, adjusting to the slower pace of life in the South of France has been surprisingly easy. I suppose it hasn't been long; only a couple of weeks have gone by, although it feels like longer somehow. I've fallen into a pattern of dog walking in the sunshine, helping JoJo out in the guesthouse, and thankfully getting quite a bit of dog sitting and dog walking work from Anton, plus a few one-off pet sitting jobs referred via Leo's veterinary surgery.

I'm enjoying all the fresh air and sunshine, and things haven't been weird with Anton since the grimoire incident. Or at least, if he did think I acted very strangely he's too polite to actually say so, and in the meantime I've really grown to love Pickle and Squeaker. Pickle is starting to come out of his depressed shell and engages in play more than he used to but still has his moments, and Squeaker is just a delight, bouncing around full of joy and wanting to do whatever her big brother does.

One day, the week following the grimoire incident, I'm dog sitting for Anton at his home and second guessing whether I did the right thing in not replying to Scott when I notice Pickle attempting to steal the new silk-cotton-blend scarf I bought at the market. I'd stupidly left it within reach along with my handbag on the arm of the sofa. I act quickly, whisking it out of his reach, otherwise he'd take the scarf under the bed and it'd be a long while before I'd get it back. Unfortunately, Squeaker chooses that exact moment to jump up onto the sofa, thinking she's joining in a game. She lands on my phone, barking excitedly. The cover is closed thankfully so she won't scratch it but the unmistakeable sound alert of a text being sent from my phone alarms me.

One I've zipped the scarf into my bag I grab my phone to check.

Seriously? No, no, no….

I blink hard at the screen, unable to believe it. How on earth did Squeaker manage to send a text? And not any old text, a heart emoji – and she's sent it to Scott. I panic. Why isn't there an instant retrieve button when it comes to texting, or at the very least an 'are you really, really sure you want to send this?' option. I shouldn't have left the text message app open on the screen but really I'm not sure I could've foreseen this.

I bite my lip, wondering how I can fix the situation. What if he thinks I've changed my mind and I'm still interested?

Well why did you save his number onto your phone in the first place? a sensible and non-panicking part of my brain questions.

Because a week was a long time ago, and a tiny part of me wanted to save his number on my phone, just in case.

Of course, now this has happened I know for sure I shouldn't have. My reaction is one of horror, not of what might come of this. Funny how it took an excitable terrier to help me work it out. I absentmindedly stroke Squeaker who's looking at little anxious that she might have annoyed me.

"It's okay Squeaker sweetheart," I reassure her and stroke her behind her ears just how she likes it. "I know you were excited to see me again. I mean, it must've been at least thirty seconds since we had our last cuddle and I understand that's a very long time when you're a little dog."

My phone beeps with a reply, making me jump.

When I look at the phone screen I see a blowing-a-kiss emoji and one word:

Daisy?

Crap. How could he know it was from me? I bet Becca gave him my phone number when Angie wouldn't.

Once, I would've done anything to receive that kind of text from him. Yet however I felt then, I know how I feel now.

Not interested.

Not interested because the man I fell for didn't really exist outside of my mind. Not interested because lying by omission is still lying, in my mind.

Not interested because I was infatuated with a mirage.

If I've learnt anything from the thing with Scott it's that just because I feel a certain way doesn't mean I *have* to act on it or that I *should*. Sometimes the figurative mad dash to the airport and the grand declaration of love simply ends in tears, and not the happy kind.

If I needed a reminder not to fall for another unavailable man this is surely it. Why did I invest so much emotional energy in a mirage anyway? Because I was bored, I think. Bored and coasting in a job that supposedly ticked all the right boxes but didn't stretch me or satisfy me in any meaningful way. Bored, with too much time on my hands to chat to him, too much time to analyse our conversations afterwards and to daydream about what might happen.

I type a quick reply:

Yes this is Daisy. Sorry, I didn't mean to text. A dog stood on my phone – I know, weird but true!

I switch my phone off rapidly, before I can get drawn into a conversation – or even worse, before he can ring me and put me on the spot. As it is, he's hardly going to believe I'm telling the truth about the dog texting him. I probably wouldn't have done, but that was before I spent lots of time with the guesthouse dogs and realised just how much trouble a pack of pint-sized pups can get into. Scott is going to assume I texted him and then simply lost my nerve and backed out.

"You have no idea how complicated it is being a human." I roll my eyes at Squeaker who stares at me wide-eyed, the picture of innocence, and then I collapse back against the sofa cushions with a sigh. Squeaker looks up at me and tilts her head to one side in the universal and very cute 'dog does not compute' gesture.

"He's never going to believe you texted him,

Squeaker," I say to her despairingly. "*I* would never believe me. He'll simply assume I'm messing him about."

Pickle wanders over to me and looks up at me enquiringly, now over his sulk at losing out on snatching my scarf.

"Yes, you're quite right, Pickle and Squeaker. Humans should take a few tips from dogs. What more could anyone want than a warm place to sleep, cuddles, and food? Time to get over myself and hand out the treats. A cup of tea and some chocolate for me and one of your favourite duck chews each for both of you."

I get up and head into the kitchen, both dogs trotting at my heel, relieved I've stopped nattering and have mentioned the word *treats*. I've got used to talking to them and don't care if it's a path to insanity. I swear they understand more than we give them credit for. I go to the fridge where Anton keeps fresh milk to go with the Earl Grey tea bags he keeps in a pretty tin on the kitchen counter for me. He always leaves out a lovely bone china mug for me to use and often puts biscuits or a cake from the patisserie on the kitchen counter with a note that says 'Eat me'. The fact that, in spite of everything he has on his mind, he still takes the time to consider what I might need during the day is a thoughtfulness that really touches me.

At least talking to Squeaker today has helped me realise one thing for sure: I came to France to get away from Scott, to end my obsession with him, and it looks like it's worked. Now I just need to steer clear of romantic entanglements and my rehabilitation will be complete. Yes, I still crave that deep heart-to-heart connection but sorting my life out needs to be, *has* to be, my priority.

The following week, I'm looking into my bedroom mirror and trying to do something, anything, with my hair. It's even curlier than usual washed in the water here and the humidity we're starting to get at times with the summer weather makes it look more than a little wild. I give up in the end and scoop all the tumbling curls up into a ponytail which will be cool at least, even if it won't win me any points on style.

I'm liberally spraying on some perfume when Poppy wanders in.

"Oh, are you on your way out somewhere nice?" she asks. "I thought maybe we could do something together. Sorry I've not had more time for you since you got here – it's just been a bit manic with the chateau gallery and also opening up the barn restaurant for lunch at the weekends. Plus I've had quite a few animal portrait commissions; you know how I love painting them and time just seems to race away from me when I'm painting."

"It's fine, honestly. Yes, I know how incredibly busy you are. I would've loved to have spent some time together today but I have to work. Another time maybe?" I check my reflection in the mirror. I consider putting make-up on but surely then it would look like I was trying too hard? At least my skin is lightly tanned and my time outside has left me looking healthy, even if I am a little more freckled than I'd like. For the same reason I'm still wearing my usual denim shorts but I've put on one of my newer T-shirts in a lovely teal-blue shade that complements my auburn hair.

I can see Poppy's reflection in the mirror and notice her narrow her eyes.

"You're putting perfume on to walk dogs?" It sounds like more of an interrogation than a question.

My cheeks flush. "Well I'm not just walking the dogs. I have to go into the centre of Mirepoix, so I thought I should make more of an effort. Anton has his dogs with him at his bookshop and he wants me to walk them from there today."

"Oh I see, yes, it all makes sense now," Poppy teases.

I consider bluffing it out but denying any attraction only seems to sound like I'm protesting too much. Also, this is Poppy, and while Poppy often comes across as scatty when it comes to anything emotional, she's far more perceptive than most people realise. Annoyingly so, if you want to keep something hidden.

"So… I might like Anton a bit. It's only natural – he's an attractive man – but really, it's a waste of time. It's not like I'm ever going to do anything about it." I shrug as though it doesn't bother me. "You know I'm trying to sort my life out, a life without romantic entanglements. And anyway, he's a client which means he's off limits. Plus, I'm here to get over an unrequited crush, not start up a new one. Also, he's clearly still grieving his wife so…"

Poppy bursts out laughing. "Daisy, just how many excuses do you need? I think you might be trying to persuade yourself, not me."

I can't help smiling wryly in return. "You might be right." We both know I wouldn't be putting perfume on during the day for a dog walk otherwise and Poppy knows me too well for me to lie to her. "But there are so many reasons why it's not a good idea. I don't even know why I'm bothering with perfume; it's just an instinctive thing, I suppose. Are there rules about how long it is deemed seemly before you can ask out a widower anyway? It's not exactly something I've thought about before."

Poppy shrugs. "I think that might depend on the widower in question. And you're right, if he says 'no' things would be really awkward…"

"And then I've potentially lost my best customer, I know," I reply glumly. "The thing is, do you remember when I went out with that guy who was still obsessed with his ex, only I didn't realise until I'd fallen for him?"

"Yes, and didn't he call you by her name during sex once?" Poppy rolls her eyes.

"Worse than that," I admit, walking out into the courtyard with her where my bicycle is leaning against a wall. "Well, not worse exactly but at least that was an in-the-heat-of-the-moment thing. He actually told me when I broke up with him that I was definitely second best and he'd been 'settling'."

"He never did!" Poppy exclaims. "You didn't mention it."

I grimace. "I was too embarrassed to admit I'd put up with it for so long. Deep down I think I knew he was still in love with his ex and I kept thinking he'd get over her and be persuaded of my charms. But in this case, with Anton, even if he likes me back and even if I decide I'm staying… well, I'd have to be convinced he was really ready to move on otherwise I think I'd be concerned that I might be being compared and found lacking?"

Then I give myself a shake.

"I'm being ridiculous and way over thinking all this, Poppy. Please forget I said anything. I like Anton, I fancy him, but there are sooooo many reasons not to go there."

"Well, I suppose that would be the sensible approach. After all, you did come here to straighten yourself out," Poppy says kindly. She's not good at being stern. "New life, new career, no moping around after a man, or I'm supposed to slap you... or words to that effect, wasn't it?"

I nod and laugh. We both know she's never going to slap me but I take her point; I did say that, and for good reason.

"You're right, Poppy." I swing my leg over the bicycle saddle. "It's not like I've not got enough to do with finding new clients and getting to grips with the French tax system."

Poppy shudders. "Don't. The very idea gives me nightmares. I just let JoJo and Leo do it for me. We all agreed it was better that way."

I laugh, full of affection for my lovely, quirky friend.

"You're a star, Poppy. Don't ever stop being you."

"Who else would I be?" she asks, genuinely bewildered.

As I cycle away, I wish I had her unswerving confidence to remain true to myself; to not hide the parts of myself that strangers often don't understand. My gran used to say I should be proud of my unusual gift and not let my mother succeed in squeezing me into her own particular version of 'normal'. Gran used to say the word *normal* as if it were an insult.

'Be your own unique and talented self, Daisy dear,' she'd say, or sometimes calling me Deedee, using my childhood nickname from rolling the two words into one. "Never feel you have to hide who you are. Own it, be proud of it.'

I'm ashamed to say I didn't always manage it. After all, teenage girls can be vicious, and following my mum's insistence that I should do my best to fit in often seemed the easiest option.

The easiest but not the best.

But maybe it's not too late to adopt Poppy's attitude. Perhaps this can be a fresh start in more ways than one.

Anton explained to me he'd be working on his book at the shop today. He seems pretty laid-back about the fact he often has plenty of time between customers as it allows him to combine the two. He said footfall doesn't matter so much nowadays when it comes to rare books as most of the specialist orders come via the internet. While he doesn't actually need me to dog sit as he's not travelling to visit a client, he apparently still wants Pickle and Squeaker to have a walk both to keep them happy and to allow him an hour's undisturbed writing time.

He's on his mobile phone when I arrive and seems preoccupied, making only brief eye contact as he hands me their leads.

I try not to let his lack of friendly greeting rattle me as I head off towards the bridge and down to the river. It's beautifully warm today – not too hot, not too humid, just lovely – comfortably denim shorts and a T-shirt weather. Pickle brightens when he sees the river and Squeaker picks up on his excitement, letting out a volley of excited squeaky woofs. It's not hard to work out where her name came from.

I feel a fresh surge of love for these dogs. Squeaker offers me such unconditional love and affection, always seeking out a cuddle when she can and even Pickle has started to creep onto my lap at times in a gesture of feigned nonchalance, as though he were just passing and fancied a sit down. We both know he's there for the cuddle though and I know not to make too much of it, just quietly let him sit and enjoy the human contact again. I love seeing these moments when he's as carefree as little Squeaker. I have a lot of affection for the other dogs I walk and dog sit too but something about Pickle's need to emerge from depression and the trust he's starting to show me, plus the life-affirming exuberance of Squeaker, touches me at a very deep level. I still get the same feeling I got that first day I met them all – a deep tug in their direction, like I have a part to play in their lives, including in Anton's.

I sit down on a rock and watch the dogs splashing around in the shallow river. Maybe this is it – helping them though this adjustment period and providing the company for Pickle that Anton just can't give him all the time. I suppose Pickle would've been used to Claire being around most of the time. A part of me hopes it's more though, that there's a bigger part for me to play. As charming as the thought of being a dog-sitting version of Mary Poppins is, I don't want to vanish off at the end. I want to stay, to keep listening to this tug inside of me.

My parents would think I've lost my mind, giving up a well-paid job to walk other people's dogs or dog sit, never mind making beds at the guesthouse like I'm only a chambermaid, which is precisely the reason I've not told them. I did things the way they advised me for a while – for too long really – and now I'm earning less than I ever have yet I feel like I'm exactly where I'm meant to be.

I watch the sunlight dancing on the surface of the water, and occasionally throw pebbles into the river for Pickle so he can scamper after them and attempt to find them again, which of course he never does. The river meanders slowly here, and there are quiet pools where it's perfectly safe for them to play. Squeaker doesn't chase the pebbles but she enthusiastically chases after Pickle. Even as I'm laughing at the antics of the dogs, Anton isn't far from my thoughts. It would be a lie to say the tug inside of me towards this family doesn't also tug my thoughts back to him. Something invisible seems to keep nagging at me that Anton needs me too, as though the tug is compelling me to do something, to take action, but it's not like it's being especially helpful. I've already decided that asking him out is not an option. Maybe it'll become clear in time.

On my return to the shop, Anton waves me in with a wide smile on his face and seems much more welcoming.

"I'm sorry I was occupied when you arrived." He shrugs apologetically. "I had a client who has not paid his bill and the dogs just wanted to go, go, go…"

"Oh it's fine, don't worry about it." I smile back, feeling charmed by his easy manner and by his apology. I feel a bit silly now for taking it personally. What was it my gran used to say? In your teens you worry what everyone thinks of you. In your twenties you stop caring. In your thirties you realise they weren't actually thinking about you at all.

At thirty-one years old, I really ought to know better. It's not like Anton is everyone… and yes, I find that I do care what Anton thinks of me very much. I can't help wondering if this strong, invisible tug inside me, whatever it's about, might be as much about me needing Anton and his dogs for some reason, as it is about them needing me. It's an unsettling feeling and one I can't quite explain given the short period of time I've known them.

I know Gran would probably say something wise at this point about not always needing to know the answer. She'd tell me to listen to the tug though, and as confused as I've been about trusting my intuition lately, I'm pretty sure this isn't a case of my hormones scrambling the signals. I still plan to be cautious though.

Pickle and Squeaker, released from their leads, bound joyfully towards Anton to greet him while I look around at the beautifully arranged books. I've often found antiquarian bookshops can smell a little musty but there's no odd smell here, just rows and rows of exquisite and rare hardback books facing cover-side out towards the front of the shop. The books towards the back of the shop are not as colourful but still interesting. I can't help reading the spines with interest and working out how many of the titles I can translate from the French; though many of the titles are in Latin.

I feel the nerves on the back of my neck prickling, sensing Anton's observation of me.

When I turn around he's much closer than I expect and I jump slightly, then smile awkwardly to cover it up. His eyes are warm and kind though. I had half wondered if he was observing me to see if I was going to touch a book and show him more of the skill I'd tried to explain so defensively before. In fact, not all second-hand books carry much of an energy signature in my experience; it often depends on how treasured they were by their owners.

Some people might think my defensiveness unnecessarily prickly but they haven't experienced the full range of reactions I have from sceptical or patronising to downright rude and scathing. I really hadn't thought that Anton would fall into one of those categories, not really, but I'm extremely relieved to be proven right.

"It's really beautiful," I say. "Quite the loveliest

bookshop I've ever been in. I could spend all day just looking around."

He beams then, as though I've admired his baby, and the wide smile lights up his eyes. I feel a slight flip in my stomach in response and try to ignore it, along with attempting to ignore the fact I'm close enough to smell his slightly musky, citrusy scent. I step away slightly as though to look at a book further along the shelf. I think he's one of those very rare men who really don't realise how attractive they are or are not conscious of the effect they might have on women.

"If only everyone who came to Mirepoix felt the same," he says, a little ruefully. "Or stayed around long enough to buy as well as just look. Fortunately, the appraisal work of documents or book collections I undertake is much more lucrative. This shop, much as I love it, barely takes enough to cover its costs."

"So… if you don't mind me asking, why do you keep it on?" I ask cautiously. "If I'm being too nosy please ignore me. I think the shop is beautiful and I would hate it to close but isn't it a lot of effort for no reward?"

"I do not mind you asking," Anton replies thoughtfully. "I keep the shop alive for much the same reason as a farmer continues to farm the land of his father and his father before him. Because it is a part of his heritage and the rewards it brings are not financial in nature."

"Oh, so it was your father's shop?" I ask, reaching down to stroke Squeaker who has put her front paws up on my legs and doesn't understand why she's being ignored.

"And my grandfather before him, yes." His smile is a little wistful and sad but still warm. "I used to help my grandfather out after school and on Saturdays. He gave me a love of books and also a passion for the folklore and traditions of the area."

He crouches down next to me to stroke Squeaker too and her tail starts wagging so hard her bottom practically wags too. Anton's fingers accidentally touch mine and warmth blossoms through me. I should pull away but I don't.

"Ah, hence the book you're writing?" I ask, enjoying the physical closeness. At that moment Pickle comes over, looking slightly affronted to be left out of the attention, and pushes himself in between us, making us both laugh.

"Yes, I suppose," he shrugs, that totally Gallic shrug Poppy says British people can never really pull off, however much they practise. And she has practised. "All things must grow from a little seed. My grandfather was sowing the seeds of the love of books and respect for our history in me during the time I spent in his shop but it was up to me to water them, nurture them, and bring them into the world."

I'm charmed again by his turn of phrase. I think of the seeds my grandmother tried to plant in me that somehow survived in spite of the attempts of my mother to deprive them of nurture. I wish she were around to talk to right now, but maybe it's time for me to work things out for myself. No family expectations, no peer pressure to conform. Gran was different from the rest of my family though as she always challenged me to choose my own values and beliefs, and gave the relentless advice to always question, to think for myself, and then question some more. Not to mention to always live life to the full, be that on an ashram in India or trekking in Peru, or ditching your safe London job to try to work out your place in the world.

"That's such a beautiful analogy." I look up from Squeaker and Pickle to make eye contact with Anton. "I would love to know about the history of the area."

"You would?" The intensity of his gaze is definitely heated now; I'm sure it's not my imagination. The energy in the room feels infused by his passion for his work. Yet that doesn't explain the reason Anton doesn't step back from me in an attempt to establish some distance.

I suppose it could be wishful thinking. After all, some people really don't seem that aware of observing others' personal space. I need to stop thinking like this. I ought to be the one who takes a step back.

Yet somehow I don't move and neither does he, and the warmth spreads to the rest of my body, in spite of the relative chill of the shop compared to the sunny day outside.

"Would you like to come out with me on Sunday? I could show you the places I'm writing about," he offers. "If you're not too busy, of course. I must admit I find Sundays difficult, you know… since my wife died."

"Yes, I'd really like that, thank you." I nod, hoping I look casual and not as though my heart rate has suddenly picked up. "I can appreciate that must be difficult and I really would love to see something of the area. Poppy and JoJo are a bit too busy to show me around."

"Wonderful." He seems genuinely delighted and by the time I've left the shop we've arranged the details.

I'm a little bewildered, not quite sure what shifted between us just now yet somehow sure that something did.

I know Anton didn't mean it as a date. It's a combination of a friendly gesture on his part, showing me around, and also a chance for him to share stories about a subject that happens to be a passion of his. It will be fun – there's nothing to fuss about. The lingering looks and casual physical contact could have been something and nothing. Time to take a breath, to rein in any premature hopes. Maybe he mentioned his wife to make sure I don't get the wrong idea. I appreciate he could be grieving yet lonely and missing physical contact. It's probably a confusing state to be in. I need to do my best to be sensitive and aware of his situation.

I have a chance of a life in a place that is really starting to grow on me, somewhere I think I might, maybe, like to put down roots. I'm not going to be blown off-course; I don't want to end up in the same kind of mess I left behind me in London.

Maybe even worse.

All before I've even had a chance to plant my seeds and water them.

Chapter Five

"To love is to burn, to be on fire."
Jane Austen

We stand beside a torrent of writhing river as it tosses and tumbles over rocks and under tree roots.

"The river Ariège is fed from an ancient glacier in the Pyrenees. If you want to understand the folklore of the old religion, there's no better place to start than here at the river."

"The old religion?" I interrupt Anton, curious. "I assume you're not talking about Christianity?"

"No," he agrees. "I mean the religion of the mountains, the forests, and the caves. Perhaps even the spiritual beings said to inhabit them or the white lady herself, Esclamonde, the source of so many of the legends surrounding Montségur."

His eyes sparkle like the sunlight dancing on the river as it twists and turns, swollen with the late-spring melted snow of the mountain tops. I love how his passion for the subject animates Anton and somehow seems to make him lighter, to temporarily lose the shadow that often seems to haunt him, weighing him down.

"Montségur? Even I've heard of it. Poppy was telling me all about it. Are you taking me there?" I ask.

"Yes, but not today. Today we look at the deeper mysteries that have been... how do you say? Woven into the history of the region."

I imagine he'd make a great teacher. I can see him following the academic route, teaching at university level and being crushed on by all his female students. Hmm, just as well he came back to take over his father's bookshop instead, and at least he's got the book he's writing to satisfy that intellectual part of himself. No, I wouldn't want to compete with a bevy of eighteen-year-old beauties. Not that I know why I'm thinking about this but it seems pointless to pretend to myself I'm not falling for this charming man with his floppy, dark hair and guileless smiles. He doesn't know how gorgeous and charming he is and that's really attractive in itself. I'll just have to remind myself this can only ever be fantasy and nothing else – window shopping for something I can't afford to pay the price for.

"In fact, the very name, Ariège, comes from the Latin for 'river of gold'," he carries on, seemingly unaware of my surreptitious appreciation. "The Romans mined this area for both gold and silver and the river still to this day carries flecks and grains of gold. You can even pan for it but you're unlikely to get rich."

"Really?" I peer down into the water and almost lose my footing on a gnarly tree root.

Anton takes hold of a loop at the back of my shorts and gently pulls me back. I lose my footing and stumble back against him, ending up in his arms for the briefest of moments, resting against his chest and fleetingly appreciating that of all the places to land, I picked the best spot.

"Thanks." I turn and smile. "Doubtless Pickle and Squeaker would be happy if I joined them in the river though."

"I expect so," Anton replies, his tone warm and his eyes crinkling slightly as he mirrors my smile. "It would be a bit cold though."

I realise I'm still standing a little bit too close to him for no good reason and step away slightly.

"Glacier-fed, yes, got it. I have been listening, I promise." I grin, doing my best to lighten the mood and not to think about how nice it would be to rest back into Anton's embrace.

He nods and the lingering look he gives me is utterly incomprehensible. I can't tell if he's just really happy to find someone who's interested to learn about his specialist subject or if he can guess what sort of thoughts I was having.

Is he having them too?

"You've heard of the Golden Fleece, yes?" he asks.

"Yes but I thought that was a Greek or Roman myth?"

"Ah yes, but as is often the case there is a real story behind the myth. The old method to collect the gold sediment from the river was by using the fleece of a sheep. You would secure it on a branch or tree root and place it in the river and just let it collect the gold. Sometimes flocks of sheep drinking in the river would come out tinged with gold."

"Really? They did that here? Are you sure it's not worth panning for gold anymore?" I peer into the river again but more carefully this time, making sure I have a secure footing.

"Well you could ask the faeries for gold." Anton grins mischievously. "It is said they live in grottos and caves and at night they bathe in the streams and rivers. The flecks of gold turn their hair golden."

He gestures at my auburn hair, lightened naturally by all the time I've been spending outside in the sun. He almost touches it but not quite, his fingers just millimetres from taking a lock of my hair to run through his fingers. Now this I'm positive I'm not imagining. From the darkness of his pupils I can tell he wants to touch me and it's a battle for him to resist. The fact he's conflicted tugs at my heart.

"You have some gold in your hair. Perhaps you are part fae?" His hand drops back down to his side.

"Maybe I am." I smile playfully and raise my eyebrows. "So, what happened in the tales?"

"They would lure the most handsome men to the river and give both the gold and themselves to the men, though the men were never quite the same again." Anton clears his throat.

"Well you have to admit it would be a hell of a way to find out if I really am part fae." I grin. "Quite a price to pay."

"I don't know, it might be worth it." Anton's returning smile is sexy and I feel my breath hitch in my chest. This has turned flirty very quickly.

"Worth it for the gold I mean," he adds, straight faced.

I swat his arm playfully and feel lighter, happier than I have done in a while. Who could be feeling low out here in the dappled sunshine beside the clear rushing river carrying gold and legends? We're surrounded by an idyll of green foliage and crooked forest paths that look like they might well be used by faeries. Not to mention the presence of my very own sexy and unexpectedly flirty tour guide, which is a definite bonus. It's nice to see Anton relaxed and more carefree than I've observed him before.

Anton smiles, and there's definitely still a cheeky sparkle in his eyes. "There were also tales of drac and salamandes who were said to influence the weather. Their loud cries supposedly let loose mountain storms. The faeries tended to get the blame for any floods."

"Totally unfair." I roll my eyes.

"So you are part fae? I really should have been warned by your hair." This time Anton does take a lock of my hair and holds it up to the light. The sunlight illuminates the strands caught between his fingers and exaggerates the natural golden highlights in my hair.

He lets it fall again quickly but my heart is beating faster from the intimate contact. It's also the first physical contact I can't disregard as probably accidental.

He doesn't meet my eye and I try to understand how odd this is for him. I know – because I might have googled it, purely out of interest – that statistically men date more quickly after losing spouses than women. This isn't even a date, but it's not just an acquaintance-ship either, not anymore. There's been a shift and we're somewhere in the no-man's-land in between, which is why I mustn't let the beginnings of a slightly flirty friendship take on a significance they don't warrant. Not just because I promised myself I wouldn't but because I don't want to get hurt, and most of all because I don't want to hurt Anton while he's poten-tially vulnerable.

"So… are there healing springs around here, like there are at Lourdes?" I ask, helping us both move on from the slightly awkward moment.

He smiles gratefully and that smile lights me up inside, the warmth of it not helping the strength of my resolve.

"Yes, we have sacred springs said to cure infertility, fevers, and even one at Loubières which is said to make you beautiful if you see your reflection in its waters. We also have many hot springs that people with disorders of the joints find very beneficial. I believe there are scientific studies available about the mineral content of the water but that is not my area. Those kinds of explanations would have been inconceivable to my ancestors so it's easy to understand how myth and legend are born. Do you see?"

"Yes, I do. I can't believe how incredibly fluent your English is when you talk about your subject."

He shrugs. "I have studied materials in many languages and what I just said did come directly from a guest lecture I once delivered in English."

He seems sheepish to admit it.

"You're way too modest," I say, genuinely impressed.

"Now, if the dogs have finished in the river I will take you to the next stop on my mystery tour." He doesn't acknowledge my compliment but seems embarrassed by it. Watching his two dogs splashing about in the river brings a big smile to his face again. Never mind the faeries being enchanting, that smile has a power all of its own.

"I'm not sure Pickle is ever finished in the river," I say dubiously. "He'd spend all day there if he could."

"True." Anton nods. "But then he would deprive you of the next part of our tour."

"Which is?"

"The mysterious caves of Ussat-les-Bains."

"Mysterious, eh? They sound fascinating."

"Please do say if I'm boring you." Anton's smile slips a little.

"Oh no, I wasn't being sarcastic," I rush to reassure him. "I really do find it all fascinating."

And I'm enjoying seeing this lighter side of Anton. I wish I could see more of it.

I help him to recapture Pickle and Squeaker and get them back on their leads. Pickle is much the harder one to catch and makes his views grumpily known on his way back to the car, making sure he's had a good and thorough shake next to both of us first to transfer plenty of river water onto our legs. I was right; it is freezing cold.

The drive is not too far to Ussat-les-Bains. There's the huge cave called Grotte Lombrives which opens to the public but Anton knows the history of the other smaller caves that are off the tourist trail and would be almost impossible to find unless you knew exactly where they were.

I shiver slightly when we step out of the car at our next parking spot as it's much cooler the further we travel into the gorge. It's good though as it means we can leave the dogs in the car in full shade with the windows open a little and not have to worry about them getting hot. They are still wet and cool from their swim anyway.

"I cannot let the dogs off of their leads here in case they manage to run into the caves," Anton explains. "Sometimes even people go in on their own and get into difficulties."

Somehow I suspect that dogs would have an easier time finding their way out using their sense of smell – not that I'd like to put it to the test. I know the dogs mean the world to Anton. I'm already feeling a strong, protective bond towards them myself, after only a short period of taking care of them.

"Would you believe me if I told you that the Nazis came to these caves hunting for the Holy Grail?" Anton asks.

"Really? I've never heard anything like that. I thought the legend linked to this area was to do with the bloodline of Christ?"

"Pah." Anton shrugs expressively. "Most of the legends people have heard of centre on Rennes-les-Bains and are the result of Hollywood and a handful of novelists, but the caves here at Ussat are far more interesting than Rennes for their history and their legends. I'm not claiming the Holy Grail really is buried somewhere in these caves, but saying that, regardless of what the truth of the Grail is or was it most certainly is true that the Nazis believed in it and funded excavations in the hope of finding it right here in these caves just before the outbreak of the Second World War."

"Really?"

"These caves have been lived in and worshipped in since the last ice age." Anton nods. "And yes, many artefacts were found. They really did hunt for the Holy Grail or Le Graal Pyrénéen, as it is called here. Some say they even found it."

I smile, sure he's teasing me now, ramping up his tourist guide role to keep me entertained.

Yet as we pick our way into the cathedral cave, Anton's powerful torch shining into the pitch blackness ahead, I feel a tremendous shiver run down the length of my spine, as though I am walking over the graves of thousands who lived and died before me. I can feel… something here and I wrap my arms around my body, determined not to touch anything.

"So what sort of things did they find?"

"Many artefacts dating much further back in time than the Cathars who lived, worshipped, and sometimes died in the cave complexes within these mountains. There are also many underground lakes and rivers that fluctuate in flow so that some call this Venus Mountain and the caves her womb."

I nod to show I've understood.

"Worship of the divine feminine goes back further

than you can imagine in this area…" He pauses. "Well you know how French men love to worship women."

He turns back to look at me over his shoulder and there's no doubting the flirtatious gleam in his eye again, even though the light is dim. I remind myself he's in a vulnerable position and I shouldn't let myself get carried away.

Unsure of what to say, I simply smile.

"Maybe that's part of the mystery surrounding Esclarmonde, who is said to have saved the Cathar treasure from Montségur when it fell to the crusaders and hidden it somewhere in this cave complex."

He gestures around him with his torch.

I shiver again. I've been in caves in England before and not found the experience a difficult one but these caves in particular have a feel about them, a powerful spiritual presence. It's not harmful exactly, but neither is it benign.

I don't voice my unease. I really don't want to spoil things, not while we're getting on so well.

"Several people have been lost down here only to emerge after some time completely… deranged." His tone is serious, as though he's sensing my mood. "It's also said that when Esclarmonde and her followers fled the northern crusaders, they were walled in here by their pursuers. There have certainly been plenty of skeletons found in the caves."

"That's horrible." I look carefully down at the ground, wary of coming into contact with anything that might make me feel something from the past I'd rather not.

"Of course, the crusaders were all from the north, so it's very possible there were tunnels and exits they were unaware of. They were too scared to follow the Cathars into the tunnels."

"Can't say I blame them," I mutter.

"They're quite safe, if you know your way and have a torch," Anton says, misunderstanding my meaning.

It's not that the caves feel menacing as such, just that they are so full of powerful emotional residue. I can barely explain it to myself so haven't a hope of explaining clearly to Anton all the things I'm picking up.

"We don't have time today but there are many other caves with special significance here. Maybe another time I can show you the cave with the pentagram and ancient altar. There are many runic and Wicca symbols on the walls, amongst other symbols, some still unidentified."

"That sounds very interesting," I reply, but the chill down my spine has returned and I'm glad to be stepping out into the sunshine where I can't feel the ghosts of the past anymore.

"Okay?" Anton looks at me quizzically. "Are you cold?"

He offers me his hoodie and I take it, glad of the warmth while we're still in the depths of the shadowy gorge.

"Thanks." I force a smile. "So where does the Grail come in then?"

I want him to continue his lecture because I love how lit up he is when talking about his favourite subject. I wish I could see more of this impassioned, animated Anton, whose cares are maybe not forgotten but at least put temporarily aside.

"A German archaeologist called Otto Rahn was initially in charge of the search for the Grail here," Anton explains. "It is said he is considered to be the inspiration for the character of Indiana Jones. He made a find of some kind at the grotto of the wild fountain. Hidden in a hollow stalagmite, surrounded by blackened human bones, he found an ancient artefact, a Celtic cup with a piece of black meteorite in it. It is an odd thing: it has the ability to emit a red blood-like substance."

I raise my eyebrows sceptically. "Really? Or is this what the tourists are told?"

"Really, it is true. Such an artefact was found – in fact, many pieces of the meteorite were found. Look around you. There are no tourists here; they all go to Rennes or to the ruins of Montségur."

"Can we see it then? Is it in a museum or something?" I have to admit I am genuinely intrigued now. I thought he was giving me a sensationalised account to keep me entertained.

"It, along with other artefacts, were briefly on display at a museum in Tarascon," Anton explains. "But the collection of artefacts found in the caves were removed from the museum one day and everything passed into private collections. There are many people who have pieces of the black meteorite though; they've found them themselves in the caves. The rock has magnetic qualities and can emit a red substance – that part is true. There is still the issue of the missing Cathar treasure, but as the Cathars didn't care much for worldly goods I think their treasure is more likely to be spiritual wisdom or writings, such as the Cathar Book of Love which has never been found. It's possible that Rahn didn't hand over all his finds to the Nazi party as he was rather pressed into their service but at heart considered his allegiance lay with the Cathars. He even converted to the Cathar religion, initiated by a local shepherd who used to live in the hermit cave."

"Sounds like a dangerous position to take."

"That is very true. He eventually resigned from the Nazi party and vanished," Anton says solemnly. "His body was never found. Anyway, I think he believed the Grail was not a cup or a dish but the stones from the sky with the power to heal."

"So when he vanished was that it? Search over?" I find myself drawn into the story. "Looking at the mountains forming the sides of the gorge and river I never would have guessed any of this history. It looks wild and dramatic but…"

"It is a region of great depths and many secrets. A mixture of legends woven with truth and the power of human story."

"I can see why you wanted to write your book. I bet it's fascinating." I say this entirely without guile but then worry it sounds like I'm gushing. I do really mean it though.

"I'm glad you find it interesting." Anton gives me one of his lovely warm smiles that seem to increase the potency of their effect with each consecutive go. "I can get carried away talking – please, you must tell me to stop when it gets too much."

"No, I really am interested," I assure him again. "So what did happen next?"

"The Nazis sent another man, who allegedly found

the Grail and sent it to Himmler who put it on a submarine to Antarctica where it was sealed into a cave of ice."

"But that's just a story, right?" I blink against the sunlight as we walk out of the shadow of the mountain.

"Well, there really is a cave and the Nazi excursions to the Arctic are documented." Anton shrugs. "Outside the cave there is an obelisk that reads 'There are more things in heaven and in earth than man has dreamt.'"

"Don't you mean *on* earth?" I ask, captivated by his story telling.

"No, it quite clearly states *in* earth."

I muse quietly as we get back into the car.

There are more things in heaven and in earth…

"What do you believe?" I ask, slightly concerned he will take a stance in a place there can be no overlap with my own beliefs and experience.

Anton holds my gaze. "Enough to know that we don't know everything. I believe that one day science may be closer to explaining those things that are still unexplained, at least partly. Who am I to say you don't feel energy when you pick up an object? I choose to admit I don't know everything and to keep an open mind."

I exhale deeply with relief.

"That's good enough for me." I smile, settling into

the passenger seat and snuggling into Anton's hoodie. A companionable silence fills the car, the dogs asleep in the back after their trip out, and I stare out of the window at the scenery.

After a while Anton turns to check I'm awake.

"Are you up for one more stop of your mystery tour before we return?"

"Yes, of course." I nod, enjoying his company far too much to consider ending the day now.

"Now, where we are going next is a reminder, I think, that we must still use our common sense too."

"Like not blaming floods on faeries?" I ask.

"Exactly." Anton nods approvingly. "Where I'm taking you next is the site of a modern myth: the Pic de Bugarach. Have you heard of it?"

"Can't say I have." I shake my head as Anton pulls out of our parking space and we head further down the valley, rocky outcrops and forest to both sides of the road.

"Thousands of people converged on the mountain in 2012, convinced the world was going to end and an alien spaceship would come up from inside the mountain to save them."

"Seriously?"

"Yes. They would climb the mountain naked to carry out bizarre rituals. There is some kind of metal inside the mountain that can interfere with compass readings and with electronic equipment," Anton explains. "Add to that the fact there is a spring coming out of the mountain that is salt water and you can see why legends evolve from unexplained natural phenomena."

"Why aliens though?" I muse.

"Sorry?"

"I mean, if it were me I would have gone with a hoard of dragon treasure in the mountain – that's the metal."

"And the salty spring?" Anton laughs.

"Dragon tears," I state confidently.

"But why are the dragons sad?" Anton is still laughing and I love seeing more of this lighter side of him.

"Because people would rather have aliens?" I grin. "Perhaps we should start our own myth: the dragons of Bugarach. What do you think?"

"I think it's a place that for some reason brings out the imagination in people," he replies. "Did you know that Jules Verne stayed in the village of Bugarach and it is said to have inspired his novel *Journey to the Centre of the Earth*."

"I had no idea this was such a fascinating area."

"And we have barely scraped the surface today.

Nearly every village has a legend, a tale of witchcraft, or a ghost story associated with it. It is making my job hard, deciding what to include and what to leave out of my book. And I haven't even told you about the thin-veil-between-worlds theory that many ascribe to – caves appearing and disappearing. People too."

I scrutinise Anton to see if he's being serious. He merely shrugs.

"If scientists talk about the probability of parallel worlds then who am I to say for sure they are all wrong? I don't believe but I don't not believe either."

His shrug reassures me that he was telling the truth about being open-minded and a deep contentment settles over me.

More things in heaven and in earth than man has ever dreamed of...

And here I'd prejudged Anton, sure that he was pure logic and would scornfully dismiss an important part of me.

Maybe I should start being more open-minded too. And maybe, just maybe, I've found my place, some-where it's okay to be myself, even the quirky, hard to explain parts of me.

Chapter Six

"There is never a time or place for true love. It happens accidentally, in a heartbeat, in a single flashing, throbbing moment."
Sarah Dessen

"I had a great day out, thank you." I smile at Anton, enjoying how easy it is to be in his company.

Pickle and Squeaker are in their kitchen baskets. Squeaker is already asleep but Pickle is fighting sleep, one eye opening now and then as though afraid of missing out on something exciting, like the fridge door opening.

I'm not just being polite; today has been great. I feel

like the relationship between Anton and me has deepened into something more… Something I'm not quite sure either of us can define or put a label on. There's a palpable energy between us that has grown stronger throughout the day and now I find myself wanting to edge physically closer to Anton so I can feel the full potential of the charge between us that seems to promise so much.

I don't want to go home yet. I don't want this day to end. I ache to reach out and touch him, to have him focus the full charisma of his personality onto me as touch by touch we explore and take the connection deeper. Is that what he wants too?

"Tea?" Anton's voice breaks into my thoughts. I catch the smile on his face and wish I knew what he was thinking.

I nod. "Yes, that would be lovely thanks."

Am I sounding a bit too super positive and over-keen? Oh, who cares. Honestly, I don't want to play games or be with someone who needs me to play them. The whole concept of playing it cool so a man will continue to be attracted to me annoys me, frankly, and surely it's a bit insulting to men to suggest they need to be played?

"I'm glad you enjoyed today." Anton's eyes are fixed on mine, intense and soulful. "This region is so rich in myth and history. Yes, I came back to the area to take over my father's shop when he died but this is where I was born; it's in my blood. Thank you for indulging my passion."

The history… right. I know he has a true passion for his subject, yet there's an intensity in his gaze that suggests today was about more than just enjoying sharing his subject matter. Or is that simply wishful thinking on my part?

"Anytime. I really had fun." I bask in the warmth of Anton's smile, willing him to take the few short steps to close the distance between us. Willing him to make the first move, to show there might be the potential of something else developing.

If only I knew what he is thinking or feeling. Does he feel this magnetic connection too? I try to locate my good intentions from earlier in the day – the desire to do the sensible thing – yet all the reasons to be sensible seem suddenly elusive in the face of the overwhelming desire to connect more deeply.

Ordinarily, in this kind of situation I'd be totally okay with making the first move myself but given the delicate nature of the situation it feels important to let Anton set the pace. If he even wants to, that is.

Squeaker rolls over onto her back in her bed and starts snoring loudly, breaking the stillness of the quiet moment so utterly that we both start laughing. Anton looks at Squeaker with such tenderness that I feel a deep stirring inside me, a breathless yearning to be a part of this circle of love. To know, one day, what it's like to be cherished... and to cherish those I love in return.

I know I'm a long way off from that. Just a hint that Anton is experiencing the same kind of magnetic pull as me would be good, even if he's not ready to date again yet.

I hurriedly bury the inconvenient question of whether Anton might not be ready to date any time soon into the depths of my mind, ignoring it, not wanting to give it thought space as though my entertaining the idea might make it more likely somehow. Need swells up inside me, the longing to be touched, to be affirmed and made love to bypassing any mental concerns.

I want to touch Anton so much but feel awkward, more awkward than I would usually be in this situation. Perhaps the more it matters, the more awkward it is. After all, the more you care about the outcome the worse the consequences if you screw it up.

"Here's your tea." He hands me a pretty blue china mug. He's even remembered to put milk in for me. His time in England trained him well. His fingers brush mine for a fraction longer than necessary, sending a shiver of sexual electricity through me.

Intentional or not?

I meet his questioning gaze and our eyes lock contact, exchanging meaning without words. The mutual holding of our gazes is the first truly open acknowledgement that we both feel a sense of connection. It's the confirmation I need that this is not one-sided, that it's not another example of me being deluded. Is it enough to act on though?

I put my tea onto the kitchen table behind me and take a tentative step towards Anton. My body has a will of its own, not prepared to wait, determined to take action.

I step even closer when he doesn't move away, when I feel nothing but acquiescence and mutual curiosity. Reaching up, I tentatively stroke his cheek, my fingers running over the stubble on his jaw. Then I take the full plunge and step into his arms, reaching my own arms around him and resting my head against his chest. For a microsecond, Anton's stance is rigid and my heartbeat picks up, pounding with anxiety and uncertainty. Then he exhales audibly and returns the embrace, clasping me to him. Holding me close.

I melt into the hug with a sigh of relief and just rest, enjoying the feeling of his warm body against mine and the way we seem to merge into each other, connected. I have been wanting this so badly. Needing this physical affection. Needing this affirmation and the sense of deeper connection that's been missing from my life for so long.

He strokes my back and runs his fingers through my hair and I feel the tension leave his body with a deep sigh of his own. I wonder how long it's been since he felt physical affection like this. His need is probably as great, if not even greater, than my own. We stay entwined like that for what seems like an eternity. Just drinking in the connection. Enjoying the hug, the sensation of our bodies pressed together, letting the desire simmer and build.

My own needs drive me to tentatively test boundaries, seeking the assurance that he really does want this as much as I do. I need to be sure and pull back a little to meet his gaze again, his dark eyes much closer to mine now and his fingers stroking my hair in a way that makes me feel like purring. His pupils are definitely dilated. He wants this. I wasn't wrong. Something has shifted between us today.

I reach up, kissing the side of his neck and his jawline and then making my way up to his lips. His own very kissable mouth parts into a soft kiss before he begins an exploration of my face and my neck, lightly nipping at my earlobes before kissing his way back to my mouth again, this time his tongue gently probing, softly opening me up. I sense a deep passion stirring beneath the surface, yet also can feel he is keeping himself in check, taking it slow. Both the self-control and the strong desire have a delicious effect on me. It is quite simply the best kiss I have ever had and I'm ready to lose myself in this, in him.

I'm unwinding, slowly, unfurling and opening to him at a deep level. I slide my hands down his back and lightly cup his jean-clad bottom, signalling my willingness to go further. Lost in the moment.

He tenses, but this time it's in a good way, the hard erection pressing against me impossible to miss. His kiss deepens as he backs me up against the table. I try to remember what underwear I put on this morning and hope it at least matches. I honestly hadn't expected… well, this. After doing my best to suppress my attraction to Anton, to convince myself this shouldn't and couldn't happen, I'd done my best to persuade myself he was only being friendly though I had suspected, deep down, especially today, that there was more to it than that.

He exhales loudly as his fingers skim underneath the hem of my T-shirt and caress my bare skin, leaving a delicious trail of sensations in their wake. When he strokes the lacy cups of my bra, I react with a sharp intake of breath and my nipples stiffen immediately. I feel… electrified. I've never felt like this before. Never.

Never felt such an incredible energy or attraction; it really is like a powerful magnet has propelled us together. I have this sense deep down, an inner knowing that I am Anton's and he is mine. Now that I've experienced the real thing, my feelings for Scott, that had once occupied so much of my headspace, feel like a mere schoolgirl crush by comparison.

I remember Gran saying when she kissed Grandad for the first time she instantly knew beyond knowing that he would be her life partner. Knew it in the marrow of her bones, beyond a single doubt. I must admit I'd thought maybe she was exaggerating, that the "we just knew" was a romantic notion to make anecdotes more sentimental. I should have given her more credit. After all, her precognition was generally pretty spot-on.

He is mine and I am his. The knowing starts deep in my core and spreads until it fills every cell, every part of me electrified with something I've never felt before, or even dreamt existed. There is passion, yes, but this is much deeper than lust. Something way deeper than sexual chemistry or a biological attraction.

I stroke his bottom in response and try to remember

to breathe. I hardly dare speak lest I break the spell I feel is being woven between us.

He responds by pulling my T-shirt over my head and strokes the bare skin of my neck and down to the swell between my lace-covered breasts. His kisses move down to my neckline, to kiss the swell of my breasts. I admit I'm surprised by how fast he's moving but I imagine it's been a very long time… and Anton must have a lot of pent-up tension. It's been quite a while for me too and this feels so wonderful I have no intention of putting the brakes on.

I move a hand between us and press against his erection through his jeans. It's then that I notice Anton catching sight of something over my shoulder. Then that I hear him take a sharp intake of breath and watch as he takes a step back away from me.

I feel the rollercoaster plunge from elation to a stomach-lurching fall. I should've known this was too good to be true. I knew Anton was in a vulnerable situation. That he was still grieving and struggling to cope with the dichotomy of longing for the comfort of a woman's arms yet at the same time believing that he shouldn't want it; that desiring it was a betrayal of Claire.

I know that's what he's feeling; the bond between us means I can pick up energy from him in the same way I can from objects. I knew it but I pushed the knowing down and still let myself get caught up in the tide of longing; let myself get swept away by the most blissful experience of my life so far. I think I deserve to share in at least some of the guilt I know Anton is feeling right now.

I can't seem to move. I just stare at Anton. I'm still feeling the internal plummeting sensation, standing stock-still, blinking back tears, feeling vulnerable dressed in only my shorts and bra.

"Désolé… désolé… I'm sorry. I…" Anton squeezes his eyes tight shut. "I cannot… I should not have…"

"It's okay. I understand," I say, laying a hand on his arm, still feeling vulnerable and confused yet driven by my overwhelming need to comfort him which overrides everything else for the moment. *But who will comfort me?* A tiny, quiet voice inside me wants to be heard but she'll have to wait.

"It's fine. I understand, really I do," I repeat. "You have nothing to be sorry for. It's complicated."

It's only half a lie. It's not exactly fine but I do understand in the same way I've learnt that life can be complicated and messy sometimes. I understand that I fucked up. I misjudged the timing. Of the two of us, I'm the one who should be sorry. I knew he was in a vulnerable position and yet I contributed to his confusion.

I meet Anton's gaze and see a different kind of guilt now, a guilt at letting things get so far before he put the brakes on. I do genuinely feel sorry for him in that moment. No matter what choice he'd made he would have experienced guilt.

It all seems such a waste, these complicated, messy emotions depriving us both of a beautiful, joy-filled physical connection that I sense would have brought healing and a deeply needed sense of connection for both of us.

I hurriedly locate and pull on my T-shirt, hastily blinking back the hot tears that gather, knowing I can only hold them off for so long. I turn and pick up my cup of tea, sipping at it so I don't have to meet his gaze. I look out of the open window to the garden and take a deep breath, inhaling the scent of lavender. Mellow evening light casts an amber hue over the hills in the distance and filters down through the canopy of leafy shade provided by the trees in Anton's garden. It gives me a moment to take a couple of deep breaths, to stop the swell of the tidal wave of emotion threatening to submerge me.

I try to get things into perspective. It's disappointment I'm experiencing, that's all. So why does it feel like so much more than that?

"Let's just pretend it never happened," I say as unemotionally as I can manage and try to shrug. I feel a rising urgent need to get out of here as soon as possible before the weight of tears pressing at the backs of my eyes overcomes my attempts to keep them in check.

"I really am very sorry, Daisy. I didn't plan…" Anton's sentence tails off and now it's his turn to lightly touch my elbow. I try to ignore the physical sensations his tenderness stirs up for me. "It is very difficult."

Yup, it's definitely difficult all right.

"Really, I understand, and it's fine," I repeat myself and feel like I'm stuck in a loop where I have to keep pretending I'm okay and I'm not allowed to leave until I've convinced Anton he doesn't need to feel guilty, not as far as I'm concerned at least. "I'd better get going and cycle back to the guesthouse while it's still light."

I'm seized by a desire to just get out of Anton's house before I embarrass myself.

"Can I give you a lift?"

Er, no. The thought of the awkward silence in the car as I struggle to hold back the tears for the duration of the journey horrifies me.

"No, I'm good thanks. It's a nice evening for a bike ride, not too hot."

Really? I'm resorting to talking about the weather? I have got to get out of here. I quickly gather up my belongings and head for the front door.

Pickle follows me while Squeaker lies still fast asleep and snoring in her bed. Pickle has his favourite toy duck in his mouth and when I crouch down to say goodbye he tries to push it into my mouth as if to say, *Here, take my toy; toys always cheer me up*.

I'm unbelievably touched that Pickle is now trying to comfort me. His eyes are kinder, more sympathetic, than I've ever seen them before. He knows I'm not okay and his desire to comfort me almost makes me blub on the spot.

"Tell you what, you keep the toy duck for now, Pickle, and we'll play with it together when I come back to look after you," I say firmly for Anton's benefit. I'm determined to show him I can deal with this and we can go back to business as usual. I don't want him feeling so awkward about today that he sacks me.

"I'll see you Monday then?" I ask Anton briskly, not quite meeting his gaze, sensing he's feeling a little shell-shocked. I hate that such a lovely day out is ending like this.

"Yes, of course, if it is still okay?" he asks hesitantly.

"Of course it's still okay," I reply, a little too briskly, maybe bordering on snappishly, but the effort of suppressing all this emotion and dealing with the disappointment is taking its toll on me.

I can still feel Anton's gaze on me as I cycle down the track to the main road and it's only when I'm sure I'm out of sight that I allow the tears of disappointment and sadness to slide down my cheeks.

Even the sight of the beautiful sunflower fields bathed in soft evening light, a sight that usually warms my soul, fails to raise my spirits. I stop briefly at the river at Moulin Neuf to pull myself together and crouch down at the riverbed to splash my face with cold water. I'm hoping to return home and slip into my room without anyone knowing or at least not looking at me too closely. After all, JoJo and Poppy weren't expecting me back, knowing I was out for the whole day.

I need the space to curl up and lick my wounds in private; they feel far too raw to expose to the scrutiny of anyone, even my friends, however well-meaning.

Chapter Seven

"You call it madness, but I call it love."
Don Byas

A week later and things are almost back to normal.

Almost.

At least, Anton and I are pretending they are. We haven't talked about it but I confess this is mostly my fault as I don't feel up to an in-depth conversation and when Anton does try to bring it up I usually change the subject or have to urgently get back to the guesthouse.

It's not very mature of me, I know, but I'm scared if we talk about it, really talk, I won't be able to hide how sad I'm feeling. I don't know why it has affected me so deeply.

Besides, I get it, I really do. Anton isn't ready to move on. End of. So what exactly is there to talk about? I don't know how to explain the irrational depth of my feelings for a man I've really not known that long. But then, I've not been able to explain the depth of the internal tug I felt towards Anton since the first time we met. Nor can I describe why what happened between us the day of the outing felt so magical. It's all so far out of my experience that I'm scared I'll never get to feel like that again. To feel that vibrantly alive. To feel that connected. To be so full of a sense of the *rightness* of the connection so that I know that I know that I know… Anton's quote from that day about there being more things in heaven and earth than man has ever dreamed of has been playing on my mind this week.

To reduce the profound sensations to words that don't sound trite or clichéd is difficult. Yet whether I should feel this sad or not is irrelevant because I do. The timing is wrong and I still don't know how much time I'll actually have here in France. I'm getting lots of one-off jobs but regular work that would allow me to project my income is another matter.

Poppy senses I'm not myself but gives me space, knowing I'll talk about it when I'm ready. Which might well be never, as far as I'm concerned. I came here needing to get away from an embarrassing situation and to get over Scott and now, despite all my protestations and good intentions, here I am tied up in knots over another man. It's embarrassing for one thing and, given that nothing is going to happen between me and Anton now, do I really have to admit to it?

I frequently catch Poppy's worried gaze on me while I'm doing odd jobs around the guesthouse and pretend to be oblivious. Pretending to be okay as well as oblivious is exhausting. I wish I could just shrug it off as something that didn't work out but that doesn't seem to be an option.

By the following Friday I'm still not feeling myself. Being in the South of France has lost its lustre a little – the temperatures are soaring and the humidity with it, making the guesthouse work much more of a chore. The humidity is getting to me today and I feel sticky and irritable, desperately in need of a positive distraction. The dogs have been especially attentive to me, sensing I'm not okay in that way most dogs have of picking up on our deepest feelings and wanting to cheer us up. Flump in particular has taken to suddenly arriving on my lap for a cuddle, often when I'm least expecting him. Once on my lap he puts a front paw up on each of my shoulders and, after staring soulfully into my eyes, he then nestles his head into my neck, as though giving me a proper cuddle. Pickle has been really well behaved when I've been dog sitting for Anton too, often creeping onto my lap or sitting on my feet and leaning against my legs as though not wanting me to move or leave without him knowing about it.

I'm not so sure the dog I'll be seeing today is going to be quite so friendly. Though I'm grateful that I do at least have a new job today, I have to walk a papillon – which literally means a "butterfly" dog – called Molly because her owner is at a hospital in Toulouse having out-patient treatment.

It's only my second time meeting Molly today and my first time walking her. When I let myself in with the spare set of keys I've been given, she appraises me coolly and then she gives the dog lead in my hand a suspicious sideways look. I've been warned she can occasionally be a "teensy bit difficult" but that she "only really snaps at you if you're trying to groom or bathe her". She has trust issues, or so her owner Ingrid informed me.

Hmmm… We eye each other up, taking each other's measure and I put on my brightest and friend-liest "who's-a-gorgeous-dog" voice but she doesn't exactly seem bowled over by my attempt.

I consider telling Molly I have trust issues too as a

bonding exercise but once I get the idea in my head that people might have secret doggie-cams hidden in their houses I can't dismiss the idea. As a result, I keep the daft, one-sided conversations I have with the dogs to when I'm walking them.

I wouldn't really want the job of grooming Molly as she's a veritable puffball of fur, a bit like a white and tan pompom with the hair around her ears resembling a butterfly's wings, hence the breed name.

After grudgingly deigning to have her dog lead put on, we set out. The first part of the walk is okay but the sky is overcast and the humidity builds until the air feels oppressively heavy. Hopefully I'll get back before it rains. Both Poppy and JoJo have warned me about the frequent and dramatic summer storms, made worse by our proximity to the mountains but I've not experienced one yet. JoJo had a migraine this morning and swore a storm was coming, though the weather app on my phone disagreed. I took over her breakfast duties so she could stay in bed and all I can say is, what she makes look effortless is bloody hard work and so I ended up setting out much later than planned.

I'm rapidly losing faith in the weather app on my phone as the first few heavy drops of rain begin to fall and then pelt us, much to Molly's indignation. When thunder rolls across the hills in the distance, she shoots me a sideways look which plainly tells me she holds me entirely responsible and there will be consequences.

By the time we reach her home we are both utterly drenched and neither of us is in the sunniest of moods. Once we're through the gate, I let Molly off her lead and pat the pockets of my shorts to find the spare door keys her owner Ingrid gave me.

Eventually I extract them and turn around to call Molly in, only to find her rolling about on her back in the muddiest patch of grass available. It's been so dry for weeks that the ground is really hard, which means we now have a mini flash flood, water pooling on top of the earth and rapidly spreading instead of being absorbed by the earth.

She stops mid-roll and turns, spotting me opening the door. She gets to her paws and makes a mad dash towards it. There is mud splattering in all directions from the flying furball and after a brief moment of panic I just about manage to shut the door before she slides sideways through the gap in a Mission Impossible style manoeuvre.

I sigh, rain still running down my neck, even though we're now partly under a roof overhang.

I can't let her in the house in this state and I've been warned just how much she hates being bathed. I regret taking her lead off her now, before we'd made it into the house. I'm not sure how to get her into the shower. Well, I'll have to try. I can't let her owner come back from hospital to a house liberally splattered with mud. I won't let a little problem like this daunt me.

I head towards Molly with her lead and as much confidence as I can muster. She instantly curls her lip at me. She knows somehow, she just knows, I have a bath on my mind.

"It's all right, sweetie. Why don't we go for another walk?" I ask brightly "Wouldn't that be nice?"

The contemptuous look she gives me for attempting to trick her would make me laugh if I wasn't quite so soggy and shattered. My hair is now plastered to my head. That approach would've worked with Squeaker any time but I suspect Molly is more intelligent.

Molly knows there is only one reason for her lead going back on and she's not having it. There's a flash of lightning in the distance. Great. I need a solution fast.

"I don't know what the matter is, Molly. I'd kill for a hot shower right now," I mutter, considering my options, looking around the garden and hoping for inspiration.

A search doesn't yield anything as helpful as a hosepipe. It briefly occurs to me that if it weren't for the thunder and lightning I could let the rain do the job, but I know I couldn't actually do that to Molly –

even if I'm not exactly her favourite person right now and she's possibly going to try to bite me. The only thing of any use I can find is a watering can. Could that work? It's going to have to work, given that the gap between the lightning flashes and crack of thunder shows the storm is getting closer and closer.

I slip into the house, narrowly managing to keep an indignant Molly outside and go in swift search of dog shampoo and warm water which I mix together in the watering can.

She had been relatively sweet and affectionate the first time I met her, though Ingrid had mentioned Molly had a few 'issues' as a result of abuse before she was rescued. She showed no signs of it that first time though, bringing me her toy tiger to play with and rubbing against my legs like a cat, asking for fuss.

Maybe the abuse was related to being bathed and groomed. Or maybe she's part gremlin and it's my fault for getting her wet.

I find as many clean towels as possible that look old and are hopefully dog towels and lay some across the hall floor and another on her dog bed. JoJo's dog, Flump, likes to roll about on towels to dry himself and I'm hoping Molly will do the same given I'm about to make myself very unpopular. Once ready, I slip out with the watering can.

I'm concerned she won't stand still to be bathed but her nose is pressed firmly against the front door; she has no intention of going anywhere in case she misses her chance to go inside again.

When I pour the warm soapy water over her Molly begins squawking her outraged protest. She shoots me venomous glances and curls her lip but doesn't actually bite me.

"You are such a good girl, Molly. I know it's not much fun but you'll feel so much better after this, I promise." I keep up a cheery patter and pretend she isn't giving me the evils and, like the reverse psychology I use with Pickle, it seems to work.

"Shall we go and find your tiger when we're finished?" I ask brightly as the last of the muddy rivulets run from her fur and she is once again a tan-and-white-coloured dog instead of a muddy grey colour.

Eventually, to the great relief of both of us, I open the front door and we both scuttle in, a bright flash of lightning illuminating the sky behind us. Molly immediately rolls around on the towels on the floor and then on the one on her bed. I manage to salvage one clean towel for myself so I can wring out my hair and dry my face. My T-shirt and shorts there's no hope for. I mentally add a towel to my list of useful items to carry around on my bike.

My phone beeps a notification of a text. I check and see it's from Ingrid. I reply that all is fine. Ha! I'll put the towels on to wash and text her later to explain. I don't want her worrying while she's at the hospital.

I give Molly some food and fresh water and play with her a bit, hoping the torrential rain will ease off in time for my bike ride back. We seem to be friends again now she's dry. Okay, so she's definitely part-gremlin; I'll have to remember that.

Unfortunately, the torrent of rain doesn't ease up, although at least the thunder and lightning have moved off in the direction of the mountains, where I can see the odd flash of lightning illuminating the sky. In the end I resign myself to a very squelchy ride home on my bike. I may as well not have bothered towelling my hair as I'm just as wet, if not wetter, by the time I get back to the guesthouse.

However, after a shower and dry clothes I feel much better and, as if mirroring my mood, the storm has vanished to be replaced by azure blue skies and brilliant sunshine. As JoJo is still laid low by her migraine, I offer to take Flump out for a walk. He always makes me smile with his antics and, despite his playful ways, is very sensitive to everyone's moods, always nearby to offer a cuddle if someone is sick or cuddling up next to anyone who's upset, human or canine. I appreciate JoJo letting me have lots of time with him. I know she says I'm helping her out but I think she also believes in his untrained but innate emotional-support-dog talents.

I decide we'll head towards the chateau and go past the donkey field. They're certainly little characters. I've realised that Poppy wasn't joking about the bicycle lock; it seems Flump isn't the only animal escapologist around here.

Paul appears from around the corner, making me start with surprise, and Flump eyes him with suspicion. Flump is right to be suspicious – Paul hasn't tired of asking me out, as Poppy and JoJo predicted.

I'd be almost flattered if it wasn't blatantly obvious that he's only still pursuing me because I'm a challenge.

"How is my beautiful English girl?"

I roll my eyes. "I've told you many times I'm not your English girl! In fact, I'm not anyone's girl."

Flump looks up at me and in that moment his large eyes seem to reflect far more understanding of the situation than he can possibly have.

"Except Flump's. I'm definitely one of Flump's girls." I smile down at the little dog. In fact, my heart belongs to many dogs since I moved here. They are so much simpler to love and to please than humans.

Paul sticks out a hand towards Flump to make a fuss of him but Flump narrows his eyes at him and backs away behind my legs, tangling me up in his lead.

Flump peers around my legs at Paul and sniffs his boots and trousers suspiciously. I can't help comparing it to the friendly way he interacted with Anton when they met.

I try to squash down all unhelpful feelings about Anton.

"You are a very strange girl." Paul shrugs. "But I will still ask you out anyway."

I laugh out loud. I can't help it. It's the way that Paul is seemingly magnanimous and yet equally arrogant in his offer that makes me laugh.

He scowls a little. "My English, it is wrong?"

Like most of the French people I've met since I got here, he is always keen to practise his English with me and takes my attempts to speak to him in French as a personal slight to the quality of his language skills. I would've thought speaking in their language was a sign of respect but it's turned out to be more of a social minefield than I first realised.

"No, your English is correct," I say. "You are right. I am a very strange girl – you are not the first to say so. If I were you, I'd stop asking me out and try to find someone a little more normal."

He stares at me, confused, and then shakes his head and walks off, muttering something that doesn't sound very complimentary about English women.

I look down at Flump. "Well that showed him, didn't it?"

I smile when I think about how much Gran will laugh when I tell her about the exchange.

I lean on the fence to the donkey paddock and watch one of the donkeys run around the field with a punctured football in his mouth, the other donkeys chasing him. I think I might have found my kind of place. It's time to get a grip and stop moping. Honestly, I'm here in the sunny South of France; the weather has been great, even if I did get caught in a summer storm today. I'm surrounded by beautiful countryside, clean air and mountains, not to mention staying with great people in a lovingly converted farmhouse, and on top of all that I'm setting up my own business doing something I really enjoy. Plus, with all this walking and cycling I'm doing I can eat some of the delicious patisserie cakes and pastries without feeling any guilt or putting on any weight.

I simply have no business being miserable. I need to focus on all the positive things in my life, on all the things I do have.

I should've worked harder at resisting my feelings for Anton.

I decide it's time to head back to the guesthouse. Maybe if JoJo is still feeling ill and wants me to keep Flump entertained we'll go to my room and I'll let Flump do his emotional-support-dog thing.

"How about we go back and see if JoJo is feeling better?" I ask brightly.

At this he perks up, his concerns about Paul forgotten. Instead, he focuses his attention on the path back to the farmhouse. I smile at him; he is such a sweet little thing, solemn one minute and playing the clown the next. Yet JoJo says he's really sensitive to her moods and always cuddles up to her when she's not well or upset. In fact, she claims he's more sensitive than Cal when it comes to knowing if she's upset. He also checks on the other dogs if they're not okay and tries to cheer them up or break up any pack disputes as a peacemaker.

I'd love to get a dog of my own one day, much as I love borrowing other people's. Maybe if I stay here in France, if I can make a go of the business, I can do. Poppy is always telling me there are lots of dogs waiting in rescue centres, dogs like Flump who was abandoned as a puppy, who'd love a proper home and loving owner. Or older dogs like Barney who is such a loving, joyful boy and who didn't deserve what was going to be his fate – euthanasia because he was going blind. It'll have to wait until I know what's happening though. At the moment I don't even have my own roof over my head and what if I have to go back to London?

I consider what going back to London and back to hotel reception work would feel like and I'm shocked by the strength of the inner rebellion I feel. I actually hate the idea of returning to my old life. I want to stay here, if I can. I need this to be more than just a long working holiday. Something about the area has got beneath my skin, it seems. I get the sense this might be somewhere where being a little bit different from the norm is accepted.

Feeling very out of sorts, I return an overjoyed Flump to JoJo who says she's feeling much better and up to cooking dinner tonight, which is a relief for me. She makes catering for numerous people look so much easier than it really is. I'm far happier being the helper and server. What's more, JoJo even enjoys it. The few times I've had to manage breakfast for the guests on my own I found it stressful trying to keep everyone happy and get the timing right for all the dishes. I suppose getting a lot of my meals at work and mostly only cooking for one hasn't really prepared me to be much use in the catering department.

I settle down on the kitchen floor, glad of the cool

floor tiles, and make a fuss of Barney who senses my presence and snuggles against me. Something about his trusting, uncomplicated affection makes me feel calmer and a little less stressed about my future.

The arrival of Poppy and her furry entourage of Peanut, Treacle, and Pickwick makes it easier to hide my emotions in the mêlée of fuss both demanded and given by the canine contingent. They are so rapturous and unequivocally happy to see the humans they love and haven't seen for ooh… at least six hours that I briefly wonder why humans have made life so complicated. They manage to bring a genuine smile to my face and I'm even laughing when Peanut and Flump together get up to dance to a song on the radio. Flump isn't as agile on his back legs so he puts his front paws into JoJo's hands instead and dances with her.

I recovered enough from my low mood to entertain JoJo and Poppy over our dinner with the tale of the storm and bathing Molly with the watering can.

The salmon salad with tomatoes and lettuce grown in the vegetable patch at the bottom of the farmhouse garden is just right for an evening that still feels a little humid, despite the storm earlier. Over fresh berry mousse cake effortlessly whipped up by JoJo using something that I can only describe as witchcraft, I decide I'm only feeling out of sorts because I've stepped out of my comfort zone. Yes, I have no idea what will happen next but isn't that the point? Surely trying new things is what coming to France is all about? And if I'm trying to do things differently then it's good that I didn't jump straight into a relationship with Anton. Okay, my heart and my head might disagree over that last point but at least I'm starting to feel slightly more positive about things.

Yet after we've finished the mousse cake I can't help bringing up Anton's texts on my phone and scrolling back to the humorous ones, the texts that made me smile. The jokey texts he sent supposedly coming from Pickle and Squeaker were so sweet. There is genuine warmth in those texts and my mind can't help straying to that kiss… God, that kiss… I want to feel like that again, like I'm floating on air, filled up with a joy that's lighter than helium. Alive and vibrant.

Connected.

And just like that the sadness is back. Flump takes me by surprise by jumping up onto my lap without any warning. I kiss the top of his head and bury my face in his fur. Then I straighten up with a sigh and stroke him with one hand while clasping my phone with the other.

"You look deep in thought," Poppy comments, and I wonder whether to just tell her and JoJo about kissing Anton rather than trying to keep it a secret. Things have a habit of coming out around here anyway, or so I hear. Apparently everyone seems to know everyone else's business around here. It's certainly different to London where I never even laid eyes on some of the neighbours in my block of flats.

"I'm okay, just thinking about something that happened the day I went out with Anton."

"Oh? I did wonder when we didn't see you that evening. I just assumed you'd had a good time and stayed out late." Poppy frowns. "So what did happen then?"

JoJo raises her gaze from her own mobile phone and fixes it instead on me, assessing me.

"It was a nice day out. It wasn't a date and I knew that. I wasn't expecting anything to happen." I shrug.

"But something did?" JoJo asks. I have both her and Poppy's undivided attention now.

"Yes, well, sort of… There was a little flirting and when we got back to his house we kissed." I speak quietly.

"You kissed the most eligible single man around and you've waited almost a whole week to tell us?" JoJo shakes her head at me, incredulously.

"So what happened after you kissed then?" Poppy asks, clearly more concerned than JoJo, but then she knows me far better and knows I've been out of sorts this week.

"He pulled away, got cold feet, right in the middle of… well, when things started getting a bit heated." My voice sounds flat, the emotion of the words already squashed further down inside me. I can share the facts but not the strength of my reaction or the tug I've felt towards Anton and his dogs ever since I first met them.

"Did he say why?" Poppy asks tentatively. The tiny crease on her forehead tells me she's worried about me.

Flump tilts his head back so he can look me in the eye. He's obviously concerned too.

"Well, no, but…" I open my mouth but no explanation makes it out. I take a deep breath and try again. "I think he saw something that reminded him of Claire and then he backed away like I was radioactive. No, that's not fair of me, that's really not fair. He did apologise, over and over. I should have realised it wasn't a good idea."

An unusual silence falls over the kitchen. Even the dogs are quiet, either cuddled up together on dog beds or borrowing human laps.

"We didn't say anything," Poppy breaks the silence, "but we kind of wondered about you and Anton. We thought maybe there was a chance of something happening there."

"I know what I said doesn't sound like that big a deal. We kissed, he pulled away, and it should just be awkward at worst but…" I sigh, hesitating, but suddenly desperate to tell someone, to try to explain. "It was more than that. It wasn't just any old kiss. It was completely amazing, out of this world, the best kiss of my life. I've never… never felt anything like that before."

My words sound foolish but the distress is real. It comes from an ache deep inside me. An ache that says unequivocally I've lost something that was meant to be. In the same way as my gran and grandad were meant to be. I had the same belief that my gran had and yet I messed things up somehow, by pushing ahead too quickly.

"So how have things been since then?" JoJo asks. "Fancy a hot chocolate? It feels like a hot chocolate kind of evening."

"Yes, thanks." I nod. "Things have kind of been awkward, but to be fair he's tried to talk about it, to clear the air, and I keep putting him off. It's just too cringey. Plus, he is my biggest client so I planned on just pretending it never happened."

"You thought pretending it never happened was the best course of action?" Poppy raises her eyebrows. "I have to admit that doesn't really sound like the best approach to me."

"She's being polite." JoJo places a mug of frothy hot chocolate down onto the table in front of me.

"I know she's being polite. Poppy is always very polite and tactful," I say, finally raising a smile. "I said it was a plan. I never said it was a good plan."

Peanut, the chihuahua, chooses that moment to take me totally by surprise by also leaping up onto my lap, practically leapfrogging Flump in the process and ending up perched on his back. From where she stands balanced on his back she plants a tiny chihuahua lick on my nose and adds to Flump's attempts to cuddle up and make me feel better.

"They always know when we're feeling crap," Poppy says.

"I'm sure I'm putting out a tonne of stress pheromones. I read dogs can pick up on those using their sense of smell. I'm sorry, doggies. I'm okay, really I am. There's nothing for you to worry about." I stroke them both, planting a kiss on the top of Peanut's tiny head. Both their presence and unconditional love, along with the supportive friendship of Poppy and JoJo, is comforting. Nothing has changed but I do feel better for sharing.

My phone pings with a text alert and my heart beats wildly when I see it's from Anton.

We really need to talk. Not at my place, but maybe in Mirepoix? Bar No. 20 at 19:30 tomorrow evening, if that suits?

I stare at the text, not having a clue what to make of it.

I read his text aloud to Poppy and JoJo and still feel confused.

"Nothing good ever came after the phrase *we need to talk*," I add, grimacing, clicking my phone back onto standby and placing it on the table, well away from me and any errant dog paws. Far, far away; Squeaker's accidental heart emoji is still fresh in my mind.

"He could be wanting to sack me," I suggest.

"Over a drink at a bar?" JoJo pulls a face. "Seems unlikely. He could just text you."

She has a point but I refuse to let myself think of it as Anton asking me out for a drink at a bar. Nothing good ever came from false hope either.

"Maybe he just wants to talk things through and clear the air," Poppy suggests.

"Why at a bar in town instead of at his house though?" I ask.

"It would probably be too awkward talking about it in the place it actually happened." JoJo sits down with her own drink and leans forward, elbows on the table. "A public space is neutral."

I think JoJo might be right. Of the three options – a potential date, him sacking me, or forcing an awkward conversation – I expect it's going to be the awkward conversation.

"Right, I think I'm going to bed. Today already feels like it's been far longer than any day has a right to be." I gently detach Peanut and Flump, my little cuddle companions.

"Here, take Pickwick to bed with you tonight." Poppy thrusts her cute miniature Yorkshire terrier towards me once I've stood up and Flump has made his way back to JoJo's side. "He really adores one-to-one fuss and cuddles."

"Are you sure you don't mind?" I ask, smiling at Pickwick who is looking exceptionally scruffy today, even though I saw him being brushed earlier. Scruffy is his signature look, Poppy says.

"Really, he does love getting one-to-one cuddles. I once borrowed him for a couple of weeks when I was having a bad time," JoJo reassures me. "He really does love having a human all to himself for a change, plus he makes a good furry hot water bottle and cuddler."

"Well, I never say no to dog cuddles." I stroke him and he instantly snuggles into my chest. "But I'm not throwing your ball all night, Pickwick, got it?"

Pickwick instantly looks up at me and sticks his tongue out in true cheeky terrier fashion. I grin. I've always had a fondness for yorkies.

"Don't take it personally − he's always doing that." Poppy laughs. "Though sometimes his timing is remarkably apt."

"Hmm, I'm sure." I kiss the top of Pickwick's head, forcing all thoughts of what exactly Anton is going to ask me as far away from my conscious mind as I can manage. Working out what I'll say to him is complicated, given I don't know what he's planning on asking me.

Chapter Eight

"Don't let the noise of other's opinions drown your own inner voice. And most importantly, have the courage to follow your heart and intuition — they somehow already know what you truly want."
Steve Jobs

The main square in Mirepoix is always busy in the evenings but especially at weekends and even more so in summer. Each café, bar, or restaurant with outside space has tables stretching out into the square and virtually all tables are taken. The air is filled with the relaxed buzz of a holiday destination. I hear snatches of French, English, and Dutch as I make my way to the bar where I'm meeting Anton. When I see him sitting at an outside table in the main central square I feel relieved that he's there already, but at the same time there's a tiny lurch of nerves in the pit of my stomach. I want to ask him why I'm here but there are social niceties to complete first.

He greets me with a kiss to each cheek, which feels odd, even though it is the conventional greeting here. He looks handsome as always, his dark olive skin offset by a pale-blue open-neck shirt. I try to ignore the stirrings of attraction.

Nothing good can come of those kinds of feelings anyway.

As I sip the kir royale, I wait for Anton to explain why we're here tonight.

I recognise Paul a few tables away, sitting with an elegant brunette. Objectively I can recognise he's very attractive – the olive-skinned dark-haired kind of guy most women would think of if asked to imagine a hot Frenchman. Yet the recognition is a dispassionate one. It seems my idea of a perfect Frenchman is still someone with slightly wild, curly, dark hair, a smart jacket teamed with jeans and an ironed shirt. One with quirks and humour and passion for the things he cares about. One who doesn't care about the dog hair on his jacket.

One who remains loyal to his wife even after death.

"What were you thinking about?" asks Anton.

"Nothing really." I shrug and smile. "Sorry, I was just relaxing, soaking up the atmosphere. It's so nice to be able to sit outside to eat in such a beautiful town. But I'm curious, why did you ask me out for a drink this evening? Usually the words 'we need to talk' are followed by bad news."

"They are?" Anton frowns. "Sorry, I didn't mean to worry you. I just think that we should clear the air after what happened to make sure there are no problems between us. I shouldn't have kissed you while I'm not yet ready to move on."

"Oh," I say. "That's okay. I'm really not in a position to start a relationship at the moment anyway."

"No?" He seems surprised.

"No," I reply firmly. "I don't know how long I will be here in France. It depends how well the business goes and if I decide I can make a go of it long-term. It wouldn't be right to start something when I don't know how long I'm going to be around for."

"Okay, well that makes sense," he replies thoughtfully. "I'm glad we cleared things up. The dogs love having you around and life is so much easier. Now we have had this talk we can be friends, yes?"

"Er, yes," I reply, a little nonplussed. "Friends would be good."

Then Anton proceeds to talk to me about the part of his book he's currently researching and some more places he could take me to show me the history and legends of the area. We talk for an hour or so, eventually relaxing back into the easy chat we'd enjoyed during our day out. When he gives me a lift back home it feels like things are almost back to normal. Almost. If it's cleared the air enough for him then I need to make the adjustment too. We are friends who have discussed things in a civilised manner over drinks and so now we have a do-over.

The following week I receive an unexpected phone call from Anton.

"Daisy." Anton's voice at the other end of the phone line sounds panicked. I've never heard him remotely like this.

"What's wrong? One of the dogs?" My mind leaps to the most obvious conclusion, the one thing I can imagine him panicking over.

"Oui. Yes, it is Squeaker," he replies breathlessly. "We were doing the training, you know the... recall training and she saw a cat. We were only on the old railway line footpath near to the house. I thought she would easily find her way back but…"

"I'll come straight over and help you look," I say, already heading for the guesthouse kitchen.

"I would come to pick you up in the car but—"

"You want to stay by the house in case she returns. I understand. That's definitely the best thing. I'll try and get a lift over, and if not I'll get there as soon as I can." I pause and try to calm my own breathing. "It will be okay, Anton. We'll get her back and at least she isn't far from home."

"Yes, I hope it." That his usually impeccable English is slipping a little is a sign of just how stressed he is.

"Okay, I'll be with you very soon," I promise, and end the call.

I'm pretty stressed too, despite my attempts to calm and reassure Anton. My heart aches at the thought of anything bad happening to little Squeaker. With her irrepressibly waggy tail and joyful, enthusiastic affection it would be impossible not to fall in love with her.

She's wriggled her way from my lap into my heart and it's almost scary to realise just how much I love her already. But then love has a way of creeping up on us, a way of working its way under our skin, despite our best intentions.

I give myself a mental shake. Now is not the time to let my feelings for Anton resurface. We've talked, we've decided it's not a good idea, so that's that.

And we'll find Squeaker. Letting myself imagine the worst even for a second is not remotely helpful. Anton has turned to me for help and I need to be the calm one.

"Ah, Poppy." I sigh with relief when I see her in the kitchen. "Could I ask a favour? I have to get over to Anton's quickly because Squeaker has run off and I need to help look."

"Of course, yes, I'll run you over there now. I was actually just on my way out." Poppy bites at her lower lip, her eyes betraying her anxiety. "Do we need to organise a search party? I really want to help but I've got a doctor's appointment. If you don't find her by the time I'm finished I'll head back over to Anton's and help with the search."

"Thanks, you're a star." I squeeze Poppy's arm briefly and follow her out to her car. She even forgoes her usual habit of leaving each of the dogs with a treat and putting the radio on for them. It's a gesture I appreciate as I know just how much she hates leaving them for any length of time; they are masters when it comes to manipulating her, often successful when it comes to guilting her into giving them extra treats for the terrible crime she's about to commit by leaving them for an hour or so.

Once in the car I get my phone out so I can see if there have been any updates.

Nothing. My stomach churns. You hear these stories….

"You really care about her, don't you Daisy?" Poppy asks gently, thankfully jerking my mind out of the dark place it went.

"Yes, I really do," I reply quietly. "Obviously I care about all the animals I look after but…"

"With Anton's dogs it's different?" Poppy's tone is still gentle, but her question implies a deeper meaning and we are both aware of it.

I acknowledge her point with a small nod of my head.

"It's not… well…" I sigh. "Nothing has changed, Poppy. He's not in a position to be in a relationship yet. It's still too soon for him and I can't… I can't commit to him and then leave to go back to England if I need to at the end of the summer. I can't do that to him."

"Or to yourself."

I don't say anything this time. There is nothing to say. We both know it's the truth. In the same way that I know both Anton and I sense that if something were to develop between us it would not be casual. The passion that simmered beneath the surface the day of the kiss, the way I feel about him… is not remotely casual. So yes, one or both of us would be very hurt if things didn't work out because it turned out he wasn't really ready or I have to give up on my dream of living in my own French farmhouse in the sun one day, like Poppy does.

I stare out of the window at the glorious fields of sunflowers as we pass. If Squeaker has chased a cat across the fields, how on earth are we going to see her amongst these giant flowers easily six or seven times her height?

An open packet of her favourite treats and calling her is all I can think of to do.

When I get to Anton's, I thank Poppy briefly and get out of the car, barely hearing her words of encouragement.

The moment I see Anton's face I know there's been no good news.

I briefly reach down to stroke Pickle, aware he's picking up on the anxiety. He doesn't react to me with the friendly welcome he has started to display now he's used to me. He's chewing on one of Anton's scarfs, regressing to his old behaviour by retreating behind the sofa.

I want to comfort him but know I need to prioritise and I turn to face Anton. I long to give him a quick hug. I have to cross my arms in front of me to stop myself from touching him, so strong is the urge to comfort him.

"Okay, so, action plan?" I ask and when he doesn't immediately take charge I forge ahead with my own plan. "How about you return to where you last saw her, given you know exactly where that was and you search around that area. I'll stay closer to the house and search the fields closest to us but within hearing if she does return home. Does that work for you?"

Grim-faced, Anton nods.

"And we both have her favourite treats with us, packets open so she can smell them. We call for a few minutes, listen for a few minutes and repeat. Okay?" I ask. "And then meet back here in thirty minutes? Just in case, because I know the mobile phone coverage is patchy in some places. You don't want to still be searching and worrying if she's tucked up safely in her bed here."

"Good plan." Anton exhales loudly and runs a hand through his hair distractedly.

"The treats?"

"In the kitchen." Anton seems to gather some strength from my bossiness. Maybe it's just what he needs right now.

When he hands the packet of duck treats to me he grasps my hand and squeezes it firmly.

"Thank you, Daisy. I…" He hesitates. "Just… thank you."

"That's okay. Of course I want to help find her and, Anton, we will find her, okay?" I squeeze his hand back.

"Okay." He manages a ghost of a smile.

I reluctantly let go of his hand, wishing I could prolong the contact, and I head for the front door.

"It's okay, Pickle. We're just going to find Squeaker. We'll be back soon, okay?" I do my best to reassure Pickle although all I can see of him is his tail sticking out from behind the sofa and it isn't wagging.

I try to smile in a suitably bolstering and encouraging way but Anton's expression is still grim as he heads off for the old railway line that's been converted into miles of foot and cycle paths.

I try to think as I walk the perimeter of the old farmhouse garden, thinking about where Squeaker may have got stuck if she'd tried to find her way home. Maybe her collar snagged on a branch or bit of fencing somewhere?

I call repeatedly and then listen.

Nothing.

I calm my breathing and refuse to panic. I do a wider circle around the property, climbing fences where necessary, not caring about any of the scratches on my bare legs beneath my shorts. This time, when I call her name I swear I hear something in the distance. It's very faint. It could be any of the neighbours' numerous dogs but my intuition tells me to move in the direction of the sound.

Thankfully I'm in an open field now so moving around is easier. I move towards the direction of the faint barking and keep calling, then stay still and listen.

Yes, there it is again, a little stronger this time but I'd swear it's Squeaker's woof. I run now, towards one of the old bridges that spans the river. I can't see her anywhere but I can hear her. It's only once I'm at the bridge that I can take a guess at where she is. There are several storm drains that help to divert the water coming down from the hills under the roads and away from the village. As we've had relatively little rainfall recently they are, thankfully, devoid of any water but I can easily imagine the cat she was chasing being able to fit through the narrow tunnels where Squeaker could have caught her collar on a tree root or something similar.

I pause at the entrance and call her name again.

She whimpers a soft reply this time, a sound that wrenches at my heart. Is she hurt? I have to get her out. I check my mobile reception but barely have half a bar here.

I curse and eye the opening. I've always been claustrophobic and normally there's nothing that would induce me to wriggle down a drain opening, even one that's partially aboveground.

This is not a normal situation though. Squeaker lets out another little whine, clearly not understanding why I'm not coming to help her.

"It's all right, sweetie. I'm here and I'm coming to get you," I announce with more optimism than I actually feel.

Yet I can't leave her while I go to track Anton. What if I couldn't find the exact same spot again? Or she's injured and needs first aid immediately?

There's another whimper from inside the tunnel that tugs at my heart strings. It's no good; I have to go in after her. I check my mobile to find I've only got one bar of phone service that disappears when I start to text. Damn. I finish the text and wave my phone in the air, hoping to catch the elusive single bar of signal.

A louder whimper makes me stop my efforts and I decide to leave my phone at the entrance to the tunnel so I don't crush it while I'm crawling in to get her. It will also give the text a chance to get to Anton, sharing my location.

I crawl in and see her, poor thing, her collar caught on a root that has penetrated the tunnel wall. Relief almost overwhelms me when I realise she's okay and apparently not injured.

"Hey Squeaker. It's okay, I've got you, sweetheart."

I reach out my hand to her and she gives it an enthusiastic lick.

I wriggle further into the tunnel, lying on my stomach, trying to ignore how cramped it is, and aware of other roots scratching my bare arms and legs. I remind myself there's plenty of air and just focus on rescuing a frightened little dog. Sweat is rolling down my face, a combination of the effort and the heat.

Closer now, I manage to unhook Squeaker's collar and she thanks me by giving me an enthusiastic licking.

"Okay, thanks Squeaker, I got the message." I laugh. "Shall we go and find Anton? I've just got to work out how to wriggle backwards, so bear with me."

It's easier said than done. I feel a root snag one of the belt loops of my shorts and try to reverse my movement to get myself free but it doesn't work and there's no way of getting my arm underneath my body because there's not enough space. I rest my head on the ground and just pray Anton got my text and I'm not stuck here too long.

Squeaker has cheered up and seems to think we're playing a game. She licks me again and I close my eyes, controlling my breathing. Anton will come. We're not far from the house. Even if he doesn't get the text, he'll retrace my steps around the fields surrounding the house.

I calm my breathing and take comfort from the fact Squeaker curls up next to my head and settles down to keep me company, even if she could easily run out the other end of the tunnel now.

It feels like ages but is probably only about five minutes before I feel Squeaker's body stiffen and her ears prick up.

"Are you okay in there?" Anton's voice from behind me echoes in the tunnel.

Squeaker woofs her response, right next to my ear.

"Just fine thanks, enjoying a nice lie-down," I shout back. "Squeaker is here; she's cuddled up to me. She's fine too, just got her collar caught on a tree root."

I'm not sure how much he understands. There's a moment of silence and then he clears his throat.

"I hate to interrupt your… lie-down, but are you coming out?"

Clearly my sarcasm didn't translate.

"I would love to but my shorts are caught on a tree root," I shout back. "I'm not staying in here for the fun of it. Trust me, it's not that great in here."

"I'm sure." He replies, more kindly now, perhaps hearing the stress in my voice. "Okay, we'll get you out."

I feel Anton's hand on my ankle and the intimate contact makes me catch my breath. I almost forget all about the confines of the tunnel.

"Which side are you stuck? Where is the root?" His voice is calm, his relief evident now Squeaker is safe.

"Umm…" I try to focus. "It's on my right side, but I can't reach my arm back to unhook it."

"I'm going to slide my hand in and try to feel for the root, okay? Let me know if I'm hurting you."

I catch my breath again, feeling his hand sliding up my bare leg. He must be scraping his knuckles but doesn't complain so I bite my lip and ignore the sensation of being squashed.

Then his hand retreats again.

"I'm sorry, I can't fit my hand down the side," he admits.

"Really?" I groan and squeeze my eyes shut. What's next? The local fire department? The whole village turning up to watch me being dug out? I try to control my breathing and the panicked desire to get out right now.

"Shh, it's okay." Anton puts his hand on my ankle again and strokes the skin. I'm not sure it calms me down exactly but it certainly distracts me.

"I'm going to try sliding my hand underneath you. The tunnel seems taller than it is wide. I'm going to… uh… undo your shorts so you can wriggle forwards out of your shorts. Then if it's clear enough you can either make it out the other side or you come out backwards once I've retrieved your shorts. Okay?"

I pause for a heartbeat. "Yes, okay."

It's just as awkward as I thought it would be. His hand on the bare skin of my inner thighs, then reaching underneath me… I feel my pulse quicken and I have never been more grateful that women don't get erections. Hopefully he'll never know the effect his touch is having on me. In this horrible tunnel of all places.

Awkwardly, he undoes the button and pulls down the zip, then he slides his hand out backwards.

My cheeks are burning, even though no one can see me. I do hope there's no one else out and about.

I opt for forwards as it's easier to manage physically and Squeaker leads the way, probably wondering what the hold-up was about but just happy to be close to us again.

Us.

I grit my teeth and try to push the surge of longing that thought stirs in me. There can't be an us. We've talked it out. There's no point letting my mind even go there.

I do manage to wriggle out now I'm unencumbered by the belt loops and thickness of my denim fabric.

I'm hoping as I emerge from the other end he'll put my red face down to the heat and exertion.

He's too preoccupied with being bowled over by an ecstatic Squeaker. He's on the ground at her level to greet her and she's jumped into his lap, one paw on each shoulder and both tongue and tail working overtime to express her joy at being reunited with him.

When he can get free, he hands me my shorts, trying not to meet my eyes, or let his gaze drop lower.

I swiftly put them back on, feeling grubby and sweaty, desperate for a shower, and unaccountably sad at being on the outskirts of the reunion.

Anton must pick up on this as he levers himself up from the ground, first re-attaching Squeaker's lead, and then walks over to me.

To my surprise, he draws me into a hug and holds me firmly against him.

"I can never thank you enough, Daisy. I am so

grateful we found her, thanks to you." He gives me a final squeeze before releasing me.

We.

We. Us.

The word resonates with my heart, no matter how I try to stop it. I am so, so tempted to pull Anton back into another hug.

"I'd er… better get back for a shower," I mumble.

"You could shower here, if you like? I could cook you dinner?" Anton's words tempt me, further stirring the yearning inside me to let myself touch him… love him… But nothing has changed, and if I stay for a shower and dinner we might end up doing something we've both decided isn't best for us.

I hesitate and then steady my resolve.

"Thanks for the offer, but I think I need a change of clothes too." I gesture at my grubby clothes. "I wouldn't say no to a lift home though."

Is that a flicker of disappointment in his eyes? Or just my wishful thinking?

Whatever it is or isn't, I'm not sure I'll know now because the moment has slipped away from us.

The next morning I find a panicked Poppy in the guesthouse kitchen.

"I can't find Peanut," she says, looking frantically around her.

Another missing dog? Though with Peanut she's almost definitely lost inside the house, just one of the downsides of owning such a tiny dog, so I won't have to do any more crawling through drain tunnels.

"I'll help you look." I pat Poppy on the arm. "I expect she's probably just playing hide and seek – you told me yourself how much she likes that. Or maybe she's taken a dog chew off to a tiny space somewhere that the other dogs can't squeeze into so she can protect it from being stolen."

"True." Poppy chews her lower lip distractedly. "Those are the most likely options."

"But you're sure she's in the house?" I ask.

"About ninety nine per cent sure, yes." Poppy sighs. "I've really got to cure her of thinking that hide and seek is a great game."

"Have you checked under the sofas and inside the cushion covers?"

"Yes to under the sofas but not inside the cushion covers. That's usually a Treacle hiding place but there's no harm in checking."

"How about you recheck this floor and I'll check upstairs under all the beds – the unoccupied ones, that is. I'm sure some guests might still be in bed in which case she couldn't have got inside the room, could she?" I make my way to the staircase.

"Unless she's with Flump." Poppy rolls her eyes. "Remember, he can open doors if they're not actually locked. I do tell— I mean, I *remind* guests to keep their doors locked but I swear Flump is a Houdini dog as well as an accomplished thief."

I can't help smiling. "Don't worry, we'll find her. I thought you'd been doing some recall training with her?"

"Yes," Poppy sighs. "But she still thinks it's a great game to hide from me. She and Flump do that a lot when they're not chasing each other. They hide behind furniture in the house and bushes in the garden and leap out at each other to make each other jump."

JoJo joins us, stifling a yawn.

"Not found her yet then?" she asks Poppy.

"No, I think we'll do another sweep." Poppy looks around her distractedly. "Is Flump with you by any chance?"

"Yes…" JoJo looks over her shoulder. "Er… no. Though I swear he was there just a moment ago. Daisy and I will do upstairs and you check the ground floor, Poppy."

Pickwick, Treacle, and Barney are all eating dog

chews on their beds in the kitchen and completely ignore us when we exhort them to "Go find Peanut". "Flump's favourite game at the moment is hide the slipper," JoJo says as we climb the stairs to the first floor. "Which basically means I walk around first thing in the morning with only one slipper on until I find wherever he's decided to hide it in the night."

"Flump is so cute though; you can't be cross with him." I stick up for the little dog who has been so lovely to me ever since I got here, always unstintingly giving me cuddles when he sensed I needed them.

"True, he's mischievous rather than naughty," JoJo admits, smiling fondly, and I know she'd defend him with her last breath.

We eventually find Peanut under one of the beds in an unoccupied room but only because we catch a glimpse of Flump's tail wagging beneath the bed.

"He doesn't seem to realise that now he's fully grown he doesn't fit in the same spaces with Peanut anymore." JoJo rolls her eyes. "Come on, you two, game over. Out you come."

Flump does a belly crawl backwards and emerges tail first from beneath the bed. He immediately rolls over on his back, all four paws in the air, and I swear he bats his eyelashes at JoJo as if to say, *Look how sweet I am! You couldn't possibly be cross with me.*

It obviously works as JoJo reaches down to give him a chest and tummy rub.

Peanut isn't so compliant and she's not ready for the game to be over. I lie on my stomach on the floor and reach an arm out beneath the bed, as far as it will go. I just manage to brush the edge of her collar and she backs away again in response so she's just out of my reach. I try entreating her playfully, then exhorting her sternly and neither approach works. She just eyes me with pity, as though recognising an amateur.

Eventually I give up and get back to my feet. Peanut immediately darts out to the edge of the bed to stick her head out then spins round and dives back in before I can catch her.

Both JoJo and I try to coax her out or grab her in vain while Flump luxuriates in being the good boy of the two. Though if we'd hoped heaping praise on Flump would draw Peanut out, we were wrong.

"I think we'll have to fetch Poppy or some treats," JoJo gets to her feet and picks Flump up.

"Or maybe even both." I join her and we leave the room, only to be overtaken by a tiny streak of chihuahua as she darts past us and dances on the landing, as though celebrating her 'win', bouncing on her hind legs like a kangaroo and waiting for us impatiently as though wondering what's keeping us.

"Little whatsit." JoJo shakes her head, laughing, as I scoop Peanut up to perch on my chest. She tucks her head in, under my chin, and I can't help instantly forgiving her. She's cheeky but she's a sweet little thing. Before I met Poppy's dogs I had no idea chihuahuas could be so entertaining.

"The worst thing is she's teaching the others it's a game," JoJo continues. "You know about Treacle taking to hiding inside cushion covers?"

"Yes, I remember Poppy telling me about it."

"Well, a few months ago he went missing and we hunted everywhere. Eventually we found him in the shower. He hates the shower. He'd taken a treat in there to eat so none of the other dogs could steal it. Who knew dogs could be that…"

"Bright?" I suggest.

"I was going to say devious." JoJo laughs and we head back to the kitchen to find Poppy sitting in Barney's bed with him, stroking his large floppy ears.

"I heard you found her. Usual tricks?"

JoJo nods.

"Peanut, honestly!" Poppy tells Peanut off in her sternest voice, which isn't actually that stern.

Peanut leaps straight from my arms to Poppy's where she stands on her chest and licks Poppy's nose.

"Hello sweetheart," Poppy mumbles absently. "I do

wish you wouldn't play hide and seek. You do get me worried."

Peanut snuggles her head under Poppy's chin and cuddles up contentedly.

"Little monkey." Poppy kisses Peanut's head. "Leo says I let her emotionally manipulate me."

"What do you say?" I ask.

"I tell him to piss off of course." She grins suddenly, her sombre mood broken. "The fact he's right is completely irrelevant."

I laugh, realising this minor domestic drama has done a good job of distracting me from thinking about Anton.

Flump climbs into Barney's bed as well but has to sit on top of Barney as, with Poppy in there too, there's not much room.

A tender longing rises inside me as I think how much I'd love this for myself. To own my own dogs, ones I don't have to hand back at the end of the day, or the next morning if I've borrowed them for cuddles. I know Pickle and Squeaker are Anton's dogs but I've spent lots of time with them and I feel the closest to them of all the dogs I look after. They've tugged at my heartstrings almost as much as Anton has, though in a different way, obviously.

And with the thought of Anton my light and cosy

mood bursts like a balloon pricked with a needle, bringing me tumbling back to earth.

I have so much love to give them all and it's heart-breaking that I can't. I wish I could understand his reasons, or at the very least feel at peace about accepting them.

"How did the drink with Anton go the other evening?" JoJo asks. "You've been very elusive – we haven't had a chance to ask you about it."

"Oh yes, that was the other night, wasn't it? How was it?" Poppy has her polite expression on but it barely masks her curiosity.

"It was okay, I suppose." I shrug. "He wanted to clear the air, and explained he doesn't feel ready to move on yet, in terms of a relationship. He wasn't odd about it."

"Oh, and what did you say?" JoJo raises her eyebrows.

"Oh, you know, the spiel about needing to focus on my career right now and not even knowing if I'll be staying in France or not so a relationship isn't on the cards." I manage a small smile. "At least he didn't ask me to meet to chat so he could fire me, so that's a definite plus."

"And has talking about it cleared the air?" Poppy asks.

"Yes, I suppose it was better than my approach of avoiding him for the foreseeable future," I admit ruefully. "And, funnily enough, I was helping him look for a missing dog yesterday – Squeaker ran off and managed to get stuck in one of the storm drains."

"Poor thing!" Poppy exclaims.

"Poor me too. I ended up stuck too while I was trying to rescue her."

"So you're on good terms with Anton now then?" JoJo asks.

"Good terms in that we've agreed we can't be anything more than friends, yes. He's not ready to move on yet and I've just got to focus on building my life here now," I say. "I can't start a relationship if I don't even know what country I'm going to be living in come the autumn."

"That sounds very sensible." JoJo nods.

Poppy is biting her lower lip, clearly wanting to say more but thankfully she holds back. It's hard enough doing the right thing without Poppy questioning if it's the right thing for me.

———————

A few days later I'm lying on my back on the rug in Anton's living room with Pickle sitting on my stomach, for reasons known best to himself, as I play tug of war with Squeaker. She's quite a scrappy little thing and adores a good play-fight.

That's how Anton finds me, when he returns from his work trip. Once the dogs realise he's home they abandon me and scamper to greet him, Pickle using my stomach as a trampoline launch pad.

"Oof!" I rub my stomach.

"So this is what you get up to when I'm not here, is it?" Anton jokes. "Why do I have to miss out on the fun stuff?"

You want to roll around on the floor with me? I suppress the very inappropriate question. My cheeks flush, suffused with heat, and I push myself up off the floor by my elbows.

"Did you have a good trip? Any interesting or valuable documents?" I ask instead, retreating to safer conversational ground as I stand up and re-do my ponytail, which hasn't survived the dog play-fighting intact.

He shrugs. "It was a job – nothing of great value except for a few rare volumes of philosophy, but an interesting collection."

I notice the bags of shopping at his feet. Squeaker is doing her best to stick her head into the bags to investigate.

"Shall I get those for you before Squeaker eats your dinner?" I move forward to take one of the bags out of her reach.

Pickle is wagging his tail happily, almost as enthusiastically as Squeaker, and it's so nice to see him relaxed. He recovered quickly from the stress of the day when Squeaker went missing and there's barely a trace of the depressed dog I met over a month ago. He still has his moments, if something triggers him, but overall he seems to be doing well and he seems happiest when both Anton and I are with them.

"Actually, it's your dinner too, if you're okay to stay?" Anton asks. "You did say you don't need to get back to the guesthouse early this evening, didn't you?"

I nod. Anton hadn't been sure how long his work trip would take and so JoJo isn't expecting me back to help with dinner prep or serving this evening.

"Are you sure you aren't too tired after your work trip today?"

"The drive wasn't too far and anyway, I still need to thank you properly for finding Squeaker and helping me out that day." He follows closely behind me into the kitchen

"Thanks really aren't necessary." I put the bag onto the kitchen counter.

"Yes Daisy, they really are," Anton says firmly,

depositing his own bag and laying his hand over mine and squeezing it. "I reacted badly. The thought of losing her…"

His voice breaks a little and I feel all the unspoken words: that the thought of losing Squeaker, after the trauma of his bereavement, was simply too much to cope with.

There's a palpable connection between us in that moment. Not just in his hand on mine but his heart and mine, communicating without words.

Connecting.

I clear my throat. "But we didn't lose her."

I wish I hadn't used the word *we*. So much for keeping an emotional distance. Who am I kidding exactly?

He doesn't appear to notice or mind.

"Yes, and you being there made all the difference. So you're going to sit down at the table while I cook for you to say thank you. No arguments." Anton's tone is much firmer now and I can hardly turn him down. It would be rude.

Not that I want to, or have the willpower to walk away from the only place I actually want to be right now.

"Okay, thank you." I sit down and let Anton tell me all about the ancient abbey he's visited, now in private hands and the assortment of artefacts, papers, and books he'd been asked to value for insurance purposes. He sears some fresh tuna in a pan and prepares a salad, which makes a nice summer meal.

We chat about his childhood growing up in the countryside, about his bookish father and schoolteacher mother. I tell him how much I love the area and how it feels right for me somehow, being here. I say that I'd needed something to push me out of a London job that was okay but wasn't what I wanted to do long-term. I don't explain what the catalyst was that moved me on in the first place.

"So, what *do* you want to do long-term?" Anton asks, fixing his serious dark eyes on me.

"Well, I feel I was persuaded into a sensible job and I liked working with people – well, most of the time anyway..." I hesitate and gaze out of the kitchen window at the sun-drenched landscape beyond. "I love working with animals, spending time in nature. I feel a lot freer and sort of... I don't know, more myself now, if that makes sense?"

Anton nods. "You seem more relaxed."

I almost laugh out loud given the low hum of sexual tension thrumming through my veins right now. The fact we are here, in the kitchen, where we kissed, isn't helping. I'd be lying if I said I didn't replay that scene every night before I fall asleep. I know it's not good for me but I can't help it.

Instead I shrug. "I feel more relaxed."

Not to mention how much I feel at home here in Anton's house. Odd given it's the house he shared with his wife but I feel strangely welcome, like the old stone walls enjoy my presence.

It's purely fanciful thinking. I'm comfortable here because I spend so much time here. End of.

Yet it would be so easy to shut off reality for an hour or so and pretend that we're a couple, relaxing at the end of the day. It strikes me that Anton is probably lonely. Too many meals-for-one. That thought tugs at my heart, at the fragile will keeping me from reaching out for Anton. The desire to connect is palpable.

Yes, I knew this would be dangerous. Too many opportunities for accidental touching as we clear the table and stack dishes in his dishwasher. Each accidental brush of the hand sends a frisson of sexual desire through me, opening up a chasm of longing within me.

Making me wish that things could be different.

Making me hope that Anton feels the same magnetic, sexual tug. I glance at him once we've finished clearing up and when our eyes lock it hits me, that sense of falling into him. The powerful force of nature I felt the first time we kissed. I need to get out of the kitchen before I do something I regret.

"It's such a beautiful evening." I break eye contact and walk towards the window, folding my arms over my chest in an attempt to stop myself from reaching out for Anton.

"We could go for a drive," he suggests. "I can put your bicycle in the back of the car and I'll take you home after a little diversion. Have you seen the view from Fanjeaux yet?"

I shake my head. "No, I haven't. Yes, let's do that."

Getting out and about seems like a good idea in the circumstances.

I automatically check the dogs' water bowl and leave them each a treat before collecting my things, relieved to be leaving the place that holds such a potent memory for both of us.

It's a beautiful evening. The landscape is mellow with sunflower fields and hills glowing gold with the slanting, early evening light. Anton takes us through tiny villages with quaint shuttered houses and picturesque churches. We climb up into the village of Fanjeaux and, once at the viewpoint, I can see why he's brought me here. The views are incredible. We are looking down over the rolling hills and woods of the valley below and can see all the way to Carcassonne and the Black Mountains. The light is iridescent and luminously beautiful. I can understand why so many artists travelled to the South of France to paint. There's the faintest tinge of rose and amber to the sky in the west, the beginnings of a beautiful sunset.

"Wow, it's a beautiful view from up here," I exclaim and turn to Anton who is watching me closely.

"Yes, it's a beautiful view," he says quietly, ambiguously.

Did he mean…? Was he talking about me? Surely not. I'm in my dog-walking outfit of denim shorts and T-shirt, my hair pulled up into a ponytail as it's the only way to stay cool when I'm walking and cycling.

I turn away, unwilling to be guilty of hearing what I want to hear and imagining the strength of his feelings is the same as mine. How many times must I remind myself we've discussed the situation as adults and decided not to take things further? I've got to let this go. Staring into the sunset with Anton is hardly a great way to do that. The glint of metal sculptures catches my eye to my right.

I walk towards them, Anton following behind me. The statues are clever, quirky metal representations of knights and holy men, some sitting and some staring out at the view.

"They represent the story of the Cathars and the

crusaders. As you can see, they are looking out towards Carcassonne." Anton slips into tour guide and teacher mode, and the moment I'm not sure actually was "a moment" has passed.

I nod. I've read about the basic history of the crusades in this region to crush the Cathars and seize their castles and lands.

When Anton drives me home we are heading in the opposite direction, so we watch the sun setting, changing the sky from hues of amber and soft pink into increasingly vivid hues of rose and magenta, framed by the Pyrenean mountain range.

Driving off into the sunset. So impossibly romantic. Yet surely that hadn't been Anton's intent? I glimpse across at him but his face is impassive. I have no idea what he's thinking or feeling.

I know that were he to make one small move, a hand on mine or a hug goodbye… Or if he were to ask me what I wanted now, tonight… Well, I know right now I couldn't find it in me to be strong and say no. I simply wouldn't be able to resist him.

So it's probably best all round that he simply deposits my bicycle at the gates to Les Coquelicots guesthouse and wishes me a good night before driving off home.

Probably best.

. . .

So why do I feel melancholy as I wheel the bicycle round to my gîte bedroom? Why does doing the right thing feel so terribly wrong?

It seems that the more time Anton and I spend together just as friends, the more the sexual tension between us grows. We often have a meal or a drink together if he gets back after a long trip and I'm dog sitting. It becomes a habit that feels normal, and because I'm spending time in his home while I'm dog sitting I feel perfectly relaxed in his house too. There are days when I'm sure Anton feels the intense desire as strongly as I do. I wonder if he also repeats in his head the reasons we said it wouldn't be a good idea, almost like a mantra we need to remember.

One particularly hot day I'm sitting in the shade on the guesthouse terrace with Poppy, while JoJo has taken advantage of a guest-free night to have a day off with Cal in Carcassonne. Poppy and I are drinking homemade lemonade with plenty of ice and she's sketching in her journal while I'm checking my messages from home. I've still had nothing from Gran which is a shame, but not entirely unexpected. Then I read a text that makes me sit up straight suddenly and sigh.

"What's up? Bad news?" Poppy asks, looking up from her sketch of the chihuahuas sunbathing on a sun lounger.

I look up from my phone, feeling disjointed somehow. Like a part of me has been catapulted back to London while the rest of me is here in the South of France.

"The friend I sublet my room of the flatshare to in London, Sonya, she's going to have to leave straight away to go home to Australia instead of staying for the rest of the summer. Her mum is ill." I rub my forehead with my fingers, feeling the beginnings of a tension headache coming on.

"And I guess you don't have a formal contract with her because it was a temporary arrangement?" Poppy asks awkwardly.

"Yep. Well, technically, according to the official lease Vicky and I have in place with the landlord, I'm still liable for fifty per cent of the rent and bills." I pull a face. "I do have a little saved up but I can't afford to pay for the empty room and council tax etc for more than one month maximum."

"What does your flatmate Vicky say about it?"

Poppy lifts up her journal to the light to compare her sketch of the sunbathing chihuahuas to the real models.

"She's not too happy." I grimace. "I'll tell her I can cover the next month but I know after that I'm either going to have to decide to go home earlier than planned or give notice on the lease so they can advertise for someone else."

"You don't want to go home early, do you?" Poppy frowns.

"No, not at all, but I wasn't planning on burning my bridges just yet either."

"Maybe you can leave it a little while and see how things go, business-wise, then make your decision when you've got a clearer picture." Poppy suggests.

"I suppose it's just a reminder that we never really know, for all our plans, just what's going to happen in life." I agree that her plan seems the most sensible one.

Later on, I'm still feeling pensive. The unease concerning the unexpectedness of the news has burrowed beneath my skin and I simply can't shake it. It's all very well thinking I could just wait for Anton to be ready but what if I have to go back to England earlier than expected? Or, what if he regrets having said 'no' and is respecting my need to focus on building a life here? Maybe he's feeling the same levels of passionate intensity and would welcome the news I haven't given up on him.

That I can't give up on him.

I'm feeling the urge to act. It's coming from my core, from a part of me my brain can't ignore or logic away.

What do I have to lose? A little more dignity? So what? I've not got much of it left and it's not so important really, in the grand scheme of things. What I might potentially have to gain, however, now that's a prize worth risking making a fool of myself for. Some may say I never learn but I think it's a case of refusing to let fear stand in the way of something potentially amazing.

To feel the way I felt in Anton's arms again. To be immersed in the sheer joy of kissing him… There's very little I wouldn't do if it might potentially lead to that soul-deep joy again.

Walking Les Coquelicot's furry pack down to the lake gives me space to think. The only sound is the lapping of the water at the shore, the birdsong, and also Pickwick doing his pigeon impression noises when he starts his favourite occupation of trying to unearth a giant stick that is doomed to fail because it is in fact a tree root and he is a miniature Yorkshire terrier.

Maybe the reason I can't let go of my certainty that Anton is the man for me is because he really is the man for me and we just got the timing wrong. I've absolutely no doubt that Anton felt that connection, that amazing joy when we were in each other's arms and the sense of being magnetically drawn to each other. It was guilt about feeling that kind of connection with a woman who wasn't his wife, I'm sure of it. Has Anton had time to process his feelings yet?

The kind of connection my gran had with Grandad. The kind of connection that we can probably survive without, but why would you want to? Who would turn down this amazing gift of joy?

The "knowing" that Gran had, that precognition that Grandad was meant to be her husband… If I'm honest with myself, I have the same certainty about Anton, despite my talk of being sensible. No matter how many times I've tried to let go of him, to talk myself out of more opportunities to get hurt, the certainty remains. I've been trying to learn how to accept my authentic self while living here. It's in my nature to go by my heart, my gut, my intuition and to trust that knowing, even when there's no evidence to back it up.

I watch Peanut and Treacle stand at the lake's edge, delight in Flump have a more raucous splash around, and smile to see Pickwick's tenacity with the exposed tree root – he's certainly determined to take that tree home, and you have to admire his optimism.

Yes, I've decided, no more wondering or trying to guess what Anton is thinking or feeling.

I'm just going to adopt the mature approach Anton showed in choosing to discuss the situation after our first kiss. No more saving face. It's time to employ clear, direct, and open communication about how I feel and what I would like to happen, with the intention to wait for Anton until he's ready to take that step, if he isn't already. I know I was determined never to be in a position of waiting for an unavailable man, but in the case of Anton… some things are worth waiting for.

My resolve doesn't weaken as I walk the dogs back to the guesthouse and release them into the kitchen with JoJo. I hang up the leads and head straight for my bike, barely exchanging two words with anyone in case I lose my nerve.

If Anton doesn't feel the same, I'm still glad for the memory of that joy and that sensation of connection. After all, if he rejects me now I'll just be in the same position I'm already in, no worse off, just a little embarrassed, which I can survive.

I can survive it if he doesn't feel the same way as me, I reassure myself as I pedal determinedly down the lane. I barely take in the sunflower fields or the new donkey foal in Angeline's paddock. All I can think about is whether my gamble will work.

By the time I get to Anton's house and ring the doorbell before my courage can fail me, my heart is pumping fast and not from the exercise. All the cycling since I got here has definitely increased my fitness.

I hear an excited volley of woofs from Pickle and Squeaker and can't help folding my arms defensively across my chest as I wait. I know closed body language isn't exactly helpful right now but the instinct to protect myself is visceral and strong. I can't hear Anton yet but his car is here. I do hope he's here; I don't think I could get up the courage to do this a second time.

Finally I hear his footsteps and him talking to the dogs.

I take a deep breath as he opens the door a crack to stop the dogs rushing out. When he sees it's me he opens the door wider so the dogs can run out and meet me and I can come into the house.

"Daisy, this is a surprise." His face morphs from confusion, sure that he hadn't booked me for dog sitting, to pleasure at seeing me anyway, whatever the reason.

"A nice surprise, I hope?" I ask casually, so glad of the dogs as a buffer, giving me something to do with my hands as I reach down to stroke them, taking some of my self-consciousness away.

No more polite chit chat and disappointment afterwards that nothing meaningful was exchanged in words, even though I've felt that current of meaningfulness pulsing between us each time we've seen each other.

"Of course, we are always happy to see you," he replies smoothly. "Sometimes I think the dogs like you more than they do me."

We. Yes, the dogs – he clearly finds them a useful buffer too.

I smile. "Well, of course I do bribe them."

"There wasn't anything planned today, was there?" Anton asks cautiously.

"No, I was just at a loose end and I thought why not come over and say hi," I say, my chest a little tight with nerves. "So… hi."

"Hi to you too." Anton grins. A moment passes when I desperately try to think of what to say next. Luckily he beats me to it. "Would you like to come in? We can sit in the garden and have a drink if you like?"

"Yes, that would be nice." I smile, relieved and able to breathe easily again.

We walk through the kitchen and I do my best to ignore the split-second memory replay of the time he kissed me just before he stepped away. Not helpful right now.

"Would you like a kir royale?"

"That would be lovely," I say, thinking a little Dutch courage might come in handy.

I watch Anton pour measures of crème de cassis into long-stem glasses and then top them off with champagne.

"Do you always have champagne in the fridge?"

"I was keeping it for when I finish my book."

"Oh, you've finished it already? That's great news."

"Just a first draft." He shrugs modestly. "I can always buy some more for the day I finish my final draft."

"That's great progress though." I follow Anton through the kitchen door and crunch across the gravel towards the wrought-iron love seat beneath the shade of an olive tree.

The dogs follow us too and flop down on the grass, under the shade of the tree.

The seat is rather snug so it's impossible to stop my thigh pressing up against Anton's when we sit.

"To your book, may it be a great success." I raise my glass in a toast and Anton chinks his glass against mine.

"Thank you," he replies gravely, his gaze resting curiously on me as though trying to puzzle me out.

I turn my face away and take a sip, savouring the fruity blackcurrant bubbles on my tongue and the warmth that slides down into my chest with each mouthful.

I get the impression he's waiting for me to reveal why I'm here, and that he can keep quiet, keep waiting, for as long as it takes. I'm sure my cheeks are growing pinker by the minute. I feel jittery but I can't bottle this now. My mind flashes forwards to how I'll feel tomorrow if I don't take this chance. The worst he can say is thanks but no thanks.

I stare down at the blackcurrant bubbles in my glass. That isn't actually the worst he could say but he's a nice guy, so I can't see him letting me down with anything but kindness.

"Everything okay, Daisy?" Anton asks, his tone warm but concerned.

"Yes… I've just been thinking… well, wondering really…" My heart starts to pound and I feel a little faint. I take a deep breath and start again. "I know that things happened a little… fast the day of our first outing."

When you kissed me, I don't say.

"And I know we both talked about it and agreed it

just wasn't right because of the timing… but, well, I wanted you to know if you ever change your mind about the timing, I've changed my mind…" I swear inwardly. The speech is going great so far. Not. "I happen to think you're worth waiting for."

Anton reaches over and gently strokes my face with the hand not holding his drink. His touch is tender and my nerve endings shiver at his touch. His eyes are dark; I can't quite read what I see in his gaze but the intensity hits me like a fire bolt.

We sit staring at each other, saying nothing, yet many invisible messages flash between us.

"I did have more I planned to say." Eventually I break the silence. "But I can't remember any of it now. You're distracting me."

He smiles and takes my drink from my hand and puts both glasses down, safely away from the dogs.

"Come here," he says, gesturing for me to come and sit on his lap.

I do, feeling strangely shy.

"I'm sure there was something else important in my speech." I giggle, a little giddy with relief and a touch of incredulity. In spite of my inner certainty that this is meant to be and that Anton wanted it too, I hadn't really got further than my speech in my mind. I hadn't let myself dream that he would respond favourably and my heart is soaring.

"That is a shame about the speech." Anton's eyes sparkle with mischief as he gently strokes my bare thighs up to the hem of my shorts. "I was really enjoying it."

"Er, well." I try to focus but Anton's continuing exploration has me even more distracted than I'd been to start with. "Did you like the bit about being worth waiting for?"

"Very much, yes," Anton replies solemnly. "I'll admit I had a few things to think about, to process… Yet the waiting has been difficult for me too. I wanted to touch you so many times."

I pause, assimilating his comments, letting the joy of the words speak to my soul and grow wings.

"Me too." I let out a deep sigh. "I think I was going to say a bit about joy not being so plentiful in life. That we should hold on to it when we find it."

Anton draws me in closer. "So I should hold on to you. Excellent idea."

"We can take it one day at a time and just explore this… connection and see where it leads us."

"Maybe it would be simpler if we stop talking and get on with embracing… the joy?" Anton raises a thick eyebrow. I know he is taking my words seriously but I suspect there is, like with me, an awful lot of pent-up sexual tension simmering just beneath the surface.

"You forgot about exploring the connection. We need to do that too." I lean forwards, my mouth close to his lips, wanting him to take charge. After all, I did the whole mad cycle dash and brave declaration thing; it's his turn to take charge. Hmm… maybe I need to apologise to Poppy – sometimes the declaration gesture does work, it seems. Making the declaration to the right man probably has a lot to do with it.

Anton pulls me in closer, his lips meeting mine, and we kiss far more passionately, more hungrily than our first kiss. Yes, I'd say I'm right that I wasn't the only one extremely frustrated by how things ended prematurely last time, however important the reason.

"You told me to embrace, yes?" There's a twinkle in Anton's eye and he puts on a fake bad English accent. "I am sorry, my English, she is not so good."

I laugh.

"Shall we go upstairs?" His tone is more serious now and the energy has shifted subtly between us from teasing to raw need. "We can slow it down if you like, but I must admit that taking you to bed has been on my mind ever since we kissed."

"Me too," I admit with a sigh of pleasure and relief,

feeling some of the residual tension seeping out of my pores.

Walking up the stairs I feel almost as self-conscious as a teenager, my nerves practically fizzing with anticipation. Yet strangely at a deeper level I feel a total calm, a knowing that this is right. I did the right thing.

And he said yes.

Once we're alone in the bedroom, the dogs hopefully asleep in their beds downstairs in the kitchen, I am seized by the desire to make the most of this moment. I hardly dared dream Anton would say yes when I cycled over, though of course I'd hoped. Hoped in a quiet sort of way though, so as not to tempt fate. I knew there was a very real chance that it would all end in mortification and disappointment.

I don't want to waste time in case it gives him a chance to change his mind. I'm not willing to take that risk.

I meet his embrace, putting my arms up around his neck and lifting my face to his, my lips slightly parted, a tide of insistent need rising up inside me.

Longing to connect.

Wanting to make love.

His eyes darken, pupils dilating as he lowers his mouth to meet mine. I press my body against his as we kiss, hungrily, passionately, our mouths signalling mutual intent, a mutual need to take things further. There is no question mark in our kissing or touching now. The energy between us has changed with the move from kitchen to bedroom – it's more intense and charged with anticipation. Perhaps Anton is afraid of losing this moment too.

I lower my arms, one hand around his back and the other on his denim-clad bottom. I squeeze and he pulls me even tighter against him, as though trying to obliterate any gap between us. I hadn't imagined the passion of our first kiss with subsequent wishful thinking. It was present then and it's most definitely here now. Passion and something more, that tug, some undefinable quality that stirs me deeper than any other man ever has.

He's delicious, this kind, funny, and quietly sexy man. He doesn't have Scott's swagger but a solid, quiet confidence concealing passionate depths – something that is far sexier in my opinion. And as he kisses me his passionate sexual energy is practically tangible.

I sense Anton is trying to hold back while we explore each other, trying to gauge my preferences, to be respectful. I've always been in tune with my own sexual energy and confident in my body, yet for our first time there is so much exploring to do. It's best to take our time, to feel things out, gradually, teasingly. Because I also crave a slow, sensuous discovery of each other's bodies with lots of stroking and kissing. I want to explore and be explored slowly, progressively, passion building until the world around us fades away and our bodies become one. Yet I'm not sure either one of us is going to be capable of taking this first time that slowly.

The need to connect pulses between us. The desire to experience sexual connection stripped down to its basic raw energy. A dance of enticing invitation as I open my mind, my heart, and my body to be penetrated to my very core. Yielding and trusting the most fragile, tender parts of myself to a man I intuitively know is good and kind, as well as funny and sexy as hell.

Sex has always been about far more than physical sensation or release for me.

I need connection. The kind of deeper connection you can't manufacture.

The kind of connection I can feel, without a doubt, I have with Anton.

I slide a hand in between our bodies and press my palm against his groin, upping the ante, exploration-wise.

He groans and exhales loudly. His cock feels hard already.

"I have been dreaming of this... so many nights. Wanting you in my bed." His voice is husky, his French accent more pronounced than normal but not in a jokey way this time. My spirits soar at his admission. I hadn't dared hope he might have been thinking of me, fantasising about me, these past weeks in the same way I've been thinking of him. He's been so reserved at times; certainly before our chat in Mirepoix there had been such awkwardness at not knowing where we stood or how to behave, all on top of Anton processing his guilt about thinking of moving on. Perhaps he's been holding himself back because he was afraid he might not be able to stop next time, if he let me close again. At least now he seems sure of what he wants, his defences are lowered and the awkwardness between us has disappeared. I don't get any sense that he isn't sure.

"Have you?" I run my fingers over his growing erection. "I've been thinking about it too – quite a lot in fact."

My skin feels flushed, my cheeks warm.

The evening sun casts a soft light over the room and there's a faint but welcome breeze through the open windows. I glance up at Anton's face to see how he reacts to my admission

"Really?" He seems pleasantly surprised and turned on by it, his eyes gleaming, his mouth widening into a smile.

"I never thought you would give me another

chance," he admits. "I thought I had ruined my chance with you when I pulled back that day… You had every right to be upset with me. I—"

"Shh. I understood and I understand. There's nothing to forgive." I place a finger on his lips, not wanting painful memories of that day to cloud this golden moment. This is now and now is all there is. Now has never felt brighter, sharper, or more vibrant.

My heart seems to beat harder, my skin is tingling, and my senses more acute: the scent of lavender on the air, Anton's own musky scent that makes me want to bury my nose in his chest and inhale long and deep, the faint blackcurrant taste of kir from his kisses, and the delicate friction of my lace underwear between my legs and against my erect nipples.

Everything is more. Brighter, sharper, and more vibrant. I drink it all in, impressing every detail on my mind so today will remain a vivid technicolour memory to be replayed when needed. If needed. I'm not going to think beyond tonight for now.

I undo the buttons of Anton's shirt, then slide my hands inside, running them over the muscled chest covered with thick, dark hair. A hairy chest is something I find to be a personal turn-on.

He pulls my T-shirt up over my head and I'm glad I wore my best lacy pink bra. His eyes gleam with appreciation as he reverently runs a finger over the skin of my soft, creamy breasts just above the lacy cups. I arch my back, an unconscious gesture that pushes my breasts towards him. I am so hungry for more, to feel his fingers and his lips on my bare breasts. To feel his tongue on my nipples as he sucks me hard. My breasts have always been sensitive and I know with the right amount of focussed attention he could tease me to the point of orgasm from breast play alone.

Hopefully we'll have many more occasions like tonight and this will be something he'll come to discover.

I stand still as he reaches behind to unhook the bra clasp, pulling the straps down from my shoulders and letting the bra fall away.

He cups my heavy breasts and I sigh contentedly as he then lightly pulls at my nipples. Sharp ripples of sexual arousal shoot through my breasts and awaken a corresponding ache between my legs.

I lean in closer, lips parted, wanting to kiss more and keen to feel my bare breasts against his chest. Skin on skin. Wanting to feel his strong arms around me.

Savouring what's to come.

I fumble with the fly of his jeans while he more expertly undoes my shorts button so he can pull them down over my hips. As they fall down to my feet, they reveal matching lacy pink knickers.

Yes, I wore matching underwear, just in case… In a very quiet, trying not to tempt fate that things might go very well kind of way. After all, I've been craving this ever since that first kiss and I knew if the opportunity came up I'd grasp it joyfully. I've also been taking my birth control pills. There's no harm in being prepared.

I feel a little shy standing here in only my best knickers, aware of Anton's close but appreciative scrutiny. I'm hungry to feel the weight of him on top of me, his cock buried deep inside me. I can't think of anywhere I'd rather be right now or anything I'd rather be doing.

We move to the bed. It's not a practised, choreographed move but it's not exactly awkward either. Just natural. Comfortable.

I feel odd to be so completely comfortable being naked with Anton already. I am reasonably confident in my body and my sexuality but to feel so completely at home naked and to be so immersed in the intimacy between us just feels right. We are connected, Anton and I, and I'm both at peace and alive with the anticipation and excitement of what's to come.

Anton has stripped down to black trunks and he beckons me to come closer towards him where he stands at the edge of the bed. Together we sink down into an embrace, an intimate tangle of limbs.

Anton strokes my breasts, my stomach, and my hips. I hook a leg over his thigh so he can stroke between my legs. The friction of the lace against my bare skin is delicious as he rubs me expertly. Expertly enough to get me wriggling and sighing with pleasure.

I reach a hand between us so I can repay the gesture, stroking his erection through the jersey fabric of his shorts, gently squeezing and feeling gratified as his cock hardens even more in response. He exhales loudly and hooks his fingers beneath the elastic of my knickers, pulling them down and off me. I don't even notice where they end up but I tug at his boxers and he helps me pull them down and off so we're completely naked.

Anton kisses me, slowly and sensuously, his hands wrapped in my hair creating a delicious tension, an awareness of his strength yet combined with such a beautiful sense of his tenderness. Such a powerful combination in a man – gentleness and strength. I press my bare breasts against his chest again and lose myself in returning his kisses, feeling the tide of sexual energy rising, flooding and overwhelming us both.

With my leg hooked over his thigh he has perfect access to resume his attentions between my legs.

"Hmm, that feels so good," I sigh contentedly as he fingers me, spreading my growing wetness over my clit. The intimacy fulfils a deep need in me, for the kind of life-affirming connection that's been absent from my life for so long.

Though, it's never felt like this before. I never knew it could feel like this, so vivid, so exquisite…

I've never known this soaring joy coupled with deep, perfect contentment. It scares me a little to feel like this, if I'm honest. We're still in the very fragile, early steps of relationship intimacy and it scares me that I'm ready to sprint ahead when I should be taking it slow. Yet I can't stop the warm, tender feelings flowing from my heart to Anton's, even though I'm aware that I'm handing him the ability to hurt me deeply, if he chooses to pull away from me.

To stop myself from overthinking, I reach down to Anton's cock, stroking gently to start with, running my fingers over his growing erection, delighting in his groan of pleasure, wanting to give him more. I swirl my fingertips lightly around the head and then take firm hold of his shaft, squeezing.

Anton groans and rolls onto his back so I can move further down his body, my long hair trailing over his chest as I reposition myself between his thighs, lowering my mouth to continue where my fingers left off. He tenderly strokes my hair away from my forehead as I lick and suck and taste him, running my tongue around the sensitive rim and then plunging him in and out of my mouth, my lips firmly around his cock. His sounds of pleasure turn me on as much as if he were still touching me. Giving him pleasure is intensely satisfying.

I want to wipe the shadow of tiredness and distant sadness from his eyes, to make sure his mind is completely in the present. I can't help thinking, of course I can't help thinking, was this the bedroom he shared with Claire or did he swap rooms to avoid memories?

Hmmm…

Clearly it's not just his mind I need to keep in the present; I need to stay engaged myself.

I look up and hold eye contact, moving to position myself above his hard cock. I guide him inside me, enjoying the delicious moment of penetration, the satisfying sense of physical completion. I stare down at Anton and smile. He reaches up to caress one of my breasts as I rotate my hips, riding him. Soon he's thrusting up inside me, meeting the movement of my hips and creating a delicious friction.

The energy between us grows in pace and potency.

I'd almost forgotten this energy, created by two people. An energy of union that soothes the part of my soul longing for connection.

I feel my muscles unclenching, tension unwinding as the hard knot inside me unravels, disintegrates to nothing. I pause for a minute and lie on top of him, chest to chest, enjoying the intimacy. He rolls me over onto my back while staying inside me, taking me by surprise. I watch him, enjoying the view and wrapping my legs up around his hips so he can thrust deeper. He does, the energy building between us again. I reach round to stroke and squeeze his bottom, pulling him deeper into me still. His strokes are rhythmic, growing ever harder, and I can feel sexual energy surging within me, the growing urge to open to Anton, to give him this hidden part of myself.

He pauses and holds himself over me, weight down onto his arms, a slight sheen of sweat glistening on his skin. On mine too, now I notice, in spite of the cooler evening breeze reaching us from the garden. It's quiet and peaceful in the stillness of the moment.

"Okay?" he asks. I can sense he's only barely holding himself back.

"Yes," I reply, a little confused until I realise that for him this wasn't planned and he's asking if I'm on birth control, if it's okay to come inside me. "Erm... I'm on the pill and I've not had sex in a long, long time so it's okay to… you know."

It seems that articulacy has left me along with the shedding of my clothes.

"Good, that is good." Relief flits across Anton's face. "Sorry, I should have asked, not assumed… before we… but…"

Yes, I understand the *but*. This thing between us is so intense and all-consuming that it's hard to remain fully aware of the practical, of the mundane. This isn't something that happens often enough for either of us to have the sexual etiquette down pat.

Am I the first since his wife? Somehow I think so but I do my best to try to push the thought aside.

"First, I would like to…" Anton pulls away from me and I feel the loss of him inside me but he makes up for it when he moves down to the end of the bed and pulls me down with him, spreading my thighs wide and lowering his mouth to my pussy.

He circles my clit with his lips and sucks hard, making me gasp. I exhale deeply, feeling the last vestiges of tension leaving me as he licks my clit enthusiastically. When he hooks two fingers inside me and fingers my g-spot at the same time as licking me I tense and shudder beneath him. My pussy clamps tight around his fingers and I quiver as he draws my climax out. I'm about to tell him to stop, that I'm too sensitive, when a second orgasm wracks my body.

My fingers tangle in his dark hair as I float back down from my high. Anton moves back up the bed and kisses me, so I can taste my juices on his lips and tongue. I reach down to stroke his cock.

"Would you… like to turn over?" he asks, his breathing laboured. "To try another way?"

I roll over and pull my knees up under my hips so I'm on all fours, then lower my head down to the mattress.

When he rubs his cock between my legs, coating it with the wetness of my arousal and teasing me, my breath hitches in my chest. Anton has seriously sexy hidden depths. I can't remember feeling this turned on… well, ever. A man who knows what he's doing in the bedroom is a definite plus.

I gasp as he enters me in one long, hard thrust, the angle deep and immensely satisfying and a corresponding large voltage of sexual electricity pierces my core.

Then he's firmly holding my hips and thrusting hard. I'm so wet and turned on that he meets no resistance. In this position I swear the head of his cock is hitting my g-spot with each thrust. The pleasure building and throbbing inside me is more intense than the build-up to a clitoral orgasm. My thighs are quivering, the soles of my feet tingling and I feel profoundly, deeply rocked. If Anton's kissing and stroking were amazing, they were merely a prelude; his more advance skills are phenomenal. I hadn't realised just how much I needed this, needed this most basic, most intimate of acts to satisfy my deepest longings. Touching my body yes, but also caressing my soul.

It almost feels too much, too much sensation, the pressure building too intense... and then I'm contracting around his cock, spasming as I cry out into the pillow. I feel Anton's grip on my hips tighten as he cries out too, groaning loudly as he comes inside me.

Eventually he withdraws and we both collapse onto the bed. He pulls me into his embrace and holds me as my body comes slowly down from a powerful orgasm.

"Wow. That was... great. Thank you," I say, snuggling into his chest. "I had no idea how much I needed that."

"Me too," Anton says, holding me close.

I don't want to ask if I'm the first since his wife and I have no intention of ruining this perfect moment. The complexities of life will intrude all too soon, and for now I want to treasure this peaceful, happy moment in time while the illusion of our bubble can be maintained for a just a little longer.

Chapter Nine

"You never lose by loving. You always lose by holding back."
Barbara De Angelis

I f I was worried that Anton might have second thoughts in the morning, I needn't have been concerned. He seems happy enough with the status quo, although I'm aware that at some point we need to talk more and I'd like him to talk more about his wife to me. I'm not sure if he doesn't mention her much for fear it might upset me, although I don't know why he would think that. Or perhaps because he does still harbour some guilt about starting a sexual relationship with me, in which case it might be a problem.

Otherwise, my life continues much as normal, except that I stay over at Anton's more often and have become even more attached to Pickle and Squeaker, who are always terribly excited to find I'm in the house first thing in the morning after a sleepover. I try to make sure I don't stay over too often though, aware it's a new relationship and that Anton has a lot more to adjust to in this situation than I do. Plus, I still have a business to grow and want to keep up providing support for Poppy and JoJo in return for my bed and board.

One day I'm dog sitting Pickle and Squeaker when Pickle wants me to chase him and play tug of war with his toy. I try to stay out of Anton's office but Pickle has no such qualms. I follow him in, hoping to limit or prevent any damage but I'm too slow. As I walk in, I'm just in time to see Pickle's rope toy flying through the air as he launches it with the hope of getting me to play with him. I watch in horror as it catches an ornate jar on the shelf. As the jar tips I race across the room to save it but I'm too late and as it slips out of my hands the lid goes flying, sending a fine powder through the air. I gasp, feeling like I've been hit with a thousand memories and a charge so powerful I stagger back, bang my head on a shelf and collapse weakly to the floor.

My senses are overloaded. I'm feeling too much, way too much, and I can't deal with it.

What on earth was…?

Oh.

Dimly, in the back of my mind, I register that these must be Claire's ashes. I suppose they could belong to one of his parents but in my heart I know they are Claire's. I could feel her.

Then it hits me that Anton may be home any minute and I have to, have to move.

I have to fix this and quickly.

Yet my limbs refuse to move. It's only when the dogs come over and starts sniffing at the ashes and trying to lick my skin that I manage to stir myself.

I get shakily to my feet and manage to shut the dogs out of the room and then have to face the perplexing problem of how exactly I'm going to get all the remnants of the ashes back into the jar without touching them or spiralling out of control again. It's then I notice there are ashes on my shirt and, oh no, horror of horrors, down my cleavage. I strip my shirt off and whip off my bra. Thankfully, most of the ashes are on the bra itself which I quickly hide in the first place that comes to mind – beneath the cushion in Squeaker's dog basket. Both dogs have beds in the study so they can be with Anton while he's working from home.

I grab some wipes from the bathroom and clean myself up, then give the shirt itself a good scrub, having to add liquid soap and water to get the marks out.

My heart rate picks up when I hear Anton's car on the drive outside and this time it's not for the usual reasons but sheer panic. I speed up my efforts, improvising with a dustpan and brush so I don't have to make skin contact with the ashes again. Just to make doubly sure, I lift the jar back into place using a bathroom towel so I have no direct contact with the jar. This gives me just about enough time to drop the towel to the floor behind me, a split second before the study door opens.

I can blame Pickle for the random towel because he's always running off with random objects to guard. I'll make it up to him, though to be fair he did have a large part to play in the urn incident.

I'm mentally crossing my fingers I've not missed anything obvious when Anton walks in, Pickle and Squeaker trotting at his heels. He's clearly bemused by the fact his office door is shut and the dogs, whom I'm supposed to be looking after, are on the other side of the closed door from me.

"I was just… clearing up." I offer lamely. "The dogs

trod some bits of dusty soil in. I shooed them out of the room so I could clear up.

"Oh… right," he replies, but his gaze is fixed on my chest and both eyebrows are raised.

I look down to see I've missed a shirt button and there's a gaping hole through which the swell of my bare breasts is extremely obvious. Even worse, the combination of the sunlight through the window and my freshly scrubbed wet shirt means I could easily be a contestant in a wet T-shirt contest.

My cheeks flush hot.

"Umm… I had to clean myself up a bit too. It got rather messy." I cringe, hoping he'll be so distracted by my breasts that this might be the end to it. *Maybe he'll never need to know?* an optimistic voice of hope suggests, along with renewed mental finger-crossing.

What's the alternative? Tell him the truth? When Anton's gaze falls to the towel on the floor behind me, I try to quell the mounting hysteria.

I might just about have got away with it but unfortunately at that moment Pickle appears between us, triumphantly dragging my still dusty bra out from beneath the cushion pad in Squeaker's bed.

Crap. I'd meant to find a bag to put the bra into once I'd cleaned up. The dog bed was only ever meant to be a temporary hiding place.

There's a surreal moment when we both stare at the bra and then stare at each other.

I have no words.

Literally nothing. My mouth opens and shuts but no explanation is forthcoming.

My bravado sags and the momentum that had been carrying me along during the clear-up effort leaves me as limp as a rag doll. There's nothing for it but to come clean, so to speak.

I cringe inwardly at the very thought of it, especially as I'm still not sure whether he completely believes me about my reactions to touching objects or has been humouring me a little…

"I'm really sorry, Anton. There is… ah, well, an explanation. I was hoping I wouldn't have to… I didn't want to upset you but I can see I'm going to have to explain." I sigh and will my tongue to unknot itself. "You know how Pickle likes to throw his toys about in an attempt to get you playing with him?" I cross my arms over my chest.

"Yes, I am familiar with it." Anton's tone is cool and amused but then the toy part of the tale isn't too extraordinary. He's seen Pickle throwing toys about the room in the hope someone will join in a game of catch. Explaining why touching the ashes practically made me pass out is going to be much harder. I mean, he did say he was more open-minded to my ability to feel or sense energy from objects, but... what if he was just humouring me?

"I'm still not sure how how Pickle throwing a rope toy led to you being alone in my office with your bra in the dog basket." He raises an eyebrow.

"I admit this part is harder to explain." I bite my lip and decide I'm just going to have to get it over and done with, like ripping off a plaster in one go. "Well, Pickle's rope toy hit that jar, the urn..."

I gesture in the general direction without meeting Anton's eye.

"I dashed across the room to try to save it, and I did save the jar but some of the contents were... accidentally spilled. I had a bit of a reaction to coming into contact with the... umm... you know, and fell and banged my head on a shelf." I still can't quite meet his gaze. "I did manage to get everything cleared up but had to rinse my T-shirt out. I sort of put the bra to one side to wash later. And that's it really. I am so sorry Anton."

"I understand, Daisy. Accidents happen and I'm sure you did your best to clear everything up." The words coming from Anton's mouth are the right ones but his tone is flat, his face white. I don't know if he's upset, shocked, or furious.

He walks across to the shelf to straighten the jar and looks askance at the towel on the floor but refrains from commenting on it.

I look at Pickle, willing him to go and fetch the towel but he has firm hold of my bra and clearly thinks it's a new tuggy-toy. I know from experience the only way to get my bra back from him intact is to pretend I'm not interested and don't actually want it back. Otherwise he'll sense a tuggy-toy battle, one of his favourite kinds of games.

While Anton is occupied I swiftly re-button my shirt. I'm fairly sure my face is as red as Anton's is white and I feel dreadful about what happened. It may have been Pickle who instigated it but I was in charge of watching him at the time. I can feel hot tears pricking at the backs of my eyelids and my head is starting to throb where I banged it on a shelf. I also feel wiped out after all the emotion that swamped me when I made contact with the ashes.

"I really am sorry," I repeat softly.

"Yes of course it's no problem." Anton turns to face me and tries to force a smile to his face without too much success. "You said you hit your head – are you okay?"

"Yes. I've got a bit of a bump coming and my head hurts but I'll live." As soon as I come out with the phrase I wince inwardly. *I'll live?!* Really? Could I have said anything more insensitive? Could this situation get any worse?

"Good. I'm glad you're okay," Anton replies absent-mindedly and I wonder if he even heard me.

I hug my arms more tightly around myself, feeling suddenly very tired.

.Anton does come towards me now and reaches out to touch my arm gently. "Please don't get upset about it, Daisy."

My head is throbbing. I rub at the lump on the back of my skull and flinch.

Anton notices and comes closer, stepping behind me and lifting my hair out of the way. His fingertips lightly run over the bump and I wince.

"It is a nasty bump. Do you feel sick at all? Shall I take you to a doctor?" His concern is genuine and some of his normal colour has returned to his cheeks.

"No, I don't need a doctor. I'll be fine."

"How did you manage to hit the back of your head anyway? If you were running towards the shelves? Anton nods towards the dogs. "I suppose the dogs wanted to help you. They are definitely what you call a trip hazard – that is the expression, is it not?"

"Yes. No. I mean…" I take a deep breath. "Yes, that is the expression and it does suit them but like I said, when I caught and touched the jar and its… contents, I felt this overwhelming sensation that wiped me out. I couldn't stand up and, well, I'm not too sure exactly what happened."

Anton frowns a little, clearly perplexed, and something of the earlier blankness has returned to his expression.

"It wasn't bad." I stare at him imploringly, lest he think his dead wife hates me and this is some kind of sign… "Well, I'd better go now."

Anton waves a hand in Pickle's direction. "I shall wash it and…"

"No, it's fine. Please don't. Just, umm, dispose of it please?" Pickle ranks several of Anton's odd socks amongst his favourite toys, stolen and hidden around the house, but I draw the line at having my bra carried around the house and presented to visitors.

And there's just no way I could ever wear it again.

"And you're definitely okay to cycle?" Anton frowns at me, following me down to the front door, dogs following at his heels. "I'm really not sure it's such a good idea if you've banged your head badly."

"I'll be fine. It's really not far." I hurry out of the house, feeling an urgent need to get away. My head really is sore and I know Anton was probably right about my not cycling but the urge to escape the intensity and awkwardness is stronger than my common sense at the moment.

———————

I'm feeling better after a shower and a lie-down. Later that evening, Cal has disappeared with Leo to discuss possibly extending the restaurant opening hours next season and I'm enjoying a late-night hot chocolate sitting with JoJo and Poppy at the kitchen table. It's a comforting ritual by now and one designed to get me to share all the gossip. Apparently I'd mumbled something about Claire and losing my bra and Anton being strange about it all. I'd made no sense and they made sure I had a sleep but kept checking on me and waking me once an hour to see I was okay when I mentioned about the bang to my head.

Now that I'm feeling more with it, they're dying with curiosity to know what on earth happened at Anton's today.

They react with horrified shock when I explain about Claire's urn and are suitably sympathetic when I explain about feeling overwhelmed and the bang to my head. Once I go on to describe the clean-up operation and stuffing my bra out of the way in a dog bed they seem to find it hysterically funny though. So much so, particularly when I get to the bit about Pickle wanting to play with the bra and presenting it to Anton, that I find myself half groaning, half laughing with them.

"I wish I'd been there to see the look on Anton's face," JoJo says, and her comment has the effect of sobering me instantly.

"Hmm, I'm worried it might affect things between us." I stare down into the cup. Not even JoJo's hot chocolate can completely rid of me the feeling of unease. "Don't get me wrong, he was concerned about my head and kept telling me not to worry and that accidents happen, but he was really pale. I think it was a real shock to him."

"So, what is the thing that's bothering you the most, Daisy?" Poppy asks. "You didn't pick up anything... bad from the ashes, did you?"

"No, not at all. There was absolutely no sense of any negative feeling or intention." I frown. "I think it was just that I felt too much at once; it was like my system was overloaded. I suppose my biggest fear is that because Claire is the reason Anton pulled back in the first place, what if this causes him to pull back again?"

"Just take things slow, Daisy. If Anton has more things to process then maybe just give him the space to do that," Poppy suggests gently. "I think it's one of those things you just have to let play out on its own. It's not exactly like any of us can know what's ahead of us, really. Sometimes we just have to take a risk."

JoJo nods her agreement. "She's right, I'm afraid. If you overthink everything you could end up sabotaging yourself or not getting to enjoy the start of a lovely relationship because you're worrying about the middle or the possible end. Just enjoy it."

"She's right, you know," says Poppy. "Save the angsting for when you really need it."

"That wasn't quite the message I was going for actually." JoJo laughs and rolls her eyes.

"Are you bothered by what happened, Daisy?" Poppy asks perceptively. "Not worried about Anton's reaction but concerned by anything on your own behalf?"

"Maybe a little." I shrug. "He hardly ever talks about Claire and it bothers me a bit. I think it would be more natural if he did mention her and healthier somehow. But I don't want to force the issue."

"I think it's like JoJo said," Poppy adds. "This is early days in your relationship. Try to just enjoy it and let things work themselves out naturally."

"Or if you really get frustrated by it and find it a problem you can just ask him outright. Make it clear you're absolutely fine with him talking about Claire," JoJo says. "If going out with Cal has taught me anything it's that men are not mind readers and they can get odd notions in their heads or operate under the influence of a misunderstanding, thinking they're doing exactly what we want. If you want to avoid that then you need to use clear and direct communication. No assuming they know what might seem completely obvious to us. No assumptions at all, just to play it safe."

"True." Poppy nods. "I'd say it's just a question of giving him time to get to know you but Leo still needs me to spell things out really clearly."

"Is someone taking our names in vain?" Leo asks, entering the kitchen with Maxi, the large Pyrenean mountain dog at his heels. Cal follows closely behind.

"It's as I thought," Cal says. "They talk about us all the time because they haven't got anything more interesting to talk about."

"Oh please." JoJo rolls her eyes scornfully even though we had just been talking about them.

"Actually, we were talking about Daisy's upcoming birthday," Poppy says, and I admire her use of a diversionary tactic.

"Does Anton know it's your birthday coming up soon?" JoJo sips the last of her hot chocolate and sighs contentedly.

"No, of course not and I'm not going to tell him." I

reach down to pick up Pickwick who's tapping at my leg asking for a lift up. He's not as nimble as Flump or the chihuahuas who can all leap quite amazing heights for their size and tend to just arrive rather than wait for an invitation. I give him a cuddle on my lap. "That would make it look like I'm telling him because I'm expecting him to do something special or buy me a present or something. It would make me feel awkward; it's too soon in our relationship."

"Well we'll have to do something to celebrate your birthday," Poppy says.

"If Cal's in the country for it we could get him to cook you a special meal," JoJo offers.

"That's very kind of you to volunteer his services but he must get sick of cooking surely. I don't want to create extra work for anyone." I look anxiously over at Cal but he just winks at me.

"I never get sick of cooking and I'd be happy to cook a special meal for you, but if you'd rather go out somewhere special it might be difficult to do in the evening but we could probably all manage to go out for lunch and then Anton could come along without it being too much pressure."

"Thanks," I say, still feeling overawed that Callum O'Connor, celebrity chef, would be willing to cook for me.

I stroke the back of Pickwick's head and he tilts it back towards me, enjoying the fuss.

"Whatever you'd prefer," JoJo says. "It's completely up to you. I don't want to make you feel awkward."

"I think after today I've set the bar pretty high for feeling awkward." I smile. "Anything else will be a breeze by comparison."

Cal and Leo look at us enquiringly but I give Poppy and JoJo a tiny shake of my head. Some stories are definitely not for public consumption.

"That's the spirit." JoJo grins.

I rub the lump on the back of my head absentmindedly. I swear it's getting bigger and it's really tender.

"Are you okay, Daisy?" Poppy peers across the table at me. "How is the head?"

"Okay." I nod and then wince, wishing I hadn't. "Maybe not quite as okay as all that."

"Maybe an early night would be a good idea." JoJo gets up and starts tidying away the empty mugs into the dishwasher. I stand up too and put Pickwick down on the floor.

"I thought you said you were feeling better?" Poppy frowns. "No nausea or any other head injury symptoms you've neglected to mention?"

"Just a headache," I say. "I'll be fine after a good night's sleep."

"Take Pickwick with you tonight then – he looks like he needs extra cuddles." Poppy picks him up and puts him back into my arms. I know she thinks I'm the one in need of cuddles, rather than Pickwick, who gets wall-to-wall cuddles and fuss as it is. He does really enjoy the one-on-one attention though and as I'm still feeling a little odd I gratefully accept.

"Okay, thanks, I'm off to bed then." I head towards the back door. "I must say I like these canine hot water bottles that stay warm all night and don't need refilling."

"You probably won't be saying that on a baking-hot night in the height of an August heatwave. We've been lucky so far and the nights haven't been too bad yet," Poppy replies. "But yes, I take your point. Enjoy your cuddles, both of you!"

The next time I see Anton is a Monday morning when I'm picking the dogs up at the bookshop to take them out for a long walk with instructions to "wear them out so they sleep all afternoon". I'm not sure it's actually possible to wear Squeaker out to that extent. She seems to have a fairly quick battery re-charge time. Anton's being perfectly friendly but is busy with some documents he's brought to the shop to appraise so it's hard to tell whether everything is okay with us given it's perfectly normal for him to get preoccupied and a little distant when he's engrossed in his work.

Monday is market day in Mirepoix, which means the place has become a heaving throng of tourists, locals, and stallholders by the time I return from the long river walk. There are so many delicious-looking treats and interesting artisan craft stalls that I'd love to browse and take my time perusing but there are also lots of other dogs and it's quite the crush so I focus on getting Pickle and Squeaker back to Anton.

Eventually I make my way through to the side street and push open the door to the bookshop, the dogs close at my heels. I love the old-fashioned tinkling sound that announces our arrival. I love the feel of the bookshop, so peaceful, especially after the noisy crowds in the square. It's nice to see so many independent shops down the narrow side streets that lead from the market square.

Anton looks up from his desk in the corner and smiles. It's that gorgeous smile, the one that always gets me, makes me feel lit-up inside. I smile widely back automatically. I really do hope things are okay between us. There seemed to be a slight distance in Anton's texts since the urn incident. I wish I knew what he was thinking and that I could get him to understand the way touching the urn and the ashes affected me. Can he really understand though? Especially if he's never experienced anything similar himself.

I've been so used to people in the past deciding I'm crazy, because they can't understand me and think I must have some hidden agenda to scam them. The fact I've never, ever tried to market my ability or charge money for intentionally using my gift doesn't make any difference to their attitude. I'm positive Anton doesn't think I'm a scammer but I never really explained to him why I ran off the first time it happened with him, when I touched the grimoire. Maybe explaining some of my history, especially surrounding how I've been treated because of incidents I couldn't control, might help him understand me better.

"It's packed out there." I bend to unclip the dogs' leads and they go to flop on the cool tiled floor behind Anton's desk after having a long slurpy drink from the bowl of water he keeps for them there.

I must admit I'm pretty thirsty too, and not particularly looking forward to cycling back to the guesthouse just yet. I look at the cool floor tiles and am tempted to flop down next to the dogs.

"Would you like to get some lunch?" Anton asks,

closing the books. He puts away the papers he was working on and gets to his feet.

"Yes, I'd love that, but what about the dogs? It's a bit of a scrum out there." I hesitate. "You know, like a rugby scrum?"

"Yes, I know," he says, picking up his shop keys. "I'll close up for a little bit. I could do with a break and I think the dogs are so worn out they're just going to sleep."

"They had a nice time playing in the river," I say, and follow Anton out of the shop, waiting while he locks up.

He nods hello to the man who owns the antique shop. The man nods back but is also gazing at me with blatant curiosity.

"Pickle is coming on so well lately and it's definitely down to you." Anton reaches for my hand and squeezes it. "I'm really grateful."

"It's my pleasure, really it is," I reply, enjoying walking hand in hand with Anton. I'm glad that things are starting to feel a bit more... relaxed between us now. "Honestly, I love seeing him come out of his shell. I know he has his moments still but they're a lot less frequent than they used to be. And Squeaker has always been such a joyful little thing but I'm sure Pickle being happier must make her feel more settled too."

"Yes, I'm sure it does. I think you're having a good influence on all of us." He squeezes my hand. The tone of his voice is gentle and I feel a soft sigh of relief escape my lips.

"So, where are we going to go?" I ask, looking around at the square which seems to be pretty packed.

"How about Le Chapelier Fou?" Anton points to a café over the other side of the main square.

"Is that the Mad Hatter, the Alice in Wonderland themed café? Poppy was telling me about it."

"Yes, it's run by an English lady. You can even get a decent bacon sandwich there – that's what Claire used to say anyway. I thought you might like it."

The grasp of his hand in mine remains firm and I'm glad he's mentioning her without it feeling in the least bit awkward.

"A bacon sandwich? I'm definitely fancying one now," I say lightly. "Do you think that's awful, that I come to France and still crave English food occasionally?"

"Well, nobody is perfect." He laughs and I turn to him, raising my eyebrows in mock outrage.

The atmosphere feels much more relaxed between us now and Anton seems happy for me to take my time looking at the stalls, admiring the homemade jewellery being sold and the beautiful racks of screen-printed silk scarves. As we cross the square in the middle we pass a stall with some eye-catching pottery for sale – beautiful glazed vases of all shapes and sizes and mostly coloured with swirls of bronze and turquoise glaze. They remind me of the ocean somehow. I stop to touch one of them, mesmerised by it. All of a sudden I'm suffused with warmth, with love and laughter and an image of running on the beach with Anton. Startled, I withdraw my hand quickly.

I glance at him to see if he's noticed I'm acting oddly and he obviously has as his face is pale. The stallholder greets him and they speak quietly in such low tones I can't translate what they're saying in French, just pick up the odd words.

Anton still has a firm grip on my hand as we make our way to a table that has just been vacated outside the Mad Hatter Café.

We sit opposite each other. Anton doesn't look at the menu but stares pensively back at the pottery stall.

"Is everything okay, Anton?" I ask, tentatively.

He meets my eye. "What did you feel, Daisy?"

Briefly I consider lying; this is too soon after the urn incident but I'm only briefly tempted. There can be no real relationship between us if he can't accept all of me, including my odder quirks.

"I felt warmth, love, and sunshine, and running on

the beach with… erm well, with you." I shrug. "I just felt drawn to that stall in particular. I can't really explain why."

"So no one told you what Claire used to do?" He runs a hand through his unruly hair, still appearing shaken.

"Used to do?" I ask blankly. "No. Why? Oh, I see, the vases. She made them? But…"

At that moment a waitress comes over to take our order. Anton orders an omelette and a coffee and I order a bacon and sausage sandwich and an orange juice, making sure to ask for ice. I really need to cool down.

When the waitress leaves we're quiet for a minute, surrounded by the bustle of the market and the conversations of people at the tables around us.

"Yes, she was a potter," he says eventually. "Though she didn't sell directly at the market. After she died I sold the rest of her stock; the pieces I didn't want to keep for myself, I gave to Francine to sell."

"She was extremely talented," I say gently, reaching out my hand to lay it on his.

"She would be happy to know her art was still being sold, going out to brighten up other people's homes," he says. "That's why I wanted her work to continue to be sold; she would've wanted that."

"They are really beautiful." I smile and he eventually smiles back.

"Sorry." He shakes his head. "It was just weird for me. You being able to… it's hard to understand."

"No need to apologise," I say. "Really, I do understand it's strange for you. It's difficult emotionally anyway, and then you've got my reactions when I touch things relating to her to cope with too. It must be odd to get your head around."

"I felt your reaction this time," he says, meeting my eye directly. "I knew you'd felt her, even though rationally I can't understand it, I knew. Maybe because I was holding your hand? Or because there's a bond between us now? I don't understand it."

"Welcome to my world," I joke.

We are interrupted again with the arrival of our order.

The cold drink is very welcome and I take several long sips while we wait for privacy again.

"Tell me about your world," Anton says, looking at me intently and I know for sure he's not humouring me. He really wants to know, wants to try to understand.

So I tell him about how awkward it was growing up with the ability. How my grandmother encouraged me and had the same gift and the subsequent rift with my mum. Then the pressure to conform as a teenager and the bullying when I wasn't able to hide some reactions when my gift kicked in.

"That must've been hard." Anton says.

"Yes." I shrug. "Confusing too. I went through a period where I just wanted to be normal. I lost friends and boyfriends because of it, because they thought I was crazy. I don't usually talk about it much but… I wanted, I want to be myself with you. Not to have to hide this side of me. Although hiding it from you hasn't exactly been an option."

"I don't want you to feel you have to hide anything from me, Daisy." Anton's tone is tender. "Hiding just creates a barrier. I don't want any… anything to be between us. I need to know the real you."

The real me? As I eat my bacon and sausage sandwich I realise I'm still working that one out.

Once I've finished I look up at Anton.

"I think I'm still a work in progress, Anton."

He smiles. "That's okay. Life is all about discovery."

And I get the feeling that the unspoken truth is that we are a work in progress too. We are still discovering exactly what our relationship is or has the potential to be.

Discovery is exciting, I suppose. But what if we come to different conclusions? I know it's too early to expect Anton to commit to me seriously. Everything is so new, so fragile, and if I force it too soon, like I did last time, I could break it.

We finish our lunch and Anton heads back to his shop while I go in search of my bicycle, feeling lighter than I have done in ages.

The mellow feeling of contentment is a welcome respite and I'm feeling more relaxed generally. I don't have any security for the future yet, but I'm learning to be okay with that.

I'm dog sitting for Anton a few days after we had lunch at the market. After our usual river walk, the dogs and I have been relaxing in the dappled shade in the garden. Surrounded by sweet-smelling lavender bushes and the soft hum of bees collecting nectar from the flowers, I feel a million miles away from my old London life. I may have less money but I also have less to spend it on. My wardrobe for dog walking is simple and practical.

I feel more myself somehow, more in touch with nature, part of a community and surrounded by a beautiful area I long to get to know better.

Squeaker chooses that moment to interrupt my musings by rolling over, sticking her legs in the air, and starting to snore. Pickle merely opens one eye, decides nothing interesting is happening, and goes back to sleep.

I smile at them both. I've had lots of other one-off jobs and still look after Molly the papillon whenever her owner has to go to Toulouse for medical treatment but it's Pickle and Squeaker I see most often and who have captured my heart the most. I love the guesthouse dogs too of course, but they already have lots of people in their lives who adore them and they are now secure in that love, in spite of having had a rough start in life. Pickle and Squeaker however, I get the sense they need me. Anton loves them, of course he does, but they've been through a big adjustment. Anton has to leave them to work and the bond I've forged with them is special.

I get to my feet to head into the kitchen for a drink. Pickle opens one eye again and watches me but doesn't bother to follow me. They've already had their post-walk treat so food is unlikely to be on the agenda.

While standing in the kitchen drinking some blissfully cold water, my eye is caught by a flash of turquoise. I look up and recognise one of Claire's pottery vases on a shelf. Strange that it's never caught my eye before but usually I'm sitting at the table or I'm

over at the dog beds and have my back to that particular wall.

Then it occurs to me, that day of my first aborted
kiss with Anton, he must've been looking directly at the
vase just before he pulled away. The reminder of Claire
must've been triggered his internal crisis.

I feel drawn towards the vase and reach up to place
the palms of my hands on it. I'm filled with a sense of
peace, of warmth, and the uplifting frequency of a day
at a beach. I relax and sigh with a sense of relief. I feel
welcome.

I hear Anton's car pulling up outside. The dogs stir
themselves and run to the front door to greet him.
When he enters the kitchen he finds me still staring
contemplatively at the vase.

"Hi," I say, turning and reaching up to give him a
big hug. "Good trip?"

"The best." He smiles and holds up a bottle of
champagne. "I replaced it. It turns out I may just have
sold my book. I've not got the contract yet but it sounds
like it's just a formality. I thought we could celebrate.
I've got crème de cassis if you fancy a kir royale?"

"Congratulations." I beam and hug him more
tightly. "That's wonderful news."

"How has your day been?" he asks, putting the

champagne into the fridge to chill and reaching down to make a fuss of the dogs.

"Peaceful," I say. "I was just looking at this vase. I'm surprised I've never noticed it before."

He comes to stand next to me and puts his arm around me.

"Did you…? You know…"

"Touch it?" I ask. "Yes, it was good. All good. All I felt was peace."

He stares at the vase pensively. "I was talking to my friend, Emile, you know, the one with the antiques place just down the street from my shop, about psychometry yesterday."

"You didn't tell him…" My stomach clenches a little, even though I can't imagine Anton would tell anyone, it seems my body has an instinctive fear of the backlash that can come from exposure.

"No, I didn't, of course not," he reassures me. "I know you don't want it to be widely spread. Don't worry."

"So what was he saying about psychometry?"

"That he once knew a woman who had the gift, a friend of his grandmother's. He certainly believes it to be a genuine gift some people possess. He said it would come in very handy in his line of work."

"Oh." I'm not sure what to say, or where this conversation is going.

"I've also been doing some research into the use of psychometry in archaeology."

I smile. I love that he's decided to take the subject seriously. To him, as an academic, taking it seriously clearly means researching it in the same way he would one of his myths or legends.

"And what are your conclusions then?" I look up at him, trying to ignore the slight tightness in my chest, trying not to let on how very much his opinion matters to me.

"My conclusion is that there have been many things humans haven't understood that science has subsequently explained," he replies thoughtfully. "I can't claim to understand it but I know you aren't lying or making it up – why would you? You don't stand to gain financially and you're clearly not doing it for the attention. You hate the attention. I can't claim to understand it but I accept it's a part of you and I would never, ever, think less of you for being you."

I rest my head against his chest, feeling close to tears.

"There are lots of unanswered questions in this universe," Anton adds quietly. "But Emile reminded me of a quote from Tesla: 'If you want to find the secrets of the universe, think in terms of energy, frequency, and vibration.' So who knows, maybe one day you'll be able to go back to all those people who bullied you or rejected you and set them straight."

I laugh into his chest. I can't see that happening in my lifetime, but I appreciate Anton making the effort to understand me and cheer me up. I appreciate that he took on board what I said about having lost people in the past because they'd rejected this side of me.

I also appreciate his honesty. He's really trying to understand and accept all of me, and that means the world to me. We move out into the garden as it's such a beautiful evening.

"You know, Emile would probably give you a job if you wanted it," Anton says, handing me a glass full of sparkling kir royale loveliness. Blackcurrant bubbles burst on my tongue, sliding down to create a gentle warmth and relaxation that spreads through my chest. JoJo and Poppy have got me into this particular drink and nothing could be more perfect for a beautiful summer evening. Anton knows my fondness for it so makes sure he has crème de cassis in the house for me.

"I don't want to use my talent or gift or whatever you call it to make money." I pull a face. "I'm happy for it just to pop up when there's a good reason, or maybe somebody needs my help."

We fall silent and I can tell we're both wondering why it's popped up so often recently and if it has anything to do with Claire.

"So what is your dream job?" Anton asks, changing the subject. "I've told you all about the family bookshop, my love of history, and my desire to write but you've never really said what your dreams are, long-term."

"It's hard to say." I take a sip of my drink and try to think how to explain. "You see, when I was growing up I had my gran on the one hand who's really free-spirited – she has the same gift as me and was always trying to encourage me into, let's say, alternative choices. She's currently staying in an ashram in India, by the way. Anyway, she had a falling out with my mother who just wanted me to be normal, whatever normal is. I wasn't really sure who I wanted to be, but after all the bullying at school for being different and then being dumped by a guy I was really into for being weird, I started to come around to my mother's point of view. I wanted to stay beneath the radar. I was good with people and enjoyed working in a hotel – it seemed like a more interesting option than office temping. It really wasn't meant to be forever but I was comfortable so I stayed."

"And then you came here?"

"Yes, you could say my gift popped up in a way that

coincided with a bit of an epiphany. Something drew me here." I shrug. "It's not just that Poppy is my friend. I feel there's just something about this area, and something about working with animals that makes me feel at peace. Like I've found what I should be doing."

"That's good. So… you are staying here when the summer is over?" Anton asks tentatively, not meeting my eye.

"I'm not sure yet. I'd like to but I've got a few things I need to work out first."

Things like whether I can make enough to live on, and finding somewhere I can afford to live longer term, without relying on Poppy's hospitality.

He doesn't ask what things I'm talking about though. If only he'd confirm he wants me to stay, or even ask me to stay, that would be nice, and helpful to know. But he says nothing else. We sip at our drinks as the sun slowly sets behind the mountains and we talk about Anton's book deal, the dogs, village gossip, and pretty much everything except whether we think we might have a future as a couple.

Perhaps it's too soon to tell. I need to accept that life is full of uncertainty. It's rarely so neat and well-ordered that we can check things off a list.

. . .

Business: yes, sort of, still growing but slowly.

Relationship: amazing potential but no idea where it's going or if Anton is truly okay with moving on in any kind of committed way yet.

Location: amazing, I don't know quite where I'm going to be living but I'd love it to be here if I can manage it.

I need to realise that if you take risks, life can be messy with infinite capacity to surprise. I've left the old, safe, and slightly boring me behind.

I have no certainties, but the potential to live the kind of life in which I feel free to be me? That's worth living with a little uncertainty.

I'm simply going to have to learn to embrace this new way of living, of discovery, and be patient.

Chapter Ten

"The deepest moments of intimacy occur when you're not talking."
Patricia Love

DAISY: *Help! I'm dog sitting as JoJo is with Cal in London to attend some event and Poppy's gone with Leo to a relative's funeral in Lyon. Looking after six dogs isn't so bad but I've made a terrible discovery: *whispers* we've run out of dog treats!!! I can't leave the house as they start howling. I don't suppose you have any dog treats to spare? Tell Pickle and Squeaker I'll make it up to them — an extra-long river walk and a treat of their choosing.*

ANTON: *Of course. Be with you in 30 mins. Anything to help a damsel in distress.*

DAISY: *My hero! Thank you for saving me from the furry lynch mob. I'll owe you a favour.*

ANTON: *I like the sound of that. See you soon!*

O f course, by the time he arrives the dogs have set off another howling chorus initiated by the chihuahuas.

"Who knew small dogs could make such a noise?" Anton's eyebrows are raised when I open the front door to him.

"Because I tried to get them to settle down by playing some relaxation tracks," I admit reluctantly.

"Okay, I'm not sure I understand." Anton frowns.

"Well I didn't think about the nature noises they put onto those tracks." I shrug. "It turns out that waves lapping on a beach and the nature calls of wildlife actually drive canines crazy as they try to find the source of the noises."

Anton laughs.

"Hey, it's not funny!" I lightly swat him on the arm but can't help laughing myself. "Okay, it may be a little bit funny. Do you have something I can shut them up with?"

Anton hands over a packet of streaky duck treats, highly prized in this house. It works like a charm and soon they are all chomping away and settled down as if they haven't been howling up a storm.

"Thanks." I exhale with relief into the restored peace of the household. "Thank God there are no guests booked in until tomorrow. You'd expect the two larger dogs, Barney and Maxi, to be the loudest but I have to say the chihuahuas have a very piercing howl for such tiny creatures."

It turns out Anton hasn't just brought the dog treats, he's also brought me some Earl Grey tea bags, a bar of Lindt chocolate, some milk, cheese, and fresh bread as well as a couple of cakes from my favourite patisserie in Mirepoix.

Warmth spreads through my chest. He's brought me a care package.

"I didn't want you to go hungry if you couldn't get out to the shops," Anton explains as he empties the contents of his bag onto the kitchen counters. "It sounded very much like you were being held hostage."

I laugh. "Kind of."

"I came prepared to negotiate your release," he adds, mock seriously. "Pickle has authorised me to use anything up to the full packet in order to secure the release of his favourite dog sitter."

"That's so sweet. I'll text him later to thank him."

"I brought the other things. You can thank me now, if you like." Anton's eyes twinkle.

I step into his arms and turn my face up to his to kiss him. It's beginning to get interesting when something tickles my bare leg and I jump. I turn to see Peanut hopping up and down on her hind legs to get my attention, occasionally tapping me on the leg to punctuate her demands.

"I'll have to give you a proper reward later maybe?" I suggest, my pulse quickening.

"I look forward to it." He grins. "I'm still surprised the dogs were howling and you needed to resort to a nature soundtrack. I thought they were normally okay to be left for a while?"

"Well yes but I don't think Poppy and JoJo have been away at the same time before and it's unsettled then. They're all rescues who've experienced being abandoned, except Pickwick who Poppy sort of inherited, so I suppose I can see why that might make them anxious." I nod to the food. "Would you like to stay for lunch? Have you got time?"

"Yes, I have time." Anton pulls a chair out from the kitchen table and sits down. "You know you happen to be my favourite dog sitter too. I'm sure they'll settle down soon."

"With bribes, yes." I laugh and let Peanut have another small piece of treat. "She doesn't understand why she only gets a tiny bit when Barney and Maxi get a whole treat."

"Quite right too," Anton addresses Peanut. "I say it's size discrimination. How are you supposed to ever grow any bigger unless they feed you more?"

Sensing a friend, she leaps straight into his lap for a cuddle.

"Don't encourage her," I laugh, bringing the bread, cheese, and cakes over to the table. "She's already tried that argument on all of us."

Peanut rolls over on his chest so her head is tucked in on his shoulder and makes her puppy dog eyes at him.

"I can't believe such a sweet little dog could be that manipulative," Anton protests.

I swear Peanut flutters her eyelashes at him.

"Ha!" I laugh, fetching some water and glasses and pulling up a chair so I can sit at the table with him. "I'll tell Poppy and JoJo that when they get back. She's incredibly cute but she's definitely playing you."

"No, surely not. I believe she is innocent in every

way." Anton strokes Peanut and she wriggles against him in sheer delight.

"You know, if you'd like me to be your knight in shining armour I could take you away from all these stressful hostage situations and dog servant duties for just a few days? Perhaps two days next week?" He raises an eyebrow at me.

"Poppy told you it was my birthday, didn't she?" I shake my head. "Really, you don't need to do anything."

"But I want to do something. And in fact, it's already booked and paid for." He grins. "Poppy checked your phone calendar for work bookings and guess what? Your only client for those two days was me. She also told me to present it as a done deal so you wouldn't feel guilty about saying yes but would feel guilty about saying no because it was a last-minute non-refundable deposit."

I burst into laughter. "Poppy looks so sweet but she can be sneaky. Okay, kindly knight, if you promise to polish your armour, I will be your willing damsel."

"My willing damsel, eh?" His eyes gleam. "I do like the sound of that."

"So are you taking me to your castle?"

"Not quite my castle, no, but it is a castle, a chateau

hotel. I'm not going to tell you any more because it's going to be a surprise."

"But what about the dogs?" I ask, alarmed, hating the idea of them being left with someone they don't know very well, especially after all the progress they've made.

"They're coming with us – the hotel allows well-behaved dogs."

"Well-behaved dogs?" I ask a little sceptically. "I love them loads but they can sometimes be a little bit naughty."

"It'll be fine. I don't think they'll give us a lie detector test and we won't exactly leave them to roam the hotel stealing objects to hoard under the bed."

"Thank you," I say, getting up and going round to Anton so I can put my arms around him and give him a big hug. Taking especial care not to squash Peanut of course.

"It's called the Château des Étoiles," Anton announces as we head towards one of the most impressive build-ings I've ever seen.

The chateau of stars… It's more traditional than Château Camon, with beautiful turrets and it even has a moat. It's surrounded by acres of immaculate grounds and vineyards.

"It's gorgeous. I can't believe you arranged this for me." I beam.

"Well why not? It's your birthday. It's worth celebrating and I wanted to make it special for you."

"Oh, oh thank you. I don't know what to say." I blink back unexpected tears. No one has ever done anything like this for me before and I'm moved far more than I could have imagined. I turn to look at the elegant wrought-iron gates, hoping Anton won't notice the tears I'm blinking back.

"Thank you, Anton. I think this is the loveliest birthday present I've ever been given."

"It is my pleasure, Daisy."

It's easily the loveliest hotel I've ever stayed in. The dogs aren't allowed in the restaurant so we put their dog beds into our sumptuous room complete with four-poster bed and luxurious silk bed covers. They seem happy enough on their dog beds but we decide to have dinner brought up to the room rather than have to leave them alone. Dinner has been ordered both for us and for the dogs too, who even had their own menu to choose from.

"So, do you think you like France enough to stay?" Anton asks as we stand on the small terrace looking out over the immaculately kept grounds that remind me a little of Versailles, though on a very small scale of course.

"Like France?" I feel caught a little off guard. "Yes, of course, I really love France but there is a lot of paperwork and it's not so simple since Brexit."

"Well, we hope that you do stay," Anton says, his gaze fixed on me in a way that makes my heart rate speed up while time seems to slow down, which is such an odd contradiction. "What would Pickle and Squeaker do without you?"

I wonder if he felt it too, the intensity of the moment and the need to diffuse it by using the dogs. In case I get the wrong idea or… I sigh inwardly at the delicate balance of what can and can't be said at each appropriate stage of a relationship.

We've had sex and yet I'm supposedly not allowed to tell him I love him because it's "too soon". How screwed up is that? That words can scare us more, make us more afraid of rejection than sexual intimacy does?

I know what Gran would say about the rules and it probably wouldn't be polite. I don't want to ruin things though, not when they're going so well so I follow his lead, dialling down the intensity and regaling him with stories of my recent language misunderstandings.

"So the doctor just said *la petite* with no context which confused me, so I replied I didn't have any children." I laugh at Anton's suppressed smile. "Yes, you've guessed it, she actually said *l'appétit* which sounds exactly the same. How was I to know she was asking about my appetite?" I roll my eyes.

Anton laughs.

"Not fair," I reply. "You have too many words that sound the same but mean completely different things."

Anton shrugs. "You have the same in English."

"Hmm, I suppose," I reluctantly concede. "And then just yesterday I spent twenty minutes talking to this man who'd come to the gate about his missing collie. He seemed so adamant the collie had been left at the gate and I was getting ready to hunt everywhere for this dog when it finally dawned on me that he meant *colis*, like a parcel delivery, and he was asking if we'd received a parcel that was meant for him."

Anton laughs and warmth fills my chest. I'm glad I'm wearing my fancy emerald-blue dress, even if we are eating in the room. It makes my cleavage look great and the way the fabric is cut and hangs makes me feel curvy rather than bumpy.

Anton seems to approve of my appearance in that way polite men have of subtly admiring you without being too obvious about it. He looks as gorgeous as ever in a sand-coloured jacket and open-neck white shirt paired with dark-blue jeans.

Then I realise I'm staring, and not in the way that polite girls do but more in an openly-feasting-my-senses way. I blush and look down at my plate, feeling ridiculously self-conscious. The food is delicious and the trio of mini desserts – crème brûlée, raspberry and cream macaroons, and fresh strawberries with meringue – all look heavenly. Normally I'd be tucking in but my hunger for Anton is growing stronger by the minute.

"*Ton appétit?*" Anton meets my gaze with an intensity I'm sure reflects my own although his eyebrow is raised and his mouth quirks with humour at our earlier conversation. How is my appetite? I feel the underlying sexual tension and wish I knew the French word for ravenous.

I could keep the joke going but the moment feels too charged, too serious for that. As though the very air around us has changed, the distance between us contracting. He reaches for my hand and holds it, circling the palm with his thumb. A shiver of sexual desire travels through me, electrifying me.

"I did buy you a present," Anton says, a slight diffidence in his tone that is unusual for him and odd given the relaxed evening. Could he be feeling any insecurity? The thought that he might be is encouraging somehow;

it helps me to relax to know he doesn't just take all this in his stride. It means it matters to him, surely?

"Did you? But you already booked the hotel. Thank you – you didn't need to but that's very kind of you."

"You might not like it, and it's fine if you don't," he clears his throat and shrugs. "I thought it would... never mind, why don't I leave you to open it while I take the dogs into the chateau gardens to settle them down. Then... well we can decide if we want dessert now or a little later on."

My heart rate is beating fast as he leaves the room with the dogs. Before shutting the door he points out a delicately wrapped package he has placed on the bed for me.

What if it's horribly uncomfortable bright-red underwear he's bought in a size too small for me because he's worried about offending me by suggesting I'm bigger than I am?

Time to take a breath. This is Anton. Sexy and smart. Not sleazy. Still, so far life has taught me that you never really know someone and that anyone can have the capacity to surprise you.

I take my time, relishing undoing the delicately curled cerise ribbon and lifting the lid off the box. It is clothing but although it's wrapped in scented tissue, I already know it isn't tacky; I can feel through the tissue that it's silk. Unwrapping it fully I find a gorgeous forest-green silk negligée with delicate straps and pretty darker lace edging around the bust and décolletage neckline. There are also a pair of delicate green silk and lace knickers to match.

Normally I might have considered a first gift of this kind to be a bit… well, forward but it's hardly our first time making love and it's so exquisitely beautiful I love it and can't wait to find out how it feels against my skin. This must have been the cause of Anton's diffidence, not being sure how I'd react to this kind of gift.

I realise he's giving me time to change and head to the bathroom so I can be ready for his return.

I undress quickly and slip the knickers and negligée on, hoping they'll fit me properly. They do, and I wonder how he knew what size to buy. Poppy maybe? The fabric feels fantastic on my skin. I've never worn anything like this before – fancy underwear, yes, and I have some nice matching bra and knicker sets but nothing this… sexy or this grown-up. It's not the kind of present any of my previous boyfriends would've bought me and it would never occur to me to buy it for myself.

The straps are thin and delicate, exposing most of my back, and at the front the neckline dips very low to the bodice which snugly hugs my breasts while the rest of the silk below flows to pool around mid-thigh.

I stare at myself, mesmerised by the sensuality of the gift, of how sexy it makes me feel. I feel grown-up and womanly. The colour brings out the richness of the auburn in my hair.

I hear the main bedroom door click shut and the pad of dog paws on the wooden floor as the dogs head to their beds and water bowl.

I gently stroke the swell of my breasts above the snug neckline and shiver.

Then I see Anton's reflection in the mirror, watching me stroking my skin, his expression inscrutable. The bathroom door was ajar so I hadn't heard him enter.

"I hope you like it?" he asks.

"I love it." I turn around and smile widely at him. I see his expression relax and some of the earlier tension vanish.

He steps forward and turns me back towards the mirror.

"I knew the colour would suit you, my Titian beauty." He runs his fingers through my hair, moving in close. "I love how it fits you… so close."

He strokes the swell of my breasts, first above the neckline, his fingertips tickling my bare skin and making me ache for more. Then he reaches lower, his fingertips lightly brushing up against my nipples so they stiffen, protruding through the thin fabric.

I watch him in the mirror, mesmerised.

Feeling sexy.

Feeling powerful.

The raw hunger in his eyes as he cups both my breasts and presses up against me leaves me in no doubt that he shares my feelings about the effect of the present.

I lean my head back against his chest and he frees one hand to pull my long auburn hair to one side so he can kiss my neck.

His erection stiffens against me and I can't help wondering if he wants to take me here and now, bending me forwards over the bathroom countertop. No man has ever been able to turn me on this quickly or made me feel quite so desirable or desiring.

His other hand slides down from my breasts to palm me between my legs.

Then he tantalisingly lifts the hem of the negligée up so he can skim his fingers over the lace knickers. He continues to stroke me through the lace, an erotic sensation that ignites a fiery passion inside me.

We've had some amazing love-making sessions but something tells me tonight is going to be very special.

Anton kisses my neck and lightly nibbles my earlobe before pressing his lips to my ear to whisper.

"We shall go to the bedroom?"

"Absolutely." I exhale my reply. I really must remember to breathe. It's difficult when I'm feeling so… so… electrified.

I feel a brief glimmer of self-consciousness return as I walk to the bed but it's quickly overwhelmed by the anticipation created by Anton's palpable presence behind me. He might not be touching me right now but still I feel him, feel his eyes on me and sense his fingers, his hard body, that kissable mouth…

I'm not really sure how I get onto the bed, only that in no time we lie face to face on top of the expensive covers and I fumble with his shirt buttons as he strokes my thigh, hip to knee, over and over in a way that both increases my sexual tension and the fumbling of my fingers.

I manage to fully open his shirt so I can run my fingers over his hard chest, then trail them down to the fly of his jeans.

Instead of undoing it though I palm and stroke Anton's erection through his jeans and am gratified to hear him moan with pleasure.

He slides a hand between my legs and again he

strokes me through my knickers, the friction of the fabric heightening the pleasure.

This is very different to our first time. I feel just as comfortable with Anton as I did that first time but there's certainly less insistent urgency and pent-up frustration this time and we know we have more time to explore.

I let him set the pace, happy to put myself in his hands, literally. When he does undress fully, I lie on my back and wait. I glance over at the dogs in their beds – Squeaker is fast asleep but Pickle has one eye open, watching inquisitively.

I giggle as Anton climbs back onto the bed next to me.

He quirks an eyebrow and I point wordlessly at Pickle.

He rolls his eyes. "Well we can't shut him out of the room this time, given we're in a hotel. Never mind, I'm sure it'll be fine."

"You won't find it… distracting?"

"Nothing could distract me from what I plan to do to you." He smiles that oh-so-charming smile of his that transforms him from sexy professor to flirty, just the right side of dominant male.

I gaze down at his hard jutting cock.

I'm not sure even the fire alarm going off would distract me either.

Part of me still can't believe it's true. That he still wants me, wants more of me in the way that I want more of him. That he cared enough about me to arrange this trip away for my birthday.

I want to make him feel lovely. To give and receive pleasure.

I reach out a hand to fondle him and he whispers in my ear.

"Let's take it nice and slow. We have all night."

So I gently skim his erect cock with the back of my hand, lightly teasing him and in return he strokes me all over through my negligée and knickers.

The growing anticipation makes the sexual tension build with sensually slow intensity.

A loud snore from Squeaker makes me giggle and Anton mock grimace, but it doesn't ruin the mood; rather, our amusement seems to deepen the intimacy between us.

Soon I can't resist kneeling on the bed next to him and lowering my mouth to his cock, licking and lightly teasing him, swirling my tongue around the head.

With a groan he reaches out and slides a hand up my negligée and strokes me rhythmically through the lace knickers. He slowly edges them down so he can stroke my bare pussy, teasing me as I teased him, before plunging a finger inside me. Then he adds a second finger, scissoring them to open me up. The more he alternates fingering me and stroking my clit, the more he turns me on and I can't help sucking him harder, plunging him deeper into my mouth as he strokes my hair with his free hand.

Then, when I briefly come up for air, he takes me by the hips and spins me round, straddling him backwards so I have a knee planted either side of his torso.

I take him back into my mouth, the different angle allowing me to take him deeper, something I know Anton appreciates from his satisfied groans.

Anton grabs my hips quite firmly and I start as I feel the delicious sensation of his tongue licking me and teasing my clit. One of his hands moves from my hip to finger me inside, rubbing in some very interesting places as his tongue teases my clit. The combination of the two is too much for me and I contract around his fingers, releasing his erection from my mouth and holding onto his cock as I come, moaning and spasming. I'm so wet I feel a little embarrassed but he's licking up every drip as though he loves it.

Once recovered, I spin round and sit down hard on him. I try to tease him, leaning forward, trailing my hair on his chest and stomach. We kiss and I taste my arousal on his lips. Then he pulls down the straps of the negligée and plays with my bare breasts, sitting up a little to suck each nipple in turn. I have never felt sexier or more womanly.

Once I lean back and begin riding him though, he doesn't want to take it slow anymore, thrusting up hard to meet me, grabbing my hips and then pulling me down on him. Then he holds still to keep from coming and deftly moves me over onto my back, effortlessly lifting one of my legs and then another over his shoulders so his strokes are deeper, harder and oh my… so delicious. I watch him, one of my hands on his chest as he takes me deep and hard; I watch his eyes flicker open and his gaze lock onto mine as he comes with a final hard thrust.

Then we lie in an intimate tangle of limbs, the negligée still around my torso. I feel… totally at peace. Satisfied too. Well and truly satisfied.

There's no awkwardness, no urgency to disengage and head for the loo on my part, and seemingly no hurry to disengage on his part either, though he makes sure all his weight isn't on top of me as we recover and our breathing stills.

"Well I knew French men had a reputation but… wow."

Anton laughs, a deep rumble laugh that reverberates through my chest.

"We are the most romantic men in Europe," he declares solemnly, but there's a twinkle in his eye that shows me he's not taking himself too seriously.

"Go on then," I tease. "Say something romantic."

"Hmmm," he tilts his head to one side. "Okay. You are the champagne that fizzes through my veins – delicious, potent, yet also intrinsically fragile. A delight to be savoured."

I giggle.

"*Les Anglais…*" he rolls his eyes. "No soul."

"Sorry, that was actually beautiful," I say shyly.

"Your turn then," he teases. "Say something romantic."

My mind goes blank. The words *I love you* hover on my tongue but I don't want to be the first to say them.

"Erm… sorry, my mind has gone completely blank." I smile apologetically. "Can we have our desserts now?"

He laughs and shakes his head with mock disdain and I grin back at him, not caring that he's smirking. I kind of like this touch of teasing arrogance in him; it's a side of him I haven't really seen before.

"I can see I'll have to teach you the soul language of

love. It's not just about words but much deeper than that. There is a reason why the words flattery, chivalry, and romantic are all words that originated from old French."

It should sound corny but the dark intent in his eyes and the sensuous way he's stroking my back and my hair sets all my nerve endings tingling again.

"The language of Love."

Love. He uses the word first. Kind of…

Phew.

Though he didn't actually say *I love you*, and he was playing around at the time.

I'll still take it as a good sign though.

Pickle and Squeaker are enjoying their walk around the extensive gardens. Anton and I follow behind them, holding hands. The dogs are investigating fresh sniffs together which is something really only another canine is ever going to truly understand.

"It's nice they have each other," I say, watching Squeaker eagerly following her big brother's pawsteps, her short, stubby tail wagging madly.

"Yes, I think it helped them, you know. When Claire died, Squeaker was still a tiny puppy so it hit Pickle harder, losing her…" He pauses and takes a deep breath.

I gently squeeze his hand and he relaxes, some of the tension seeming to leave him. The more time I spend with Anton the more I'm starting to feel his emotions. Even if he's not in the same place as I am, I still get a sense of his energy just before he sends me a text. It's one of the reasons I'm so sure the connection between us is something special. I've not felt an energy bond of this depth before.

His thoughts though, they remain a mystery to me.

"Pickle looked after Squeaker," he adds, his mind still with the dogs. "Even if at first he wasn't sure about us getting a puppy, he soon became fiercely protective of her."

"That's really sweet."

"I think you're good for him, you know," Anton says. "For Pickle. He's definitely less depressed since you came into our lives."

"Oh, I'm glad."

My heart beats wildly. Dare I ask him?

"And you?" I ask quietly, my eyes fixed on the dogs, not daring to look at Anton directly. I don't want him to feel like I'm forcing him into complimenting me but I need something from him, to know if this means something to him in the same way as it does to me.

We don't have to be on the same page yet, but at least the same book would be a promising start.

"For me too, yes. You are good for all of us."

This time he squeezes my hand and I exhale with relief. JoJo is right; I only need to take this step by step. Even if it's not forever, at least for now we are both brightening up each other's lives.

I want it to be forever though. The stubborn, insistent "knowing" inside of me argues. *This is meant to be. Just for now will never be enough for you and you know it. You're scared to commit in case you get hurt but bone-deep you know this is meant to be more.*

Despite my mind's acceptance of JoJo's common sense, I know it's true. This joy, this energy connection, it's not just because we're lovers. I've never experienced it with anyone else but Anton. The fact I can feel his energy while he's texting me and before I actually receive the text has to mean something, surely?

The voice sounds an awful lot like my intuition. I am starting to trust it again, tentatively.

What happened in London muddied the waters and stirred up a lot of silt so I couldn't see clearly anymore. Once all the sediment finally settles and my equilibrium is restored, I hope I'll be able to trust myself again.

If it turns out I'm wrong about Anton I think it will be an awfully long time before I ever trust myself again.

The dogs see a squirrel and race to the bottom of a large tree, disrupting my thoughts, and we have to put them back on their leads.

I force myself to take a deep breath and stop getting ahead of myself.

One day at a time.

I feel like I need to get one thing clear though because although we've talked about my gift we haven't really discussed the urn incident.

I clear my throat as we circle around the grounds and back towards the chateau.

"I've still been feeling really awful about that day in your office." I glance sideways at Anton to register his reaction.

To my surprise his lips quirk into an amused smile.

"There's no need. It was an accident," he says.

"But you looked so shocked. I felt really awful."

"It was a bit of a shock but it's okay, really. Please stop worrying about it," he says seriously, then lightens his tone. "It was the sight of Pickle with your bra in his mouth and your audition for a wet T-shirt competition that really threw me."

He laughs.

"Oh, I have no memory of those details. Are you sure you weren't taking mind-altering substances at the time?"

"Definitely not. But you did bang your head that day so maybe you have a little amnesia?" he suggests.

"Yes, amnesia," I agree. "And I have a feeling I'm never going to recover the full memories of that day."

"Very convenient." He grins.

I relax a little. If he's joking about it then maybe he's genuinely okay about what happened.

"What did you feel?" he asks suddenly, and my stomach tightens again. I turn to look at him but he's not meeting my gaze, just staring into the distance ahead of him.

"Feel?" I ask cautiously, though I'm fairly sure I know what he's talking about. This is my own fault for bringing it up, I know. I have only myself to blame.

"When you touched the container and…" He can't seem to bring himself to say *her ashes*.

"Everything good," I reply honestly, because he deserves a proper answer. "It was just so intense that it overwhelmed me. I felt her. Claire. Her essence and her personality. I felt too much. Normally I'll just pick up a strong emotion and maybe a sense I can't shake of who an object belonged to or something about its history, but this was different."

I pause, sensing this conversation needs to be driven and directed by him. I can tell he's finding it difficult so if he wants to leave it there and move on that's fine.

"She likes you," he adds softly, so quietly I barely hear him.

"Sorry?"

"Claire likes you," he says with more conviction. "I meant it when I said back then that although I wasn't sure about some of your experiences I was willing to keep an open mind, remember?"

I nod.

"Well, I had a dream that night, at least I think it was a dream, yet it felt so vivid, so real. Claire and I were both standing next to the river, the same place where you and I had talked, remember?"

"Yes."

"She said she'd wanted to visit me before but until you came on the scene I'd been too closed-off for her to reach me."

"Oh."

"She said you were really good for me and also that she's been talking to the dogs and apparently they are also huge fans of yours."

Tears well unexpectedly in my eyes and I blink them back.

"You don't think I'm crazy, do you?" he asks anxiously. "Maybe it was just a dream. I know most people would say it was but… it felt like so much more. It was her. She was there and I can't explain it away."

"*Me*, think that *you're* crazy?" I ask incredulously. "Of course not. It's a bit like that for me. I know it's real and sometimes information will come to light that backs up what I sensed but not always. I know I can't prove things but I don't feel the need to."

"So you didn't see her then, that day? In the office?" he asks.

"No, I only tend to feel things and sense things, not see anything."

"She found the whole incident with the urn really funny, by the way," he adds unexpectedly. "That's what she said. It's one of the reasons I felt so sure it was her. It was exactly the kind of thing she would have found amusing. So if you're asking if we're okay about what happened that day then yes, we are. You have nothing to worry about. And if I'm right then Claire's okay about it too."

"Good, thank you for telling me that." I squeeze his hand tightly again before letting go so Anton can hold the door open for us to get back into the hotel.

I feel rather emotional but considerably better than I did and I say a silent thank-you to Claire for helping me out.

Chapter Eleven

"They slipped briskly into an intimacy from which they never recovered."
F. Scott Fitzgerald

DAISY: *Help! Pickle has stolen Squeaker's favourite rabbit toy and won't let me take it back. Any tips?*

ANTON: *You need to do a toy hostage exchange...*

DAISY: *Umm...???*

ANTON: *Get hold of Pickle's favourite duck toy and offer it as a swap!*

DAISY: *Thanks. Got it!*

After we get back from the hotel and slip into our usual routine, I can't help wondering if my feelings are stronger than Anton's. He doesn't ask me about how my future plans are going and despite the emotional intensity of our hotel break, I would still feel better if he would make it really clear that he wants me to stay, and not just for the sake of the dogs.

"So you don't think it's a bad sign he hasn't said 'I love you' yet?" I ask early one morning, pulling up a chair at the kitchen table and pouring a cup of tea from the pot. The kitchen definitely seems to be the hub of the guesthouse, where all the important discussions take place.

"Definitely not," Poppy smiles sympathetically. "You see, the French have the verb *aimer* but you can use that to say you love chocolate or sport… There is only the one word so it's not all that special if you also apply it to a person. Leo told me that's why you don't hear people saying *je t'aime* very often as it doesn't mean that much."

"So, how do you know then?" I ask, perplexed.

"The French are more into romantic gestures, and nicknames can tell you a lot about feelings."

"What's Leo's nickname for you?" I ask.

Poppy's cheeks redden "I'm not telling. But don't be

surprised if you get called a little flea or a cabbage – they really are terms of endearment, not insults."

"You're having me on, surely?"

"No, really, they're popular nicknames." Poppy grins.

I'm still not entirely sure I believe her but this is Poppy; she's not really the kind of person to wind people up.

"Or there is *ma mignonne*," she adds. "That's a bit like 'my cutie' in English. Or maybe 'sweetie'."

"Ah, so that's why I keep hearing people saying *mignonne* about chihuahuas or Pickwick."

"Yes, exactly. But honestly, don't worry about it if he hasn't got a nickname for you yet. He took you to a gorgeous hotel for your birthday – I'd say that's a pretty good sign as signs go. Actions are better than words any day.'"

"Yes, I know that," I say, biting my lip. "It's just I'm getting a bit stressed about applying for residency here. It's a big deal and I want to be able to grow my business a bit more, to find a way to be independent. You've been so kind and I know I've helped you out in return but we both know once the gîte renovations are completed you need to rent out the room I've been using."

"Oh, we're still a way off of worrying about that,"

Poppy says. "And if Anton wasn't in the picture you'd still want to stay, wouldn't you? You seem quite happy here."

"Yes," I reply with certainty. "I love it here and would be very happy to live here. I'm a bit anxious about what might happen if my income drops, and moving country is a big deal, but you're right; I'm happy here. It feels like home."

"So what's the problem?" Poppy asks. "You know we can give you paid hours here to make up the shortfall if necessary, at the restaurant or gallery even."

"That's very kind of you. Are you sure?"

She takes my hand in hers and squeezes.

"Absolutely," she states. "So, any other roadblocks in the way?"

I take a deep breath and prepare to share the real reason I'm scared about making such a big decision without knowing where things are going with Anton.

"Well, the thing is, what if it goes badly with Anton? He'll be really close by, and it could be really awkward." I shrug. "I hadn't considered the huge difference between dating in a city compared to a small, rural community. There would be no way to get away from him or get over him."

"And what if it goes really well?" Poppy smiles. "When I came here I had no idea if I could make the guesthouse work. My ex had left me in a financial hole and I took it one day at a time. Maybe it will work out and maybe it won't, but half the adventure is trying."

"Yes, you're right." I let out a sigh of relief, my mind made up. "I only get tied up in knots when I listen to anxious thoughts and ignore my intuition… and my intuition says I should stay."

"We both know your intuition is worth listening to."

I hope so, I really do, because my intuition has never been stronger than when it comes to Anton.

Just one day later I'm sitting at the table in the guesthouse kitchen, cradling my early morning cup of tea, my mobile phone in my hand. I'm barely aware of the dogs crowding around me, asking for fuss.

Peanut decides not to wait for an invitation and leaps up onto my lap anyway.

I put my phone down and cuddle her, absentmindedly kissing the top of her head. I'm still feeling distracted from the email I received from my London flatmate, Vicky.

"Hi Daisy, how's things?" JoJo comes into the kitchen laden with fresh vegetables from the vegetable patch.

"Um, I'm a bit stressed actually. Do you remember me saying that the girl I was subletting my room to went back to Australia because her mum wasn't well?"

She abandons the vegetables on the kitchen countertop and comes to sit at the table opposite me.

"Yes, I do remember. Didn't you decide to pay for a month's rent and council tax and then decide what to do?"

"Yes, but now Vicky's told me she's been offered a great new job in Manchester so she's given notice on the flat and I'll have to either go back and find another flatmate or give notice myself.

"I thought you were definitely planning to make a go of it out here?" JoJo frowns.

"I was. I am. I…" I pause to attempt to un-jumble my thoughts. "I suppose I hadn't wanted to burn my bridges just yet."

JoJo laughs but not unkindly. "That might be very sensible, Daisy, but I think sometimes you need to burn your bridges. Can you really commit to your new life if you're still looking over your shoulder at the old one?"

"I suppose. But as I said, it was short notice and the rent still had to be paid. It seemed like a good option. It would've been a good option if it had worked out as planned."

"Hmm, but you still need to decide what to do

about the flat share?" JoJo nods. "I understand. Is it a time-sensitive decision? Would you have to go back to get your stuff out or is it in storage?"

"It's in storage thankfully but yes, I really need to decide now. It's a nice flat but…"

"It's not where you want to be?" JoJo says pragmatically.

"No, and I know it hardly seems like much of a dilemma but I wasn't expecting to have to decide right now, by tomorrow. I thought I'd have more time. It feels like a bit of a risk, burning that last bridge. But then, I suppose setting up a new business is always going to be risky. There are no guarantees and I am getting new clients via my advert at the vets' surgery."

"There are never any guarantees about anything in life. I turned up here with nothing but my car and a vague hope of getting work somewhere no one would recognise me. You know Poppy and I are very happy to have you around. Plus, it's only one bridge. There'll be other bridges, other places to live if you need them."

"Thanks," I reply and try to smile.

Yet I know, deep down, that my anxiety is to do with what I discussed with Poppy the other day. My decision doesn't have so much to do with financial worries as it does with where I stand with Anton. If he were to break up with me I couldn't just get on a plane and go back to my old life to get away from the pain of having to see him all the time. Maybe even having to see him with someone else one day.

I know deep down what I have to do tomorrow and I'll just have to find ways of managing the anxiety of uncertainty. Maybe some more yoga sessions with Poppy? And with the dogs of course. I smile as I remember the furry mayhem of our last yoga session. Poppy and JoJo have made their new lives work here so I'm going to do my best to make sure things work out for me.

Anton is unexpectedly tender this evening. He's obviously picking up on the undercurrent of my disquiet, even if he doesn't understand it. He's asked me once or twice what's wrong, to which I've replied, "Nothing."

I know it's a really annoying answer to give but I can't share the real anxiety I'm feeling because if I tell him what's really on my mind it will force the issue. I don't want to put pressure on him to tell me how he sees our future.

If he sees our future.

In an ideal world, I could let things develop naturally. There would be no pressure, no time-sensitive decisions to be made. So I need to deal with that decision on my own and just let things carry on developing as they have been.

At least instead of pressing me to find out what's wrong he's being extra gentle, extra thoughtful, which I really appreciate about him, the fact that he doesn't conform to any male stereotype but often surprises me. Who knew that I would find his intelligence as sexy as his tousle-haired sexy-professor look? He has a depth that intrigues me,

In his bedroom we lie on the bed facing each other. I'm still wearing my sundress, though my sandals I've kicked off on the floor and he's in cargo shorts and a collared T-shirt but our legs are bare and intertwined in a casual intimacy that feels natural between us now; as though our bodies naturally navigate towards each other, happiest when in physical contact.

With the back of his hand he casually and almost reverentially strokes the swell of my breasts cupped by the bodice of my dusky-pink sundress. Where his fingers trail over bare flesh my nerve endings spark to his touch.

It never seems to get old, this dance between us. Not just between our bodies but our souls, our minds, the energy that makes up the sum of us… It delights in the natural ebb and flow of the tide and the paths of our respective tumbling waters and tributaries as they navigate rocks and force a route through branches and sundry debris in order to reach each other again, to converge into one body of water.

The dance is at once an eternal mystery and yet at the same time the most natural, instinctive thing in the world.

I gaze into Anton's eyes and in the stillness of the moment I swear I can see deep into his soul. The longer I keep my gaze fixed on him, the more I see.

On the surface he has a warmth and a richness with the complexity of dark chocolate and coffee. Beneath that though lurks the wildness of the Ariège landscape and his storytelling troubadour ancestry of old. He has taken up the mantle to keep the old stories alive, albeit in print not in song, but the vocation suits him. Beneath the wisdom and the academic knowledge lies the dreamer, the boy who clamoured for stories from his grandfather when he helped him in his shop. The shop he lovingly maintains even though it barely turns a profit and his real income comes from document appraisals. The love of story and of books is rooted deep in his soul.

I swear I see flecks of gold in his irises I've not noticed before. I'm reminded of that first day out together with Anton's tour that started by the Ariège river. The day he told me the tales of silver and gold mining in the area and of how fleeces were laid in the river, hooked by branches, to collect the gold in the river sediment. And shared the more whimsical tale of the water fae with gold in their hair who lured handsome men into its watery depths.

He strokes my hair now, as he did then, as though remembering the same day, one that somehow cast a spell over both of us. A spell I never want to be broken.

Though we're past summer solstice, the sun still sets late and now it casts a beautiful slanting amber light over the vine-covered hills and fields of sunflowers in the distance.

Everything is golden.

Through the open window, the scent of warm earth and lavender from Anton's garden fills the room, a faint breeze disturbing the muslin curtains.

It's as close to a perfect moment as I've ever known. If only I could freeze time now before any decisions are made and paths irrevocably taken.

I'd hoped his recognition that I didn't want to talk about it would ease the pressure I'm feeling but I'd forgotten how much can be said in silence; how our eyes reveal and our body language and micro expressions communicate far more than if words were added, almost as verbal distractions.

I feel close to Anton. Intimately close. Scarily close, but the fear only comes from how it might feel if I were to lose this intimacy.

Anton slips one of my dress straps over my shoulder and tugs it down. He breaks the locked gaze to glance down with surprise and pleasure. The bodice of the dress is suitably fitted and supportive enough that I don't need to wear a bra underneath.

He strips me reverentially, stroking and kissing my breasts. I remove my knickers while he shrugs out of his shorts and shirt and we resume our quiet contemplation of the moment.

Relishing the anticipation.

Knowing we have all the time in the world. All of tonight at least. I mentally shut thoughts about the future and decisions to be made behind a steel door.

Not tonight. For tonight, tomorrow does not exist. The real world does not intrude. I've never been much of a fan of it anyway.

Tonight is me and Anton and this room.

And in this space where nothing else exists and there is no fear or doubt, I'm free to love and love freely, without limit.

I love you, I love you, I love you. My heart sings it to Anton, my body sings it, a song so strong, so vibrant he must hear it surely? And yet my lips stop short of declaration. Is there anything worse than saying the words only to be met with silence? Plenty I'm sure, if I thought about it properly, but not now in this moment when I'm aching for him to tell me I'm his in the same way that he is mine… Not my everything but at the very least the shooting star in my night sky, the compass in my heart that points me to home, the joy that makes my soul want to dance and do cartwheels.

You are my love.

The words pulse through me tonight as we begin to make love. We've had fun sex, affectionate sex, exciting sex, and we've had sex in a way that awoke passions in me I never knew existed… but tonight feels like the first time we've truly made love. Tenderly, passionately expressed our feelings with stroking and kissing and teasing. Exploring each other's bodies with the passionate attention of cartographers mapping each other's erogenous zones and mentally recording the information.

I never knew how amazing it felt to have the sides of my breasts stroked, or the small of my back caressed at the same time as Anton tenderly brings me to a state of such arousal I'm praising him with each exhalation of my breath.

My hands slide over his chest and down his abdomen until I'm stroking an already hardening cock.

I tease him gently, cupping and palming his balls, teasing his shaft with my fingertips. Deliberately taking my time.

His hands shift down to my bottom, stroking me, lightly squeezing my buttocks and pulling me harder against him.

I reach round to stroke the backs of his thighs and his bottom, gently squeezing his buttocks as though he were already inside me and I'm pulling him deeper.

Because I need him deeper, need him piercing me to my core. In me, part of me, joined to me exquisitely in a way that reminds me why we do all this angsting and put up with all this uncertainty… Why so many songs and films and plays are devoted to the pursuit of this connection… and almost as many describe the sadness of its loss.

It's not just an evolutionary biological drive. It's not just a case of compatible pheromones. It's about the joy of remembering, for even just a little while, that we are not alone, that though we are infinitesimally small in this extensive universe somehow we are connected.

A part of the whole.

And in sex we have chosen to remember this with someone who fills our soul with joy.

That's why it matters so much to us. Why we're

afraid to be the first to declare our feelings… Why love can make cowards of us all.

We're closer now. Close enough that my hard nipples are firmly pressed against Anton's chest and I feel his very stiff cock pressing against me. We're kissing, tongues meeting with joy and growing need. I know I'm more than ready for him; I can feel the wetness of my arousal like an aching need spreading to fill my every cell.

And yet, despite our growing mutual need we stop kissing and lock eyes again.

The dark pools of Anton's pupils reflect the depth of his desire me. Or perhaps they're simply reflecting the desire in mine. Yet it's more than that. I'm aware of a deeper layer of stripped-back soul in the windows of his eyes now and I'm sure my own naked soul is equally revealed.

I'd thought that not talking would be the emotionally easier option tonight. With another less perceptive man perhaps, but not with Anton.

As he rolls me onto my back and my legs automatically wrap around his hips, the age-old merging of two into one has never felt so mindblowingly intense. I reach to guide his cock in but I'm so wet, so open for him, subsumed in the lowering of my defences for the most intimate of all acts that he barely needs my help.

In the past, I've loved him taking me from behind, loved the... new things he introduced me to on my birthday, loved the unexpectedly erotic side to my sexy professor, yet tonight this feels the most perfect of all – the weight of him on top of me, the slow and steady build-up of sensation and skill that has me climaxing without additional stimulation. The satisfaction of him coming inside me, and holding me afterwards.

It feels like heaven.

As Anton drifts off to sleep, I lie motionless and wide awake in his arms, all the thoughts I had earlier resurfacing. I can't help wondering if Anton has been holding back from saying he loves me, from committing to me more deeply just in case I'm planning to go home to London in the autumn, my French adventure completed.

It's possible I suppose, but in the other scenario, in which I am more loving than loved and I stay and build my life here – something I really want to do – he will always be on my doorstep if things go wrong between us. It's a crucial difference between rural and city dating I'd never considered. This is a small community and he's also one of my best clients.

If this goes wrong I'll end up in a similar situation to the one I came to France to escape. Not exactly the same because Anton is a far better man than Scott and my feelings for him are the real deal this time.

I could be happy here, but not if I end up living my life in the limbo of unrequited love. Always hoping, longing for a sighting or a word or two. Or worse still, waiting and hoping he'll change his mind.

Unable to move on…

I hate that this matters so much to me it scares me.

Matters so much I can't ask him.

My earlier thought returns unbidden: love makes cowards of us all.

Chapter Twelve

"We are most alive when we're in love."
John Updike

FROM: *Gran*
TO: *Daisy*
SUBJECT: *Apologies*

Darling Daisy,

I'm so sorry I've been out of contact. Getting access to an internet café hasn't been as easy as I'd hoped. There are frequent power cuts in the only town that has a place with reliable internet and I only make infrequent visits when we have to get supplies for the ashram community.

Imagine my surprise when I read your emails! I've been having a great time but it sounds like you're the one having all the exciting adventures! Leaving your job, moving to France, setting up your own business… If I'd left replying any longer I might have found you married and pregnant!

I know you've always struggled with listening to your intuition when it comes to men but the problem is, when our hormones are involved it's not always our intuition sending the messages. It can easily get mixed up with what we want to hear.

With Anton I'd say ask yourself how he makes you feel. Is the feeling joyful and expansive? Do you know that you know that you know? If the connection is joyful but things aren't moving forward as quickly as you'd like, I'd say it probably is a case of timing. Be patient; some things can't be forced before their time.

It sounds like you're staying in France for all the right reasons and I hope you enjoy your adventure, sweetheart. I would love to come and visit you when I make it back to Europe.

Don't worry about being normal and sensible. Sensible is no fun at all and normal is definitely overrated, no matter what your mother says.

You're different. You're special. Own it and learn to trust your inner knowing again.

I hope your next email brings even more exciting news, and don't worry, I'll tell you all about my adventures when I see you again in person.

Lots and lots of love from,
Gran xxx

"Have you got a second, Daisy?" Poppy is biting at her lower lip and there's a tiny crease on her forehead that gives me a moment of misgiving.

"Yes, of course." I sit down at the kitchen table, the place we always seem to end up talking. "Is something wrong?"

I cross my arms and lean forward on the table.

"Kind of. Well, you see…" Poppy doesn't finish her sentence. "Have you decided yet if you're staying on here?"

"Please just say it. Do you need the accommodation back that I'm staying in? Am I in the way?" My heart sinks a little.

Poppy looks instantly stricken. "No, of course you're not in the way. You've been an incredible help since you got here. It's just we've had a wedding party wanting to block book all the accommodation for two weeks in September and we'll need to get everything finished in the barn gîtes to accommodate everyone."

"That's fine. It's okay, Poppy. It's your business and you were only supposed to be helping me out for a bit." I try to smile but it feels a bit forced. Inside, I'm panicking. I thought I'd have a bit longer to sort myself out. I've been picking up a few new clients here and there but I don't think I'm making anything near enough to rent a small flat in Mirepoix yet and I've already handed in my notice for my flat in London.

I'd got used to being a part of life here in St Quentin and things have been good between me and Anton but we haven't really talked about the future and I'm not sure how committed he is, or wants to be, yet.

"I'm sure we can help you sort something out." Poppy reaches forward and gently lays her hand on top of mine.

"I'll find something, I'm sure. I'll find a solution," I say as brightly as I can. "It's not your problem, Poppy."

"Don't be daft. You're not a problem, you're a friend." She smiles. "Well… there may be one solution but I'm not too sure you'd thank me for it."

"Why not?" I ask, wondering what could really be so bad.

"Well, you know how lots of people around here need house sitters when they can't be in the country all the time."

"Yes. I looked at pet sitting as it obviously fits in with my business but mostly the opportunities that come up are too far away or too time consuming so that I wouldn't be able to fit in my regular clients."

"This isn't too far away, still within cycling distance. And there aren't any pets, just very large gardens. The owners need someone to sleep there overnight to keep their insurance premium down. They were burgled once – completely cleaned out. Furniture, the lot. It's very remote."

"That sounds perfect." I eye her suspiciously. "What's the catch? Surveillance cameras in the bathroom and bedroom?"

Poppy giggles. "Nothing like that. I've heard the owners can be a bit, um, difficult."

"But they won't be there most of the time, will they?" I ask, my enthusiasm rising. No rent in return for looking after a house and gardens? I'm sure I can manage that.

"No," Poppy says, but still seems a little reticent. "Why don't I get Leo to arrange a meeting for you with them at their house? Then you can make up your mind once you've met them."

"Okay, thanks, that would be great." I'm surprised she isn't more enthusiastic. Poppy generally thinks well of everyone. Whatever they're like, I'm sure I can put up with the situation in return for free rent.

How bad could it be?

My enthusiasm has been dented a little by the time I've cycled over to Chateau Laurent, the very grandiose title the owners have given their house. Admittedly it's a large one, but it's not a castle by any stretch of the imagination. Also, the grounds are worryingly quite a bit bigger than I'd expected. But it's not like they've advertised for a full-time gardener.

I don't mind the isolation of the place and the views across to the mountains are fantastic, but every single person I've mentioned the interview to has pulled the same rather-you-than-me face which has me concerned. Still, I've not exactly got many options on the table and now I'm definitely sure I want to stay I'm just going to have to suck it up and deal with whatever the elephant in the chateau is, the one no one seems to want to describe to me. The woman on the phone, Evelyn, sounded nice, fairly charming even. Whatever the catch is I'll deal with it.

Evelyn greets me in a friendly enough manner although she can't help commenting on the fact I'm a whole three minutes late and is looking rather sniffily at my bicycle. Her husband, Marcus, just nods at me rather curtly as they give me a tour of the grounds and explain exactly how much work it takes to keep every-thing neat and tidy and how much strimming I'll need to do from now through to autumn. Plus, watering all of the plants by hand each night from the rain butt, not by hosepipe.

"It's also very important that you put everything back in exactly the same place in the sheds," Evelyn lectures, reminding me of my old headmistress.

"Of course," I say, sure my cheeks are going to hurt from all this faux polite smiling. I'm trying to ignore the sweat running down my back under my shirt and can't help wondering when, or if, they're going to offer me a drink. Some water would be very welcome right now. I had a few unexpectedly steep hills on my journey so even though I left in plenty of time the hills had eaten up all the extra time I'd allowed. Well, all that time plus three whole minutes, obviously.

"No, I mean exactly the same place." She looks at me sternly. Yes, she must've been a teacher in a previous life. "Marcus has photographed everything in its place and measured the gaps between everything so he'll know if anything has moved. The same goes for inside the house too."

"Right." I try to maintain my can-do attitude as I remind myself how much I need this accommodation.

"If any of the plants die we'll expect you to replace them at your own expense, though of course we will let you use our tools and even provide you with your own pair of nail scissors," Evelyn adds, as though this is a particularly generous offering.

"Er, thank you," I reply, but my confusion must show because she gestures towards the borders of the lawns.

"After strimming and mowing we trim the borders with nail scissors to give them the perfect finish."

Not quite sure how to respond to that I just nod. Is that even a thing? Surely she's winding me up; it's a prank they pull on all the new house sitters. Yet looking at them both now I can tell they are not prankster sort of people.

After a tour inside the house, which is very nice but there's still no offer of a drink, Evelyn – who is clearly the boss, or at least the spokesperson of the relationship – decides the interview is over and says they'll be in touch.

Okay then.

I briefly wonder if it might be easier to just buy a tent and wild camp somewhere. Maybe it'd be best to save up for a campervan. Which I might be able to do if I take this housesit for a while.

As I make my way back to St Quentin I decide I'll just have to make it work. I want to stay and I want to be close to Anton. I want my own French escape to go as well as Poppy and JoJo's has.

In the meantime, my own news has been eclipsed by the news of the route the Tour de France is taking, namely that it's coming through St Quentin sur Aude on its way to the big climbs of the Pyrenees. There are guests coming to the guesthouse especially for the event, which JoJo is preparing for with military precision.

"I don't want any dogs in the kitchen while I'm preparing the picnic." JoJo stands with her hands on her hips looking rather formidable. The farmhouse dog pack look utterly unabashed but she puts the fear of God into me, and Poppy too from the looks of it.

"I thought we had to keep all dogs, donkeys, and animals of all description under strict lock and key today after that incident with the woman who moved past the barriers with her sign and caused a huge pile up of contestants?" I say. I have been primed on the news coverage from what happened that year in another part of France and the following court case, and I have no desire to go to prison. Let's just say they take the Tour de France very seriously here. It's totally understandable when riders are injured because of someone's carelessness but Madame Dubois, in her capacity as St Quentin's mayor, has lectured the entire village on the subject and said if anyone puts so much as a toe, a paw, or a hoof out of line, the reputation of the whole village will be trashed. Leo was translating for me, but I got the gist. Also, as it's the first time in thirty-five years that the Tour de France has travelled through our village on route to the climbs of the Pyrenees, we do not want to give them a reason to ban us for eternity.

So, the fact that I'm expected to keep the dogs out of the house but away from the race sounds like a bit of a contradictory order.

"Yes, but the actual riders don't come through until hours after it starts," JoJo explains. "I've checked the itinerary. We have all the floats, like a parade giving out goodies and sweets to the crowd. Then there's a long gap during which everyone will get out their picnics, and you know how seriously the French take their picnics."

Poppy and I nod at this. It's not unusual to find tablecloths and wine coolers at picnic benches in motorway service areas.

"I need all dogs out of the house for the morning," JoJo continues. "Flump has grown incredibly long in the past few months, and what with his ability to open doors we can't leave it to chance. Some of our guests are here purely for this event and we must give them the full experience, complete with all the lunch that is meant for them."

"I can manage them all if you need Poppy here," I

offer. The relief of having made my decision about staying is making me feel magnanimous. I haven't told anyone yet though; I want to tell Anton first and gauge his response in person.

"Are you sure?" Poppy nibbles her lower lip. "Leo is on duty at the clinic so he can have Maxi with him, and Barney will be happy sleeping in the barn for the morning, particularly if I get him a bone from the butcher's and put the radio on for him."

"I've taken the four dogs on my own before. It'll be fine." Though saying it will be fine does make me worry I've somehow tempted fate.

"Great, thanks, Daisy. Then I can just focus on the food." JoJo smiles at me with obvious relief. "If you keep them until after the parade then bring them up here and lock them all in, you can come back down and join in the picnic and we can watch the race without the fear of anyone going to prison for disrupting the race or running the risk of incurring the wrath of Poppy's mother-in-law."

We all smile at that. Madame Dubois is a lovely woman but kind of old-school French. Think Chanel-clad, a stickler for formalities and polite etiquette, and thoroughly dependable in a crisis.

"It sounds like a good plan…" Poppy says, a little

uncertainly, eyeing up the quartet of tiny trouble makers.

"It is a good plan," JoJo replies firmly. "This time nothing is going to go wrong."

I notice Poppy subtly touching the wooden table, presumably for luck, and wonder if I should've done the same. Sure, I've heard all the stories about previous animal-related disasters here, but they were exaggerated for comic effect, weren't they? Plus, I'm sure I heard the donkey enclosure has been reinforced even further with every security measure possible so a repeat of the donkey raid on the village refreshments should hopefully never, ever be repeated.

Hmmm. Maybe I'll enlist Anton's help with the tiny trouble makers. And maybe, just maybe, I'll tell him my decision this morning. Or at lunch. Or maybe later.

At some point anyway.

Anton seems happy enough to accompany me with Flump, Peanut, Pickwick, and Treacle to watch the floats come through the village. I've absolutely no idea what to expect so the carnival-type atmosphere takes me by surprise. The floats are mostly sponsored by local companies and are ingeniously formed in the shape of the products so they look like egg boxes or branded sweet boxes. Handfuls of goodies are thrown out to the crowd and children scurry through the legs of adults to get to the sweets. Those closest get baseball hats and bandanas from the various team floats. One float comes through in the shape of a giant water bottle advertising a mineral water brand. The people on the float spray water over the hot crowd, taking particular care to get the police and firemen staffing the event as wet as possible. Everyone laughs though and takes it in good humour.

In fact, everything is going fine and by the time a float approaches the village in the shape of a giant dog biscuit box with an enormous dog biscuit on the top, I've relaxed my guard. Then I realise, a tad belatedly, that they are throwing out free samples of dog treats to the crowd.

Unprepared and lulled into a false sense of security by their previous good behaviour, I'm taken totally off guard by Flump's sharp tug on the lead which manages to yank the lead away from where I looped it around my wrist.

The chihuahuas and Yorkie try valiantly to follow but thankfully have the pulling power of rabbits so Anton has firm hold of them.

Flump, on the other hand, has raced through the

crowd to the float and taken a flying leap up onto it, scaling the box and sitting atop the giant fake biscuit with a look of modest pride on his face. The crowd are laughing and taking pictures. Worse still, I hear the helicopters with the television cameras circling back round so they can get footage of the cheeky dog who has joined the float procession. I can see this going viral on the internet by this evening.

JoJo is going to kill me.

Anton hands me the triple lead coupler for the other dogs and has leapt into the fray before I can make it past the other dog owners trying to scoop up the goodies that have landed at their feet.

He leaps gracefully onto the slowly moving float which thankfully slows and comes to a stop so he can grab Flump and manhandle him from his pride of place as the dog biscuit float mascot. There are good natured cheers as he jumps down, Flump tucked firmly under his arm.

All the same, my cheeks are burning hot when he returns and I suspect my face is the colour of beetroot.

"Thank you, thank you, thank you," I say. "Could you maybe hold onto him, like, really firmly, all the way home and we'll just go back and hide out in my room until the dogs are allowed back in the kitchen?"

To my relief he agrees. Only as we're walking away

and the crowd and helicopters are far behind us can I actually breathe properly.

"After the dogs are allowed back in the guesthouse, we'll go back to fetch Squeaker and Pickle and make our way back here to join in the picnic and enjoy the riders coming through. Don't look so petrified. I've got a jogging lead so I can attach both Pickle and Squeaker to my waist and we'll stay well back. You have to see the cyclists. You can't say you attended a stage of the Tour de France if you don't actually stay for the main event."

"If you say so," I agree doubtfully. "That jogging waist lead might've come in handy earlier, like this morning, you know!"

"I thought these dogs were so tiny they'd be unable to pull away. It turns out I was wrong." He shrugs. "But I have redeemed myself, no?"

"Yes, you saved the day, my hero." I smile and almost blurt out my news but then decide to wait until later in the day. It's going so well and it would be awful to end up ruining the rest of the day if he doesn't respond as I hope he will. Otherwise the rest of the day could be spent in an awkward silence.

Only once we're all ensconced on a picnic blanket beneath a shady tree, with the guests all on their own blankets with personally packed hampers, do I confess to JoJo what happened earlier. To my relief she laughs.

"Someone already sent me the YouTube clip," she says. "Don't worry, Flump can be very tricky. He looks so innocent and then once your guard is down, he's off on one of his adventures. It seems everyone took it in good humour."

"I think Peanut will have competition for her YouTube channel," Poppy says. "If we start Flump a channel too, of all his misdeeds and cheeky behaviour, she's going to have to up her disco-dancing moves and widen her repertoire."

Over warm, crusty French bread and delicious pâté, followed by French pastries, fresh strawberries, and chilled mineral water, I finally feel the tension seeping out of me. I'm leaning back against Anton and he's gently stroking my back, Pickle and Squeaker curled up at our feet, safely attached to a waist lead. I'm happy, I realise. Really happy for the first time in I can't remember how long. Happy being part of a lovely community, living somewhere so amazingly beautiful, not to mention sunny, and most of all being in love with a man I'm mostly sure, well pretty sure, feels the same way about me.

After the lunch we split off to find good places to stand to watch the race competitors come through. We've found a little shade for the dogs beneath a tree as the sun is now high in the sky and the temperature is soaring. There's an air of restless anticipation. Everyone has finished their picnics and packed away the remnants, waiting for the main event, and the atmosphere is making me jittery.

I think that must be the first time I've called it *my* village in my head. Up until now it's been *Poppy's* village or *where I'm staying*. The realisation makes me impatient to tell Anton my news. I simply can't wait any longer. I've got to get my words out now, here in the moment, so I can't lose my nerve.

"You know you were asking about my plans for the future? Well, I've decided I'm definitely staying here. I want my life to be here." I blurt out my decision.

"That's fantastic news," Anton pulls me into an embrace and whispers in my ear, "I've been waiting for you to make the decision before I asked you my question: would you like to move in with me?"

"Er, yes!" I say, shocked. I couldn't ask for greater confirmation that he's serious. "Thank you. Of course, I'd love to, I mean."

"Well I couldn't ask you before you decided." Anton grins. "I had to know a life here was what you definitely wanted. Also, imagine if I'd asked you just before you announced you were going back in the autumn."

I shake my head and decide that love doesn't just make cowards of us all but it can make idiots of us too.

"Are we certain we one hundred per cent have the dogs attached to your waist and also have our wrists double looped through their leads?" I ask.

We both look down to check and then, as if by mutual consent, move in for a kiss. Squeaker and Pickle are behaving themselves for once, in spite of all the other dogs and cyclists bringing their own bikes to watch the Tour de France riders come through the village.

"I love you, Anton," I whisper in his ear, no longer caring that I was the one to say it first.

"I love you too, Daisy." He holds me to him, so close I swear I can feel his heart beating in tandem with mine.

After all that fussing about the words, they slip out easily, naturally, as if there had never been any doubt.

When the actual cyclists come through it's a blur of Lycra, toned thighs, spinning wheels, and cheering from the crowd and the whole event is over in a matter of moments.

I have a brief odd sensation, sort of half-shiver, half-thought, about how short our lives are and how much time we waste in worrying and misunderstandings and miscommunication. Holding back out of fear when what we really want is this: hearts pumping, joy soaring, and putting our all into living our best possible life.

Over in but a moment.

Well, if that's so, I plan to make the absolute most of every single one of them.

Oh, and also I will never, ever use sodding nail scissors to trim grass borders.

ANTON: *This is from Pickle and Squeaker. We're so happy that you're joining our pack. We need to ask a very important question though: do we continue to get double dog treat rations? That's the ones Anton gives us and the ones you give us that you think he doesn't know about? Urgent response required.*

DAISY: *Dear Pickle and Squeaker, I am honoured to be joining your pack. Of course you'll still be getting double treat rations. Should Anton give you any trouble, just remind him that after I move in he'll be getting free dog walking and doggie day care and that should shut him up pretty quickly. See you soon sweethearts, all three of you that is (heart emojis)*

Epilogue

"If I had to live my life over,
I would start barefoot earlier in the spring
and stay that way later in the fall.
I would go to more dances,
I would ride more merry-go-rounds,
I would pick more daisies."

Nadine Stair

Anton and I are standing on an old stone bridge that spans the Ariège river, not far from the spot where Anton first talked to me about elemental water spirits and the history of the ancient caves. Although the old stone gorge is often cool, being overshadowed by mountain on both sides, the sun is high today and sunlight dances on the river, like it did that day.

329

That perfect day which ended with me sobbing my heart out, sure I had ruined something wonderful forever. I suppose it just goes to show we never really know what lies ahead of us, around the next bend in the river.

Squeaker and Pickle stand next to us. I'm holding both their leads just in case, although for once Pickle isn't pulling to get into the river. They both seem to know what we're doing is important and are behaving far more sombrely than usual.

Anton has hold of the urn. We both agreed it would be best if I didn't come into contact with it today, even if Claire would've liked the idea of me joining her for a swim in the river, I'm not sure I'd enjoy it. That water looks cold.

I shiver involuntarily.

"Okay?" Anton looks at me.

I nod and long to put my arm in his or at least on his back to show my support but it's not a good idea and anyway, this is Claire's moment. Hers and Anton's and Pickle's and Squeaker's.

"I was thinking about that old folk song 'My Life Flows On', I'm sure you know it, or maybe you've heard a modern cover," I say, the words coming so vividly to my mind I'm sure I'm meant to sing them.

"My life flows on in endless song
Above earth's lamentation.
I hear the real though far-off hymn
That hails a new creation.
No storm can shake my inmost calm
While to that rock I'm clinging
It sounds an echo in my soul,
How can I keep from singing?"

When I finish singing the verse there's a peculiar silence. A silence deeper than the gushing river, deeper than the bird calls or the rustling sounds of tiny creatures in the undergrowth. As though the forest and the river of the area's "old religion" as Anton calls it, and the spirits of the river and the trees are observing the scene with us, solemn out of respect and sympathy, yet singing the old verse with me and filling the place with a peculiar peace.

"That was lovely, thank you, Daisy," Anton smiles at me and then he closes his eyes, lowering his head and saying his final goodbye. And then the dogs and I watch as he empties the ashes into the dancing river. We watch as they are carried away by the rushing waters and mingle with the flashes of golden sunlight and maybe flakes of real gold from the river silt too.

"Thank you."

I turn around, startled to hear a woman's voice.

"Did you… hear that?" I ask Anton tentatively.

"Hear what?" He's wrapping up the urn in several layers of packaging so I don't accidentally touch it again and doesn't look at me. I'm glad.

"Nothing. I probably just imagined it," I say quietly, knowing that I didn't and also knowing that those words were meant for me. Claire thanking me for taking care of her family. My heart whispers its own thank you to her in return and I watch until the last of the ashes must surely have passed the next bend in the river, wherever that may take her.

Then we walk, hand in hand, dogs at our heels as we make our way to the car so we can drive home to the elegant old farmhouse with green shutters that will now be my home too. This is my next bend in the river and I choose to make the most of every minute of it.

ONE MORE CHAPTER

One More Chapter is an
award-winning global
division of HarperCollins.

Sign up to our newsletter to get our
latest eBook deals and stay up to date
with our weekly Book Club!
<u>Subscribe here.</u>

Meet the team at
<u>www.onemorechapter.com</u>

Follow us!

 <u>@OneMoreChapter_</u>
 <u>@OneMoreChapter</u>
 <u>@onemorechapterhc</u>

Do you write unputdownable fiction?
We love to hear from new voices.
Find out how to submit your novel at
<u>www.onemorechapter.com/submissions</u>